PIIA NYKANEN

Fear and Love

Contents

Acknowledgments

Writing, to me, is about connection, which is not measured by perfect sentences, but by the ability to awaken feelings, to reach into another life and leave a mark. To stir emotions that linger long after the final page is turned, that is the true weight of words.

The greatest turning point in my creative journey came when I understood this truth: the most powerful writing is born in the places we are told not to go. It lives in confronting taboos, in breaking silence, in daring to speak aloud the things others bury. That is where honesty becomes art, and where words transform into something dangerous, beautiful, and unforgettable.

There was someone extraordinary who entered my life at exactly the right moment. He carried a magic that lit a fire inside me. His openness, his uniqueness, and his willingness to be my muse became the force that breathed life into these pages. Between us stretched an invisible leash; delicate yet unbreakable. I held it as a writer, drawing him closer, and he surrendered to the pull. That leash was passion itself, binding muse and writer together in trust, desire, and creation, keeping this story alive when I might have let it fade.

At times, writing this book felt like writing a love letter. I felt the spark, the devotion, the raw magic, the kiss of life he gave me when my own world had dimmed. To my muse: I am endlessly thankful for your generosity, your light, and the way you awakened the fire in me. Without you, this story would not exist. I only hoped this book could be as rare and unforgettable as you. Never change, because it is in your truth, your presence, and your passion that I found the courage to create.

To my dear friends, thank you for listening to fragments, reading little snippets, and encouraging me when doubt crept in. Your faith in me kept me going, and I love you all for it.

Writing is a gift I will never take for granted. Finding your own voice is a strange and wonderful journey, but the true magic happens when your words finally find their people, the ones who recognize themselves in your story and feel less alone. That is when writer and reader truly meet.

With love, passion, and endless gratitude,

Piia xxx

The undeniable limerence shook her core as she listened to one of his old voice notes. His words came onto her like the shivering snow. She closed her eyes, not wanting any of his words to escape her. In her vision, he was fully clothed, in the same black t-shirt, perfectly framing his body that she adored from the moment she laid her eyes on his picture. And the moments that followed when nothing would give her greater pleasure than receiving his message when on the outside her world was so shaky. She was hailed with bombs, but his presence gave her shelter. She didn't want to become a girl made from the darkness, but a girl made from millions of flavors, and vibrant colors.

With each passing moment, she felt him close, even though he couldn't have been further away. How was this possible? She felt his fingers adjusting behind her ear and taking a piece of her hair, staring at her.

Her heart was a fireplace, all her books thrown in, all her writings in flames. And only the feelings remained like ashes you couldn't get rid of. Black, like his t-shirt, black like the night they met.

It was the darkest moment before dawn when she opened her eyes.

The voice notes echoed through her bedroom, his voice so intimate, warm, and mellifluous it soothed her right back to the beginning when her eyes landed on the lonely rabbit. "It's not like this is a postmortem or anything" he kept talking. "We are continuing…"

She remembered his hand on her breast, his teeth gently biting her, and her thoughts so wild. "Bite harder, so I can remember you longer".

Her legs locked him, his white gold, warm liquid running down her legs. There is nothing I could promise her. Love is not guaranteed. She knew it. Just like she knew the painful part of her life; breathing didn't mean you were living.

The invisible armour she imagined was stopping the Fear from haunting her. I tried to fight. I tried to stand in Fear's path and laugh. I tried to be so radiant. And I had found him to stop the Fear for me. To bring her back.

Twice from the depths of the ocean, just as her lungs were filling up with salty water, she started to feel peace by letting go. She felt his hands grasping her hips and pulling her back, his brown puppy eyes with so much life in them guiding her back to the shore. Once when she snorted so much cocaine it burned her eyes, but it was the time with the knife in her hand, that I guess I could take credit for most, because she remembered the fleeting moment of the energy flying her to cloud nine, right into his apartment, forgetting all the bad that happened to her. That moment, a little spark that there is a life worth living. She felt his hands taking the knife away. Placing it on the table, with the same soft hands that he held her breasts and hips when she felt like floating on top of him. His eyes were on her even from a million miles away.

At times she felt like she had met an extension of herself, her match in so many ways, disturbingly dark even.

She remembered the snow falling on her phone screen and his name popping up when the rabbit was fully alive and in action, staring right through her across the dark road. But now, the rabbit, the extension of everything, was slowly dying.

That white rabbit was me, the Love, and her name was on my list as the very last human to save. I was energy, and they were flesh, and needless to say, the best story was saved for last. When small puckers formed on her flesh and chills down his spine, we could overcome the Monster, and Fear would no longer laugh at me. And I was going to try because the physical world and mine are like the space between the words you read.

Chapter 1

Sydney, Australia, January 2023

Shivering, Harriet leaned into the balcony glass.

"Let go. Let go," she whispered to herself. Emerging from the shadow of the moon, I tried to enter her mind, desperate to pull her back. I shouted. Her breath fogged the pane, her body trembling in the wind, fourteen stories above the garden below.

"Let go," she repeated, almost testing herself. Moonlight carved her fragile figure in silver. I strained, pushing against the boundaries of her mind.

"Harriet!" I cried. "You don't understand how radiant you are. Your soul, your being—" Her wide eyes stared into the night, strawberry-blonde hair whipping across her face. The blue-and-white dress clung to her—the same one he had pulled up as though her body belonged to him. She could still feel his freckled hands, still hear his voice:

You're codependent. Useless. You let yourself go.

His malice crawled over her, sharp and cold, biting into her flesh and embedding itself in her very being, until every nerve and every thought quivered with its weight.

"It isn't your fault!" I screamed, but she leaned further out, toes curling over the edge. Below, I stood on the lawn, ears erect, whiskers stiff with dread. I loathed myself for witnessing her torment, for arriving too late. With my last ounce of will, I summoned Him.

"Fear," I whispered. "Come." The clouds swallowed the moon. Darkness thickened, choking the air. Then I felt it: Fear, alive and crawling, coiling around Harriet like a predator. His laughter rolled across the night, deep and merciless, vibrating the very air.

It didn't just mock her; it hit her like a fist, shoving her backward. She staggered, body trembling, toes slipping off the edge. Fear whispered her worst doubts, dredging up every lie he had told: *You're weak. You're nothing. You can't survive without him.* I surged forward, energy flaring, locking into the shadowed presence. It hissed and recoiled at my intrusion, claws of darkness scraping against the edges of Harriet's mind. I pushed, twisted, struggled, our battle invisible yet brutal, tearing at the night itself. Fear shrieked, writhing like a living storm, its weight pressing down on the balcony, rattling tiles, rattling Harriet's body, rattling the very air.

Harriet's chest heaved. Sobs tore from her throat. I fought harder, forcing the shadow back, pulling her trembling soul toward clarity. Her pain was jagged glass, cutting her from within. She did not want death, only silence, only release, but he had trapped her in a labyrinth of lies. I could still hear his cold, triumphant words:

No one will believe you.

But I believe you, Harriet. I have seen the Monster. I know what he is. She was not meant to fall. She was not meant to try to end her life. This was not her fate. Before him, she had been alive, joyful, untethered, her future wide open. Then he arrived, circling her like a predator. Outside the bar, jealousy flared when another man offered her a cigarette. He sent her stumbling home, drunk and alone through dark streets, punishing her for imagined sins. He waited in her apartment when she arrived. A week later, another woman was murdered along that same route, at the same hour. It could have been Harriet. Still, that was only the beginning. He drained her joy, feeding on her despair. He caged her in servitude: caretaker, cleaner, slave. And she stayed. Until the new girl appeared. Harriet had endured years of lies and whispers that twisted reality like smoke. Every broken promise, every distorted truth, carved deeper into her. She had cried herself to sleep countless nights, her pillow soaked with tears no one would see. Her pain was in her body as well as her heart. Black eyes hidden beneath careful makeup, bruises she tried to explain away, trembling hands, a constant reminder of his cruelty. He had perfected manipulation. Not only anger, not only lies, but gaslighting. *You're overreacting. You're imagining things. You're too sensitive.* Every bruise, every raised voice, every broken promise became her fault. He twisted her memories, rewrote moments, and made her doubt the truth her own body shouted at her. Yet sometimes, fragments of clarity broke through. She remembered what she had seen, felt in her gut. This was abuse. It wasn't her fault. And yet the echo of his words tugged her back into doubt, making her waver between fear and resistance. Every word, every look, every cold blue stare made her question herself. She blamed herself for his violence, for the emptiness behind his promises. She had loved him, tried to reason with him, tried to save the man who was never there to be saved.

And then the new girl appeared, bright, ignorant, untouched by his darkness. Harriet felt fresh betrayal, but a small part of her knew: this girl had no idea what she was stepping into. She hadn't met Harriet. She hadn't seen the trail of pain, the nights spent crying into nothing. Harriet had been broken, humiliated, gaslit, and erased. The new girl wasn't chosen because she was special. She was chosen because she was next. Another soul to break, another life to hollow out. I watched her fling herself into his arms at the airport, mistaking the devil for a prize. Dark hair spilled over his steroid-swollen muscles as she smiled for the cameras. Cheap jewelry glinted like chains. She thought she'd won, blind to the truth. But before Harriet escaped, he had to break her one last time. His cold blue eyes locked on hers as he hissed again: *No one will believe you.* Then he forced himself on her. For years, he whispered poisoned promises: *If you do this, maybe*

I'll love you. He drugged her, toyed with her, hollowed her until she was a ghost. Migraines, blurred vision, her body rebelling against unseen toxins. Sometimes she woke to his weight crushing her. And no one listened. Not the police. Not the world. He remained invisible, a nobody who thought himself untouchable.

But I will not give him eternity here. Monsters like him deserve no name, no story. Only this truth: what he called love was cruelty, dressed in flesh. Fuck him. Let him rot.

Harriet's toes curled over the balcony edge, breath shallow, body swaying in the wind. For a heartbeat, I thought she would fall.

Fear's laughter cut through the night, low, merciless, alive. It struck her like a hammer, rattling her balance, rattling the tiles, rattling the world itself. I threw every ounce of myself into the struggle, pushing against the shadow, clawing it back from her mind. Fear shrieked, twisting, writhing, its weight slamming against us. Every hiss, every echo of doubt it sent toward Harriet, I met with defiance, with light, with force, until the air snapped with energy.

Finally, Harriet collapsed onto the cold tiles, sobs tearing through the silence. Not strength, not clarity, just exhaustion. The fight to die was the same fight to live, and she no longer had energy for either.

Anna, her friend, found her hours later, knees pulled to her chest, eyes vacant. Without question or hesitation, she moved fast. Bags were packed. A flight was booked. By sunrise, Harriet was walking through the airport on autopilot, clutching her passport like a lifeline.

On the plane, she stared blankly at violent films, drowning herself in wine, silent and hollow. But she was gone. Gone from him.

Anna had seen what others refused to. She booked the flight herself, knowing the risk, knowing too well the headlines filled with women lost to men like him. She had sensed the danger from the start.

Now, Harriet was free.

And I—I could work again. Not as a hero, not as a savior, but as what I am. Sometimes clumsy, reckless, even drunk on my own strange energy, but unlike Fear, I have no hunger for destruction. I stumble, yes. But more often than not, I land where I'm needed.

This time, I will land beside Harriet.

Chapter 2

On the plane, January 2023

Harriet stared out the tiny airplane window, the vast expanse of the huge ocean, a cold, grey mirror reflecting the turmoil inside her. The long-haul flight was a blur of recycled air, stale coffee, and the constant, gnawing pain that had become her unwelcome companion. It wasn't just physical pain, though the phantom ache of his grip still lingered on her arm. This was a pain that dug deeper, a pain that whispered insidious doubts, a pain that nearly, chillingly, drove her to the edge.

She never forgot that glass balcony. It loomed in her memory, a shimmering, malevolent stage set for what Monster, she refused to call him by his name anymore, had so meticulously orchestrated. His perfect plan. Push her to kill herself. He'd paint her as unstable, and mentally ill. *"She was crazy,"* he'd say, his voice dripping with false concern. *"I did everything I could. Poor Harriet, such a fragile state."* And everyone would believe him. He was perfect, after all. Always calm, and composed, the picture of a loving, if slightly burdened, husband. He never did anything, not overtly. It was all her fault, her imagined slights, her irrational fears.

He had chipped away at her, day by day, year by year, like a relentless sculptor shaping her into a reflection of his twisted desires. He isolated her from everyone, subtly undermined her confidence, and meticulously controlled her finances. He told her she was worthless, incapable, that no one else would ever want her. He made her believe it.

The balcony was the crescendo of his masterpiece. She remembered standing there, the wind whipping through her hair, the dizzying drop blurring below.

He'd backed her towards the edge, his blue eyes glittering with a cold, controlled fury that she knew intimately. That's when the thought had taken root, insidious and dark: maybe he was right. *Maybe she was a burden. Maybe everyone would be better off...*

But even as she teetered on the precipice, a sliver of something stubbornly refused to break. A flicker of defiance, a primal survival instinct. It whispered, *"Not like this. Not for him."*

She didn't die. Instead, she backed away from the balcony, her legs trembling, her body shaking with a terror that transcended fear. She spent the rest of the night in a catatonic state, staring at the ceiling, replaying the scene in her mind. But through the haze of fear and despair, a new clarity began to emerge. She saw his plan, his meticulous manipulation, the venomous web he had woven around her. And she knew, with a terrifying certainty, that staying was a death sentence.

The next hour, she acted. It wasn't a grand escape filled with drama.

Her friend Anna helped, and she packed a small bag with essential documents and a few changes of clothes. She needed to go as far away as possible. Quickly. But that meant going back to her *mother. She already felt the reverse culture shock taking over even thinking about it. Still, better than dying.*

Leaving behind the life he had so carefully constructed, the life that nearly killed her happened in the blink of an eye.

Now, thousands of feet above the ocean, Harriet had caught the flight to safety. She was still alive. The journey was far from over. She had a long road ahead, a road filled with therapy, healing, and the slow, arduous process of rebuilding her life. But for the first time in years, she felt a flicker of hope ignite within her despite still feeling the numbness of it all. *She had chosen life.* She had saved herself. And that, she realized, was the most powerful act of defiance of all.

Chapter 3

New York, February 2023

Arden was sitting on his black couch, the only splash of "color" in his otherwise greyscale apartment, swiping on the app. The rhythmic flick of his thumb was the soundtrack to my anxiety.

"Hot," he muttered, pausing on a profile with a pouty-lipped blonde. "Yeah, maybe…" he said.

I sighed internally. We were running out of time. Harriet was getting closer to deleting the app, her ex, the absolute evil Monster, had installed on her phone. I needed her to see Arden's notification, the one I was about to engineer before she purged her phone of his digital poison.

Then Harriet's photo appeared: an awkward smile, a slight tilt of her head that always made my nonexistent heart ache. "Hmm, interesting…" Arden drawled, his tone devoid of any genuine feeling.

"SWIPE RIGHT!" I screamed into his consciousness, willing the command to override his apathy.

Arden, the banker. In his mid-thirties, he was undeniably sexy in a rugged, "corporate little bit of a sleazebag" sort of way. The grey around his temples added a touch of maturity, and he had mastered the art of the flattering selfie. More importantly, he was the best I could find on this damned app.

Again, it may not be my best choice, but the options were dwindling. If we were to believe his bio, *"One of those finance guys who will give you the attention you deserve,"* it was the attention Harriet desperately needed to claw her way back to life. I owed it to her. I had failed to protect her from the Monster. The very least I could do was orchestrate a distraction to her pain.

I continued to observe him in his apartment, a minimalist space that screamed "player". He put the phone on his coffee table, its screen now displaying a match with Harriet. Then he opened his laptop, adjusting the camera with unnerving precision.

"What on earth are you doing?" I wondered aloud, even though he couldn't hear me. This wasn't part of the plan. He took off his light blue boxer shorts. I gasped, my spectral form momentarily stunned.

"WOW," I breathed, involuntarily impressed. If anything, there were a few extra inches for Harriet.

In all my years of intervening, of nudging fate and whispering suggestions, this was the biggest and the most…ahem…beautiful cock I had ever seen. And, as the song goes,

"What's love got to do with it?" Well, I had everything to do with *that.* And, seeing something like Arden, well, I could say I had the best job in the world sometimes.

And Arden's big package was something I had to deliver. As a matter of urgency. His hand went slowly up and down the swollen, oh-so-perfect, pinkish seven inches. He was staring at the laptop, a self-satisfied smile playing on his lips.

There was something mind-bending watching his intimate moment, a voyeuristic angle I wasn't quite comfortable with until I realized I wasn't the only one watching. There were a lot of people on his laptop screen. It was hard to make out exactly what they were saying, but he was certainly confident and charismatic in front of the camera, performing for them and for himself. I could feel my eyes narrow.

What the hell was this? This wasn't a dating app, this was some kind of…cam show? And his video? It wasn't just on his regular dating app. He'd used it to… market himself?

The blood ran cold in my non-existent veins. This wasn't a distraction. This was a disaster.

Chapter 4

Arctic Circle, February 2023

The wind howled like a hungry wolf, clawing at the windows of the small flower shop nestled deep within the isolated woods, almost at the Arctic Circle. February had sunk its teeth into the landscape, painting everything in shades of white and grey. Inside, however, a splash of vibrant color bloomed in the form of "Easy Flowers", a sanctuary of floral artistry run by Rebecca, and currently unwillingly assisted by her daughter, Harriet.

"Constructing flower arrangements individually is an art," Rebecca whispered, her striking blue eyes, a shocking contrast to her what you would prefer to call a weather-beaten face, but it was an alcohol-beaten face, peered at Harriet. Rebecca looked like she was in her element here, surrounded by the heady scent of roses, lilies, and pine. Harriet, bundled in layers of wool, felt only the biting chill that seeped through the shop's aging walls.

"Look, here is what we call a Lovers Only Package," Rebecca declared proudly, holding aloft a partially assembled bouquet as the snow fell thicker outside. "He can afford a lovely arrangement, my long-time regular customer." She carefully placed a hand-picked red rose, its velvety petals a stark contrast to the surrounding greens, in the bouquet. "Matt, he no longer writes a simple celebratory message. This time it's real love."

Harriet leaned on the counter, its surface worn smooth with age and countless flower deliveries. She watched Rebecca pick a variety of stems from the water-filled buckets, her hands moving with a practiced grace born from years of dedication.

"What he wants to say with this bouquet is that meeting her is like meeting a twin flame. He is crazy about her, but in a mature way."

'Twin flame, more like a dumpster fire...' Harriet thought quietly. The words stung, echoing a truth she desperately tried to bury.

Rebecca knew the ins and outs of her customers, which was as important as knowing the seasons and terrains in the flower business. She understood their unspoken desires, their hidden hopes, and their tangled webs of relationships. Harriet, on the other hand, only saw the wilting reality behind the pretty facade. She imagined Matt clutching the striking arrangement close to his chest, determined, but happy, standing behind a door, ready to knock, smiling ear to ear.

"This is for a delivery and needs to be ready in five minutes," Rebecca declared, grabbing a roll of brown string and starting to wrap the bottom of the bouquet together. Her wrinkly fingers worked fast, securing the stems with practiced ease.

"Oh, so it gets delivered to his love interest today?" Harriet asked, her voice carefully neutral as she erased the earlier scenario in her head.

"What if no one is home?" Harriet asked the question laced with a nervousness she couldn't quite conceal.

"It has instructions to leave it at her door," Rebecca replied, scanning a piece of paper on the counter. Her focus was entirely on the bouquet, oblivious to the swirling emotions within her daughter.

"Well, someone will be very pleased today." Harriet tried to smile but felt the piercing pain in her heart. She remembered always receiving extravagant flowers from Monster after the worst lies. He had been with her hot and cold. Every time she caught him lying, the flowers arrived or other gifts. Sometimes he beat her up without a word, without flowers. No, sorry, nothing. It was justified. She had exchanged words with him, argued with him, or looked at him the wrong way. The bouquets were always magnificent; apologies whispered in the language of lilies and roses.

And she, a fool, had always accepted them, mistaking fleeting beauty for genuine remorse.

He will get away with it, won't he?

Harriet forced herself to breathe. This was different. This Matt, if Rebecca was to be believed, was genuinely in love. He wasn't using flowers as a weapon but as a genuine expression of his feelings.

The bouquet was finished, a riot of color against the stark white of the Arctic winter. Rebecca held it out, admiring her handiwork. "Right, all ready for the delivery van."

Harriet stared at the arrangement, at the rose that symbolized a love so different, so healthy, from the one she had known. A love that was now blooming for someone else. The smile she forced felt brittle and fake. This time, there would be no flower deliveries to patch up her broken heart.

"Wouldn't it be lovely if we all had Matt in our lives?" Rebecca laughed.

Harriet could sense the sarcasm. She hadn't asked about Monster yet. Rebecca had never expressed an opinion about Monster. It was like another thing in Harriet's life she couldn't care less about.

"It's over," Harriet finally said.

"I gathered. Since you flew to the world's end and landed here."

They chatted for a while, but it was clear their mother-daughter relationship wasn't typical.

Harriet was eyeing up the keys on the counter.

"Is it OK if I stay at the cabin for a bit?"

"Just don't steal my painkillers and vodka". Rebecca slid the key across the counter towards Harriet. An older man walked in, eyeing her up and down.

"He is here to pick up the flowers for delivery".

"This is Harriet. My daughter."

"She is staying here for a while."

Harriet nodded and walked out to the snow, taking a step forward. Her left foot gave way, and she slid on the ice, having no time to balance.

"Oh My God, no." She fell backward, and the ice underneath the snow felt like a ton of bricks hitting her bottom.

She sat on the ice watching the snowflakes fall.

Nature could be deceiving. Beautiful snowflakes glistering on top of killer ice. *This is like men, you admire them for a minute, and the next minute they beat your ass.*

Harriet dragged herself into the cabin. As she closed the door, the darkness of the room made her feel strange. Fear stood at the corner, with a smirk.

Vivid and scary flashbacks of Monster's fists on her, his cold blue eyes staring deep into her soul, were back. He was far away, but the Fear made his presence known. Harriet grabbed her phone.

She googled what to do when you feel suicidal. Her hands shaking, she read: *"Postpone any decision to end your life for 24 hours".*

The pain she felt in her chest was unbearable, sharp, piercing through her slowly beating heart. She wanted nothing more than to die. It would be the easy way out. She could write that one last letter. Tell the truth. It didn't matter if no one read it.

Chapter 5

rctic Circle, February 2023

Harriet bit her lip and grabbed a towel. *"At least have a sauna, take a moment."* She told herself, feeling dizzy, her past filling her head again with nightmares. *"What difference would 24 hours make?"* she wondered, the question echoing in the hollow chambers of her mind.

As she ran cold water on her wrists in the bathroom, the icy chill doing little to soothe the burning memories, her mind recounted the past with cruel clarity. She had met him at a hotel pool, dazzling, charismatic, a whirlwind of charm that swept her off her feet. The red flags, she knew now, had been there from the start, waving frantically like desperate pleas for her attention. Even his ex-girlfriend had reached out, a ghostly figure appearing in her inbox with chilling warnings, whispering words like "psychopath" and "compulsive liar." But Harriet, blinded by "a love" she now recognized as a carefully constructed illusion, dismissed them all. He was so convincing, so adept at twisting truth into whatever narrative suited him. She believed him, blindly, foolishly, falling after him like a love-struck puppet.

He had wanted everything to happen quickly, impossibly so. Marriage proposals arrived within months, followed by insistent demands to move in together. He took over her finances, seamlessly integrating her accounts into his own, promising combined security and future prosperity. Harriet had possessed a valid visa allowing her to stay in Australia, but he had subtly, meticulously, convinced her to switch to a partner visa, binding her residency to his good graces, making her utterly dependent on him.

Then, it happened. The day the facade crumbled. They were in the car, arguing about something trivial, the air thick with unspoken tension. He was driving. His hand lashed out, a sudden, brutal blow that landed squarely on her face. The impact sent a shockwave of disbelief and searing pain through her. Her ear rang a high-pitched whine that amplified the silence that followed. She covered the blossoming black eye the next day with makeup, a pathetic attempt to conceal the truth. At work, they noticed and questioned. She concocted elaborate excuses, a child's wayward kick in the park, a rogue ball, anything to avoid the shame, the humiliation of admitting the Monster she had invited into her life.

The second time it happened, the authorities intervened. The aftermath of the assault was a chaotic blur of flashing lights and stern faces. They charged him with assault. Harriet, even with a split lip and a face swollen with bruises, begged them to let him go. He worked for the military, she explained, and his career would be ruined. He was stationed away often, and the time apart always seemed to cauterize the wounds, both physical and emotional. He would return, contrite and charming, promising never to repeat his mistakes. And for a while, everything would be almost…good.

Until the cycle began again, slowly, insidiously, tightening its grip like a constricting serpent. He installed spyware on her computer, monitoring her every move. He told her to quit her job, claiming he wanted to take care of her, but it was a calculated move to isolate her further. He made insidious comments about her friends, subtly poisoning her relationships, and categorizing them as "good" or "bad" based on their perceived loyalty to him.

When Harriet dared to wear a dress that showed her knees, he called her a slut, his words dripping with venomous judgment. He bought her razors and demanded she shave, telling her she was disgusting "down there." Then her breasts were too big, and she was forced to wear minimizer bras, her body becoming another battleground in his twisted game of control.

He, meanwhile, was a master of hypocrisy. He was on social media, flirting with other women daily, jetting off for "work" all the time, his explanations becoming increasingly implausible. Harriet had long ceased questioning his extramarital affairs. The fight had been drained from her, replaced by a numb resignation. She was existing, not living, trapped in a gilded cage of her own making.

She stepped into the sauna, the dry heat enveloping her like a suffocating blanket. The sweat beaded on her skin, mirroring the tears that streamed down her face. *What difference would 24 hours make? Could it erase the years of abuse, the erosion of her self-worth, and the suffocating weight of her choices?* Maybe not. But perhaps, in that small pocket of time, she could find the sliver of courage she needed to reclaim her life, one shaky step at a time. She wasn't sure how, or when, but she knew, with a newfound clarity that burned brighter than the sauna's heat, that she couldn't, wouldn't, live like this anymore. 24 hours might not be enough to fix everything, but it was enough to start.

Harriet bit her lip and grabbed a towel. *"Breathe."* She told herself, feeling dizzy, her past filling her head again with nightmares.

He was a compulsive liar, maybe even a pathological one. What was the difference? Harriet was too tired to think, to Google it. It didn't matter anymore. He lied. Full stop. He lied to everyone and about everything. The barista, the landlord, and his mother. He lied about the weather, the color of the sky, and the price of milk. And he never faced any consequences. Harriet thought maybe it was due to her. She was always protecting him, smoothing things over, explaining away his inconsistencies.

He had a long criminal record, a tapestry woven with threads of assault, fraud, and criminal damage. Yet she protected him. She excused his outbursts, paid his fines, and lied to the police. She told herself she was helping him, that he was a wounded bird who just needed her to mend his broken wing. But the wing was a lie, and the bird was a predator.

The emotional abuse was constant, a dripping faucet of insults and belittlement. He called her useless, a burden. "You can't even drive a car," he sneered, "You're completely codependent. You need me, Harriet. Nobody else would put up with you." And she believed him.

Then came the day the dripping faucet overflowed. He pinned her onto the bed, the blue and white summer dress suddenly too tight, too restricting. He pulled her hair back, his eyes cold and empty. He pulled the dress up, and everything went black.

Rape.

Harriet wiped her tears, bit her tongue until she tasted blood, and went numb. Her feelings, her body. She felt nothing. She was numb all over, a block of ice in a searing desert. He walked to the kitchen, the clatter of the blender a jarring intrusion into the silence that had swallowed her whole. She could hear him making a protein shake. He then left for the gym like normal, the sound of the door clicking shut echoing through the apartment. Normal day.

Harriet walked around the apartment in a state of shock. She put on a mindless TV show, a sitcom with canned laughter, and stared at it with a blank face. Each joke landed with a dull thud in the vacuum of her mind.

The next day, he said he was leaving. Out of the blue, unceremoniously, he was gone with his bag. No explanation, no apology, just a slammed door.

Harriet felt a mixture of panic and pain, a twisted knot in her stomach. The panic was for the unknown, the pain for the loss of the delusion she'd clung to for so long.

She walked around the apartment, her mind blank. *"Was she this stupid?"* she would ask herself, the question a relentless, self-inflicted wound.

He then started messaging her. He was staying with a friend, he told her, someone who understood him. That he might love her again, he added, if she did something for him.

He wasn't staying with a friend at all.

The messages became more frequent, more insistent, and more bizarre. The instructions were clear; find a guy on a dating app and arrange to have sex in front of her "husband." All communication with the chosen man should go through him, he dictated. No kissing. He would be the puppeteer, and Harriet, his unwilling marionette.

He kept pressuring her. "Hurry up, you're running out of time!" he would message her, the urgency in his words a sharp sting on her raw wounds.

Then came the message that shattered the last fragile remnants of her sanity. He told her to "be nice to my girlfriend!" as if this was some game, some twisted performance for his amusement. *Why didn't he ask his girlfriend?* The question echoed in her mind, a beacon in the fog of manipulation. Why was he putting her through this? *His wife of so many years?* The answer, clear and simple and terrifyingly obvious, struck her like a blow. He didn't care about her. He never had. He enjoyed hurting her. He enjoyed controlling her. And this… this was the ultimate act of control.

Harriet's head was spinning, and she felt sick. The numbness evaporated, replaced by a wave of nausea and a burning anger that threatened to consume her.

She had had enough. She had endured enough. She had been pushed, prodded, and broken down for far too long. She looked at the downloaded app, a digital gateway to her humiliation, but she couldn't go through with it. Her fingers hovered over the delete button.

All the threats of force and coercion to engage in sexual performance for him made her stomach turn, but she was so numb to it all.

He kept coming and coming at her, trying to break her to pieces. He would *never* stop. He came back again and raped her again. And, after that, she escaped to the balcony. Numb, again. She had given up everything to be his nothing.

She wanted to throw herself down. All she heard was his voice calling her again *stupid, useless, couldn't even drive a car, let yourself go, and no one would ever believe you.*

Her fingers were barely touching the glass balcony as the wind threw her hair in her face. *"Jump,"* she heard him say.

Chapter 6

Arctic Circle, February 2023

Harriet sat in the sauna, the dry heat clinging to her skin like a second layer. She stared at the steaming rocks, their ancient faces seeming to mock her with their silent wisdom. She rose, the heat a tangible weight lifting from her, and walked outside into the crisp, unforgiving embrace of the Arctic winter.

The snow crunched under her bare feet as she exhaled. The water vapor in her breath billowed out, condensing into a fleeting cloud of tiny droplets of liquid water and ice, a miniature spectacle blooming and vanishing in the frigid air. It reminded her of life, her life, a fog dissipating, leaving only a cold space behind. *She felt betrayed, adrift.* Maybe she had no intuition, blind to the signs. Maybe that's why it all happened.

The app on her phone beeped, a jarring intrusion on her bleak contemplation. *"You are safe,"* she whispered, the words tasting like ash in her mouth. She grabbed her phone, the screen a cold rectangle in her trembling hand.

"You have a match!" the app proclaimed.

She retreated inside, seeking solace in the flickering flames of the fireplace. The fire crackled and hissed, a counterpoint to the churning turmoil within her. *"I bet you can't trust anyone ever again,"* Rebecca had mentioned at the flower store, her voice laced with a knowing pity. Harriet had ignored her, but the words had burrowed deep under her skin.

Something inside of her was brewing, a slow, simmering defiance. *"I can't let him destroy everything,"* she told herself, the words gaining strength with each repetition. She opened the app, the bright interface clashing with the darkness that clung to her. Still, she heard Monster's demanding voice echoing in her head. *"If you do this..."* He had always used threats, veiled and explicit, a constant current of manipulation and abuse. She could see it now, the puppeteer's strings, so cleverly disguised as what she thought might have been "love and concern".

She stared at the very first guy on the phone screen. *"Are all men bad somehow?"* she wondered, a question tinged with weariness and lingering fear. She stared at the profile of a man she had never met, a stranger who held the potential for either salvation or destruction for a woman.

"I am just trying to give you the attention you deserve," he had typed, followed by a spark emoji. A pathetic attempt at charm, perhaps, but it had worked, piquing her interest. She swiped through his photos. He looked up at the camera, a glimpse of the world stretching beyond the plane window behind him. Another time, he was caught randomly laughing at an event, wearing a tie that looked slightly too tight. And another, bundled in hired ski gear, walking up a mountain in the snow, his face flushed with exertion and joy.

He lived in New York. It wasn't like he was down the road, a potential threat lurking in her immediate vicinity.

He was 6300 kilometers away, an impossible distance, a safe distance.

Harriet looked at his photos again. Intrigued. His dark, curly hair, the strong line of his neck, and the quiet confidence that seemed to emanate from the screen. *"Who are you, Mr. New York?"* she wondered, a flicker of curiosity igniting within her.

The distance only amplified the attraction, considering her vulnerability. She felt a sense of depth, a greater intelligence lurking beneath the surface. "What would I do if he were standing in front of me?" Run? Approach him? She had no idea. She felt like she had been a caged animal, wearing a restrictive minimizer bra for years that had hurt her chest. Now, even her breasts were free, unbound by the constraints of expectation, with no bra in sight.

What did it matter anymore who she spoke to? Maybe she… maybe she was ready to take a chance. Maybe she deserved a chance. Maybe, just maybe, this stranger from New York could be the key to unlocking the cage she had been trapped in for so long.

Chapter 7

Arctic Circle, February 2023

"Maybe she could speak to this stranger for 24 hours," she mused aloud. "Give him 24 hours and pretend that he is a normal *husband.*" A shiver of exhilaration and guilt ran down her spine.

"Hello, husband," she typed jokingly and waited, half-expecting silence or a crass reply. A moment later, a notification popped up. "Hello, wifey."

Harriet hadn't smiled in a long time.

They exchanged a few more messages. Small talk. She felt an unexpected light creeping into her chest.

"You look like you have good energy," she typed in impulse, instead of deleting the app, maybe stupidly, giving it a go on her terms.

"Better experienced in person," he typed back, a hint of playful challenge in his words. She hesitated. "Let's move this conversation over to WhatsApp," Arden suggested. He gave her his number, and she saved it, her fingers trembling slightly.

Harriet stood in the doorway to the sauna now, wrapped in a white towel. The heat was already making her skin prickle. "Hello wifey", lit up on WhatsApp, as promised.

First time in months, she smiled and saved his number as "Husband".

Harriet adjusted the towel and in the spear of a moment snapped a selfie standing in front of the wooden door to the sauna. She sent it without a second thought.

Her cheeks were warm and had a natural rosy glow. Her eyes, which had been brimming with tears for weeks, were now dry. She looked around her and felt this new, exciting possibility. Even though he was sitting on his black couch in New York, miles away, she felt him near. *How crazy.*

She let the white towel drop on the floor.

She let him see her breasts. Her legs, her ass. The vulnerability was liberating and terrifying all at once.

And she let him hear her voice. A voice she hadn't realized she'd been holding back for so long. She talked about her day, about the memories that still clung to her, about the fear that she'd never be happy again.

He listened. He didn't interrupt. He didn't offer platitudes. He simply listened. And when she was finished, he asked gentle, probing questions that made her think, that made her feel seen.

She would let him be her husband for 24 hours. A temporary husband, a virtual husband, but a husband, nonetheless. And, hopefully, this time, it was a better husband. One who listened. One who saw her. One who didn't treat her like the Monster had.

Chapter 8

Arctic Circle, February 2023

Harriet felt the electricity flowing through her veins again.

She was having six orgasms a day, all in those 24 hours she had given to her new "Husband".

It could have easily been more. In the dark bathroom with the phone in her hand, she played Arden's video again. Again. And again.

She paid attention to his black t-shirt; it was a perfect fit. He wasn't too muscular, not the Monster, a narcissist who spent all his spare time at the gym staring at the mirror, only caring about likes on social media, cheating, lying, abusing, and injecting Melanotan.

He, in contrast, looked fit, and what turned her on most was that he looked normal. She craved normal like nothing else. Her eyes glanced down at the t-shirt; it was perfect for her; the size, the form, the way his hand went up.

She imagined dropping her silky underwear on the floor, lifting her leg over, and slowly squeezing herself into him. Her eyes lit up as she measured his size. It wouldn't all go in without some pleasurable pain, gently tearing her skin. She felt the tingling in her fingertips as the excitement took over her body once again. She would press her thighs onto him, throwing her head back, enjoying every inch of him.

"Stay, right there," he would whisper in her ear.

He would look her in the eyes, pressing against her.

The urge she felt was almost painful, the cold air pushing her to any secluded corner to touch herself and to think about him. She was dripping sweet, thin honey, gasping a little louder.

She would kneel in front of him, and it would feel like the most normal thing.

"Open, let me use it," he would whisper. "Wider," and she would smile ear-to-ear, because it would feel like the most normal thing in the world.

Intense, but normal, Harriet would feel like a lioness being fed.

He would be making a mess on her face, and she felt warm red hues bypass her heart; her head was spinning as she came, thinking of his black t-shirt, his hand squeezing himself. Breathless and hardly on her feet, she licked her sweet-tasting fingers.

Maybe she started to love herself again slowly. She leaned on the wall and massaged her round breasts, feeling her wet fingers leave a sticky mark on her nipples.

The time had flown by when all she did was cry with the pain shaking her core, piercing and twisting her heart. Now, it was being slowly replaced by incredible, breathtaking pleasure. She knew she had been extra sensitive to emotions and energies around her ever since. She never expected to feel the intense euphoria zoning her out like this. It was as if her soft, pulsating lips were whispering a little thank you, sending it to the normal guy behind the phone screen. *Her 24-hour husband.*

It was more than innocent, sudden butterflies kicking in. It was electricity, a good sign she wasn't emotionally dead after all. The very important 24 hours showed her that her capacity to feel love, lust, and sexual energy was equal to her capacity to feel pain, and that kept her alive.

I felt like winning. *This is working! I* don't know if I have earned my title as Love yet, but you could give me a little nickname for now, Lust. Maybe this lust can lead to love. Or at least save Harriet.

And, one thing was certain at this point, that Fear had taken the backseat. A text message from Anna popped up on her screen.

"The detective would like to have a Zoom call with you."

Another text.

"I can join too!" Harriet didn't think there was any point in trying to get Monster to face justice for what he had done. He would get away again like he always did.

"I don't know". Harriet responded.

"Is it worth it to talk to her and see what she says?"

"The only downside is that she suggested 2 am your time. Will you be OK with that?" Anna typed back.

"Sure, I'll talk to her."

"Her name is Emma. She is quite young, but she was already talking about covert operations and everything."

"Log in at 2 am, see you then. Love you, and hope all is well!", Anna texted. Harriet could think of something to keep her busy until then. A visit to the sauna. And perhaps message Arden back.

Now that would certainly take her mind off things.

The biting wind whipped at Harriet's cheeks, stinging them as she hurried towards the promise of the sauna. But even before she could feel the welcome heat, Rebecca had intercepted her, blocking her path with a frown etched deep into her face.

"Harriet," Rebecca began her voice a low rumble that seemed to vibrate with unspoken tension. "You know all these memories are coming back now that you are here."

It wasn't a question. It was an accusation, delivered in a tone that resonated with the echoes of shared history and, Harriet suspected, simmering resentment. Pleasant memories? Far from it. This place was a repository of the ghosts Harriet had desperately tried to outrun.

Harriet tightened her grip on the towel clutched in her hand. "I just came for a few days of peace."

Rebecca scoffed. "Peace? Here? That's rich."

Harriet didn't want to remember much of her childhood. It was a tangled mess of shadows and anxieties, a landscape she preferred to keep buried. But Rebecca was relentless, determined to excavate every painful detail.

"Come inside for a bit," Rebecca commanded, turning without waiting for an answer. "The sauna can wait."

Harriet sighed, defeated. She knew arguing would be futile. Inside, Rebecca steered her to the worn sofa, the same one they'd sat on countless times, the same one that smelled faintly of woodsmoke and unsaid things. Rebecca switched on the television, the flickering light casting dancing shadows on the walls. Harriet stared blankly at the screen, the mindless chatter of the show doing nothing to distract her.

Her mind, against her will, began to wander. It drifted back, further back, to a time when her father was still alive. Harriet remembered the tension that hung in the air, thick and suffocating, the constant feeling of walking on eggshells.

Memories, dark and unwelcome, surfaced: her father's sharp words, her mother's averted gaze, the unspoken understanding that certain behaviors were not to be questioned. These were the memories she had tried so hard to suppress, memories that could perhaps explain why she had ended up with Monster.

Maybe she had felt, deep down, that she had to put up with it. Maybe she had learned, in her formative years, that this was just the way things were: that women were supposed to endure, to be silent, to absorb the pain. Maybe she had subconsciously chosen a partner who mirrored the dynamics of her childhood, a twisted sense of familiarity.

The television blared, but Harriet didn't hear it. She was lost in the labyrinth of her past, trying to untangle the threads of cause and effect, trying to understand how she had ended up where she was.

Finally, Rebecca turned off the television with a snap. The silence that followed was heavy, pregnant with unspoken questions.

"Why did you even come here?" Rebecca asked, her voice laced with a hint of accusation.

The question hung in the air, a challenge. Harriet looked at her, her face etched with worry and a lifetime of painful history, and suddenly she didn't know the answer. Was she here to find peace? Or was she here to confront the demon she had been running from?

Chapter 9

Arctic Circle, September 1989

The air inside the house smelled of pine, smoke, and something heavier; fear, though Harriet didn't know how to name it yet. Dinner was spread out on the table: moose meat, steaming vegetables, and thick soups. Her father ate slowly, deliberately, praising each bite in a booming voice that didn't match his greedy, sharp eyes. Her mother smiled, hands trembling slightly as she poured wine, her gaze flicking toward Harriet with something unspoken and tense.

Harriet, ten, stayed still. She noticed everything: the scraps of vegetables left untouched, the half-empty jar of cranberry sauce, the way her father's plate gleamed clean while her portion sat barely touched. She ate slowly, savoring the food, noticing textures and flavors he ignored. The room was quiet, but the silence pressed against her like a weight, coiling tight in her chest.

Then the tension broke. A plate crashed into the wall. Fists flew. Her mother fell. Blood spattered, bright and shocking against the pale walls. Harriet froze, throat tight, unable to scream. She watched, knowing the rhythm of violence she'd learned too early: the rising anger, the snap of a neck, the fall of a body.

Her mother tried to rise, staggering to the bathroom. Harriet saw her gently wipe her face, the bruises forming shapes she didn't know how to name. Every movement, every sound, echoed in Harriet's small body. She felt heat climb her arms, fear and anger twisting together, her fists clenching as if they could fight the world for her.

She pressed herself against the wall, ears straining for each step, each exhale. When the front door clicked, she flinched. Her father returned, smelling of liquor and control, eyes cold. Her mother kept busy with laundry, pretending nothing had happened. Harriet's gaze caught the floor, the neat shirts, the ordinary life that barely covered the chaos.

She remembered the voice in her head: *"Not a word. To anyone."* She nodded, tears burning, staring at herself in the hallway mirror. The reflection was tense, small, furious, scared, but alive. She was the child who survived.

Later, alone in bed, she prayed, not the soft, public prayers of her grandmother, but one of her own making. She begged to survive, to keep fear at bay, clutching her tattered pink bunny, burying her face in its soft fabric. Sleep came in fragments, haunted by the echo of shattering glass and fists. When morning light spilled through the blinds, she dressed carefully, masking the chaos in her chest, stepping into the world again. Outside, the wind was cold, the woods indifferent. Inside, the memory of that night had settled into her body, a melody of terror she would carry forever.

Chapter 10

Arctic Circle/ New York, February 2023

As Love, I drifted, ethereal and unseen as usual, sometimes a rabbit on the grass, sometimes just here above, and now above Harriet's bedroom in the cabin. The scene was stark: an open suitcase on the floor, promising departure, not that she had just arrived. The room was cloaked in quiet darkness, the blinds drawn back to reveal the pinpricks of distant stars in the inky canvas of the night. A melancholic beauty hung in the air, underscored by the unspoken weight of an impending change.

Then, a notification flared on her phone, a tiny beacon in the dimness, and the melody of the night shifted and became something more complex and undeniably charged.

I felt a twinge of unease, a hesitation, the familiar tug of morality that I, as Love, am often forced to ignore. My purpose is to witness, to understand, not to judge. But as I saw Harriet slowly, almost reverently, reach inside her knickers while simultaneously holding her phone, I was acutely aware that I was intruding on something profoundly intimate. Overhead, the night sky erupted in a breathtaking display of vibrant green Northern Lights, a cosmic ballet of light and energy. But Harriet was oblivious, her focus entirely inward, consumed by the glow of the screen in her hand.

I zoomed in, my very essence drawn to the electronic dance. The screen illuminated her face, painting it with flickers of anticipation and a raw, almost desperate, desire. She was gasping softly, her hand moving with a rhythm that mimicked the pulsing aurora above.

Simultaneously, in New York, in a sleek, minimalist city apartment, Arden was sitting on a black couch. A small pillow propped him up, and he stroked his erect penis with a slow, deliberate rhythm. The simplicity of the scene, the stark contrast to Harriet's hidden touch, somehow fueled the desire pouring off her. She came, a quick, sharp wave of release that mirrored the ephemeral flash of the Northern Lights, a silent explosion witnessed only by the stars and me.

Then came the words, etched in glowing pixels.

Arden typed: "Mmm… yes, I want your vagina to take the exact shape of me while I'm inside." I narrowed my eyes, forcing myself to focus, to understand. I had to see the rest.

The message continued: "I want to push myself deep and release once… only to soon become erect again and start pumping inside you while feeling the load I just left inside you."

Harriet, still flushed, typed back, her fingers flying across the screen: "I think I'll be gasping for air at this point…"

A beat of silence, punctuated only by the hum of the cold air and the rustle of Harriet's sheets. Then, another message from Harriet: "Are you going to tell me when I get to come? Release me…"

Arden's response was almost a taunt, laced with an intoxicating power: "Do my words have that much power over you that when I say you can release?" I could almost see the self-satisfied smile playing on his lips as he typed.

Harriet's reply was immediate, desperate: "Yes, only then I can."

The conversation continued, escalating the tension, painting a picture of controlled release and fervent submission. "Eye contact and then telling you when I am ready to have *you* orgasm. Or more like whisper it in your ear?" Arden asked.

Harriet's breath quickened, the words a visible force in her small room. "Both, keep me going, deep, intense, multiple… whisper in my ear, and eye contact when you tell me, and I wrap my legs around you."

For a heartbeat, both sides erupted into a distant, dreamlike ecstasy. Arden leaned his head back against the couch, his eyes closed, lost in the image. Harriet was panting, her body trembling with anticipation. I focused on Arden, a compulsion pulling me towards him. For the first time, he got up from the couch, pacing restlessly.

Then, Harriet typed a single, shattering word: *"Husband...?"*

The word hung in the air, heavy with unspoken questions, regrets, and the precarious balance of a life teetering on the edge. I needed to know what was happening in New York. A noise, faint but distinct, came from his hallway. The sound of a door opening, perhaps. The sound of another presence.

Fear, a cold, invasive tendril, coiled around me. Fear that I had misjudged, that I had allowed this to escalate too far. Fear that my presence, my constant observation, had somehow influenced this unfolding tragedy. *If I messed things up again...*

Harriet thought her internet had gone down and kept trying to log back in. Suddenly, Arden reappeared: " I need sleep. Video tomorrow?"

"Sure, let's see tomorrow", Harriet added a kiss emoji.

It was close to 2 am, and Anna and the police detective, Emma, would be calling her soon. Despite everything, the world felt a little lighter again for Harriet.

I wasn't so sure about Arden now. I didn't expect him to be perfect, but maybe I rushed into things again in the name of Love.

Chapter 11

Arctic Circle, February 2023

Harriet scrolled through Instagram, the cool glass of her phone doing little to soothe the rising heat in her cheeks. She knew she shouldn't. She knew it was a form of self-torture. But Monster's account was still public, a pile of curated lies she couldn't resist peering into. A knot tightened in her throat as she clicked on his stories.

Then, the image. He was holding a woman, a large woman with dark hair, in an airport. Someone had tagged them both, a casual digital breadcrumb that shattered Harriet's world into a million jagged pieces. So, this was the "other woman."

The one he had spoken about at the end. The words that went right above her, when he had violated her. Not a friend he was visiting, not a work colleague, not any of the endless pretexts he'd spun for a long time.

Her hands trembled, the phone nearly slipping from her grasp. Manipulation, she realized, was his second language. He'd built a fortress of lies, brick by brick, and she, blinded by... by what? Hope? Naivety? … had willingly walked inside. He had been with her, then back to her, and then violated her. The realization struck her with the force of a physical blow. He wasn't just a liar; he was deeply, disturbingly unwell.

Harriet still had the messages. The chilling instructions: scenarios she was meant to follow if he arranged for her to be with another man. He would be watching, he'd insisted. No kissing. Just… submission. The shocking memory so vividly recalled curdled in her stomach. She bolted to the bathroom, the bile rising in her throat.

As her cold hands gripped the porcelain rim of the toilet bowl, her breathing shallowed, then intensified. The need for air felt desperate, a primal instinct battling the waves of nausea.

She remembered Fiji. The sapphire water, the blinding sun, and the growing panic as she struggled to keep up with Monster on a dive. She wasn't a strong swimmer. The diving instructor, a woman with sun-weathered skin and knowing eyes, had seen that something was wrong. She'd swam Harriet away from Monster and guided her back to the boat as Harriet gasped for air. But she had to return to the hotel room with Monster. And she woke again, with him on top of her. The memory of the pink flowers on the island caught her eye. She remembered staring at the flowers, standing tall, beautiful, unbothered.

Sitting on the cold bathroom floor, Harriet felt like she was descending into the dark abyss of the ocean, staying there as long as she needed Monster to float away from the distance. He was there, everywhere.

Why? The question echoed in her head, a relentless, tormenting refrain. The diving instructor, a stranger, had sensed something was deeply wrong. Why couldn't *she* see it enough to escape?

The truth was brutal. Even when Monster's words were lies, woven with cunning and deceit, a part of her still looked at him with… desire. No. Never. With *hope*. She hoped that there would be something better. That he would become the man she had somehow imagined him to be. She waited for him to change, to become the man of her imagination, believing against all evidence that things would eventually get better.

Why did she let him treat her so brutally? Why did she allow him to chip away at her self-worth until she felt like nothing, a hollow shell filled with his toxic narratives?

Now, the large woman at the airport. The final, damning piece of the puzzle. Harriet suddenly wanted to reach back through time, grab her younger self by the shoulders, and scream, *"Imagine being involved in..."*

Imagine being involved in something beautiful. Imagine being involved in a relationship built on trust, respect, and genuine affection. Imagine a love that builds you up instead of tearing you down. Imagine a life where you are valued and cherished for who you are, not manipulated into someone else's twisted fantasy.

Imagine being involved in something that brings you joy, peace, and a profound sense of self-worth. Imagine choosing yourself, your well-being, and your happiness above all else.

Harriet swallowed hard. It was too late for that version of herself. But she could choose now. She could build a new life. A life free from the shadow of Monster and all his lies. A life where she was the architect of her happiness, the captain of her ship. The pink flowers of Fiji, standing tall and beautiful, never became a symbol of her renewed strength. She now wished they had, and she would have *seen it all back then.*

When she questioned all this, why did she let him treat her this way, make her into a worthless nothing?

And now the large woman at the airport?

I pushed this thought into Harriet's mind, loud and clear:

Imagine being involved in breaking up a family...which essentially this woman was doing. But then realize that the person you were cheating with was a complete asshole, abuser, narcissistic liar. Harriet, it is "finders' keepers".

And that woman at the airport may have thought she was getting Prince Charming, but ended up with King Henry VIII.

Finder's keeper, Harriet.

Harriet threw the phone on the bed, angry. *"He can fuck off. And fuck off again to Mountain fuck off, and keep going. Cunt."*

I would rather see Harriet's anger than fear. I wanted her to bounce back and show no mercy, but she needed to find that spark of life again.

Chapter 12

❦

Arctic Circle, February 2023

Gleaming eyes stared back at Harriet from the path next to the cabin. She took a step back and glitched her eyes, blinking rapidly, trying to make sense of the apparition in the fading light. She could see the outline of an animal, a long-eared silhouette against the snow-dusted trees. It kept staring at her, peacefully standing on its hind legs, a creature of pure white against the darkening forest. As she took a step forward, the rabbit felt completely safe, as if she posed no threat at all.

They both felt the same comfort breathing in the cold air, feeling alive in the stillness of the woods. It was a shared moment of peace; a connection forged in the silent language of nature. Then, the rabbit leaped forward, a sudden burst of movement that startled her. It felt purposeful, like it wanted to tell her something, its nose twitching, its eyes bright with intent.

A single push from the rabbit's back legs left only a shadow behind as it darted away, disappearing into the undergrowth. And in that fleeting moment, she understood. An unspoken message, a silent urging to leave, to escape.

She walked back to the cabin, the creaky old door slamming behind her with a reverberating thud, her winter boots making a loud noise on the wooden floors, shattering the illusion of peace. Harriet was tired, bone-tired, from the all-night phone calls with the Detective. She had counted every violent attack, every instance of sexual assault, and how she hadn't fought back. How she froze, how she complied. She let him abuse her, in the name of "Love," a twisted, sickening parody of the word.

She picked up her lacy underwear off the floor, a flimsy reminder of a life she no longer recognized. She gathered her skincare, the potions, and lotions she'd meticulously applied in a vain attempt to maintain a facade and threw it all in the open suitcase that she had left open since she first arrived there, a promise of escape hanging in the air.

She waited for the fire to die in the fireplace, the embers glowing like angry eyes, before playing Arden's video in the dark. It was a shallow, fleeting pleasure, a temporary escape from the gnawing reality of her life. It distracted her, and for one orgasmic moment, she forgot about everything else, forgot about the detective, forgot about the rabbit.

As the video ended, the silence of the cabin enveloped her once more, heavy and suffocating. The shadows danced across the walls, and the fire crackled ominously, echoing the turmoil within her. Harriet felt the weight of her choices pressing down on her chest, a reminder of the life she had escaped.

The rabbit's eyes flashed in her mind, a beacon of innocence amidst her chaos. *What did it want to tell her?* The thought gnawed at her, intertwining with the memories of the detective's voice, smooth and persuasive. She had been so lost, so desperate for love, that she had ignored the signs, the warnings that had come in the form of bruises and broken promises.

As the darkness deepened outside, Harriet felt a surge of determination. She couldn't let fear dictate her life any longer. She had come to the Arctic Circle seeking solace, but instead, she found herself trapped in a prison of her own making. The rabbit's message echoed in her mind, urging her to act, to break free from the chains that bound her.

With renewed resolve, she rummaged through her suitcase, pulling out the essentials. She grabbed her warmest clothes, a sturdy jacket, and her boots, the ones that would carry her away from this nightmare. The cabin felt like a tomb, suffocating and cold, and she could no longer bear its weight.

As she stepped outside, the crisp air hit her like a slap, invigorating and alive. The moon hung low in the sky, casting a silver glow over the snow, illuminating the path ahead. She took a deep breath, inhaling the freedom that awaited her. The woods were no longer a place of isolation; they were a sanctuary, a refuge from the darkness that had consumed her.

With each step, she felt the rabbit's spirit guiding her, leading her away from the memories that haunted her. The trees whispered secrets of resilience and strength, and Harriet embraced them, letting go of the past that had held her captive for too long.

As she ventured deeper into the woods, the shadows receded, and the weight of her burdens began to lift slowly. She didn't want to be a victim; she was a survivor, reclaiming her life one step at a time. The rabbit had shown her the way, as if ready to follow its path toward freedom.

She had left her phone behind, a decision that felt both liberating and reckless, but the solitude was too intoxicating.

The trees loomed like silent sentinels, their branches swaying gently in the wind, casting eerie shadows that danced along the ground.

She paused, the silence pressing in around her. It was too quiet. The usual sounds of the forest had vanished. A shiver ran down her spine, and she turned to head back, her heart racing. The cabin was only a short distance away, but the darkness seemed to stretch on endlessly.

Suddenly, a rustle broke the silence, sharp and jarring. She froze, her instincts kicking in. The sound came from the underbrush, and her mind raced with possibilities. Was it just a rabbit again? She squinted into the shadows, straining to see through the veil of darkness.

"Hello?" she called, her voice trembling slightly. The only response was the wind, howling like a distant wolf. Panic surged within her as she took a step back, her feet crunching on the snow. She needed to get back to the cabin, to the safety of its walls. She hated the familiar feeling of Fear. No matter how hard she tried, Fear followed her. Everywhere, it seemed.

Chapter 13

Arctic Circle, February 2023

Douglas had made flower deliveries all day, a mundane task that felt increasingly hollow. He went home and put on a TV show, a mindless sitcom that failed to hold his attention. He drank a bit of whiskey, the burn doing little to soothe the unease that had settled in his gut. He couldn't get Harriet out of his mind, her face a haunting image in his thoughts. He went for a drive, a restless urge pulling him towards her.

It was snowing when he jumped in his old black Jeep Cherokee. Douglas certainly hadn't counted on such a sudden downpour of heavy snow. His windshield wipers struggled to keep up, blurring the world into a swirling white chaos.

He kept driving along the quiet forest road, the isolation amplifying the inner turmoil that churned within him. And then, as quickly as it had arrived, the heavy snow disappeared. The road cleared, the window wipers slowly returned to a languid pace, and Douglas felt sadness as he approached Harriet's cabin.

Douglas believed he shared a private line with God. A low, commanding voice often visited him in his dreams, assuring and insistent. Recently, it had told him that Harriet must believe that she needed guidance. The voice never argued, never explained. It simply repeated one word: *Believe.*

Douglas had something else to tell her, too, something heavier, a truth that would break her heart.

Harriet wanted to return to the sauna one last time and stare at the steaming rocks. The thought of the enveloping heat, the cleansing sweat, was appealing. But the mean words that Monster had repeated in her ear for years made her pick up her trainers instead. *"You let yourself go." "Look at you, you put on weight!" "Stop snacking!"* The insidious voice, a cruel echo of her ex-husband, still held her captive.

It wasn't snowing anymore, but she knew she had to hurry and not wait around for another sudden downpour if she wanted some exercise tonight. She pulled her thick blonde hair into a ponytail, knowing that the humidity indoors, followed by the cold snow, would spell disaster for her hair. The roads near the cabin felt safe at night, usually deserted. She thought about the rabbit, staring at her on the road, its eyes reflecting the moonlight. A pleasant encounter. But now she felt different.

She got a funny feeling someone was watching her, and this was not a rabbit. The hair on her neck stood out as she glanced back.

A black Jeep Cherokee was parked on the curb, but Harriet couldn't make out if someone was in the driver's seat. She kept walking, her stomach churning with a nervous energy that had nothing to do with exercise. She nervously dialed Rebecca, and with a quiet voice, she left a short voicemail. "It's Harriet," she tried to sound casual, projecting an air of normalcy she didn't feel. Her head was screaming, *"Keep checking back, be alert, and go home."*

She tried to make out the license plate of the Cherokee. The dark clouds closed in, swallowing the last sliver of the moon, as her jaw dropped. She suddenly saw a man's face through the windscreen, illuminated by the faint glow of his phone, staring back at her. His smile widened, a slow, deliberate, unsettling grin, bringing his whole face into play until he slowly slinked down on the car seat, deliberately disappearing as their eyes met.

For a moment, they both stopped and watched one another. Harriet felt panic rising in her throat, a suffocating wave that paralyzed her feet. She couldn't move forward, couldn't breathe properly. Like the insidious game had been set in motion, the game Monster used to play.

Douglas gripped the wheel, his mind circling the same thought, steady as prayer.

She must hear it. She must know.

Harriet needed to leave. Not only was Rebecca drinking again, a spiral she blamed herself for, but she had a stalker. The Fear had found her again, the same icy grip that had tightened around her years ago, leaving her breathless and trapped.

She ran back to the flower shop, the scent of pine and damp earth filling her lungs as she fled.

Opening the flower shop door, not even the strongest smell of peonies, Rebecca's favorite, could hide the fact that Rebecca was drinking again. The cloying sweetness of the blossoms was overwhelmed by the stale reek of cheap bourbon. Rebecca sat hunched behind the counter, a half-empty bottle nestled beside her elbow. Her eyes were red-rimmed and unfocused.

"What's the real reason you are here?" Rebecca slurred, her voice thick with alcohol. "Go back." The words were laced with a venom Harriet knew all too well. It was a familiar refrain, a bitter song of resentment and self-loathing sung on a loop.

Harriet's heart sank. She had hoped for sanctuary, for a comforting presence. Instead, she was met with hostility and blame. She stammered, "I… I just needed to see you."

Rebecca laughed, a harsh, brittle sound. "See me? Or use me? Go back, Harriet. You can only blame yourself for staying with him." The words hung in the air, heavy and accusatory. The flower shop, once a refuge, suddenly felt like a prison. The smell of peonies, once comforting, now suffocated her. She was alone, more alone than she had ever been. The Fear had not only found her, but it had also driven a wedge between her and the only person she thought she could trust. And somewhere out there, in the darkness, Douglas was watching, waiting to tell her *something important.*

Inside, Rebecca stood framed in the doorway, a frail silhouette against the warm, artificial light. "I will order the taxi," Harriet said, placing the cabin key on the table, breaking the silence. She didn't think she would see her ever again. There was no point. Rebecca didn't love her as a child and certainly didn't care for her now. There were a lot of mothers like this in the world, but it wasn't often discussed. I guess people would rather not talk about it.

"Tell that weirdo delivery driver of yours that he was stalking me for nothing." Harriet felt a sudden shiver down her spine that had nothing to do with the cold. She never closed the blinds in the cabin. She had been too occupied staring at her phone and Arden.

"Wait, I have something for you," Rebecca almost ran after her, a surprising burst of energy in her aging frame. Harriet had a sudden glimmer of hope in her eyes, which she quickly suppressed. "What is it m…mot…" she almost said "Mother".

Rebecca took Harriet's right hand, her touch surprisingly cold. She placed a Kinder egg in her palm. "Thank you, very kind of you," Harriet said, managing a half-smile. Rebecca must have lost her mind. She couldn't wait to leave.

The biting wind whipped at Harriet's face as she dragged her suitcase through the snow. *"I only said what needed to be said,"* she muttered, the words a fragile shield against the storm within. Harriet bit her lip and noticed her mobile phone battery was getting low again. She risked a glance back at the cabin, a knot of dread tightening in her stomach.

As Harriet pushed through with her suitcase in the heavy snow, her phone vibrated in her pocket. "Husband" flashed on the screen. She had been engaging with Arden for more than 24 hours. With a surge of defiance, a black leather glove between her teeth, she dropped the phone in the snow. She felt wet in her underwear as soon as she was holding her phone again, as if she was holding *him.*

The teasing, when he told her to hold off. When he whispered to her ear and let her come, she felt like she was tripping, her thoughts getting beyond inappropriate.

"What would you do if I were in front of you?" Arden had asked. She could feel his substance, his deeper intelligence reaching across the space between them. Her loneliness seemed already dissolving, replaced by the certainty that his self-confidence would etch itself onto her heart. He was sharp, magnetic, irresistible, and what she felt went beyond excitement. It was a raw need to pull him close, tear his clothes away, and then...

She forced her mind away from the precipice of those thoughts, the image too potent, too dangerous. Focus, she told herself. Just focus on getting to the taxi.

The Kinder egg felt heavy in her gloved hand. A childish offering after years of neglect. A hollow gesture. But as she trudged on, the wind biting harder, she couldn't bring herself to throw it away. Maybe, just maybe, there was something inside worth holding onto, even if it was just a cheap plastic toy.

The snow started falling again, fat, wet flakes blurring the already hazy twilight. Standing out in the cold, waiting for the taxi to arrive, her mind was filled with images of Arden's beautiful cock, her wearing his sweatshirt, and deep-throating his big cock, without gagging, just letting it go so deep in her throat, she felt she was swallowing his soul. She wiped the phone screen dry with the cuff of her coat.

So, what would she do if he were standing in front of her right now? He wasn't. But the thought, the mere possibility, sent a shiver through her that had nothing to do with the temperature. She felt the primal need to pull him close, rip his clothes off, and moan louder than Meg Ryan in When Harry Met Sally.

"I would...." she started to type.

She felt like she could completely surrender to him and let him take her in any way. The power he held over her was a big turn-on. Or maybe he wanted her to be on top, in control of how deep and fast she would be penetrated. The possibilities were endless and intoxicating.

She gasped and continued to type, "...grant you three wishes. Please exploit it to the full means," she was hoping he would make full use of her message. The audacity of it thrilled her. She wanted him to understand the depths of her desire, the willingness to relinquish control. She wanted him to know that she was his for the taking, in almost whatever way he desired.

The message sat there, gleaming on the screen, awaiting his response. She chewed on her lip, picturing his face, trying to imagine what he would say. A smirk, perhaps? A suggestive reply? Or maybe just a simple, "Tell me your wishes." Her suitcase stood behind her, a silent testament to the life she was living now.

She waited. The snow intensified, swirling around her like a silent, relentless dance. The taxi was approaching, but she ignored it, her focus locked on the glowing rectangle in her hand. She refreshed the screen again and again.

No reply.

Minutes stretched into an eternity. The taxi driver honked impatiently in the distance. Still nothing.

Frustration bubbled within her, a bitter counterpart to the earlier anticipation. *Had she misread the signals? Was her message too forward, too desperate? Had she scared him off?*

She kicked the snow around her to make a way and kept going towards the approaching taxi. The tires crunched on the freshly fallen snow as the car pulled up beside her. She heaved her suitcase into the trunk, the metallic clang echoing in the quiet air.

She didn't look back at the cabin. As the taxi sped down the snowy road, she finally put the phone away, the unanswered message a weight in her pocket. The image of him, of their potential, remained in her mind, a tantalizing ghost in the falling snow.

The snowstorm followed her all the way to the airport. Harriet sat rigid, watching the snow blur past the windows, her phone a dead weight in her pocket. The unanswered message to Arden burned like an ember she couldn't stamp out. She forced her eyes forward, away from the rearview mirror, away from the feeling that something, someone, was still behind her. Douglas hadn't left. She could feel it. And she was right. He was still out there, the black Jeep crawling along the same road, headlights dimmed against the curtain of snow. He kept his hands steady on the wheel, his mind repeating the same thought over and over, like a prayer.

She has to hear it. She has to know.

For days, the voice had pressed him on, commanding, insistent. He had tried to ignore it, tried to drown it with work, with whiskey, with meaningless television. But it always came back, whispering the same truth. Harriet could not go on in ignorance.

It wasn't a message he wanted to deliver. It was one he had to. But as Harriet's taxi took a turn to the airport, he knew it had to wait.

Chapter 14

Up in the Air, March 2023

Harriet walked around at the airport, the sterile air a stark contrast to the suffocating atmosphere she'd just left behind. She messaged Anna, telling her she was on her way back. The flight had been delayed two hours, but soon she would be wheels up.

"You can stay in my room. I can stay at my sister's," Anna typed back almost immediately.

"Or I just chill on the couch. Doesn't matter," Harriet replied, trying to sound nonchalant. The last thing she wanted was to inconvenience Anna, her lifeline in this mess. "Sorry, it didn't work out with your mum." The message popped up a minute later.

"It was always like that," Harriet responded, a familiar ache settling in her chest. The visit had been a disaster, a reiteration of everything she was trying to escape.

She wandered, trying to kill time. The airport tax-free store, a haven of overpriced perfumes and gaudy jewelry, caught her eye. In the window, an amethyst necklace looked ordinary, almost lost midst the glittering diamonds and polished gold. But then a shaft of sunlight hit it, and the purple hues exploded, shifting from a milky white to a vibrant pink, a deep blue, and finally settling into a calming lavender.

"Find the extraordinary from the ordinary," she used to tell herself when she wrote poems. A long time ago, before the Monster, before the suffocating routine. Now, she felt like she was living in a parallel existence, changing colors like the amethyst, trying to blend in, to survive.

She examined the purple hues, thinking about their associations: healing, wisdom, air, and intuition. She imagined Anna wearing it. Anna, who had helped her pack, who had listened to her cry for hours on end, was letting her stay in her house without a second thought. The Monster left her homeless and broken. Anna was helping her rebuild her little life again.

The sound of copper bells hanging on the storefront door made a gentle noise as she walked in. The scent of expensive leather and synthetic fragrances filled the air. She tried to focus, but the Monster's presence still clung to her, a phantom limb she couldn't shake. She imagined him walking straight into a jewelry display and knocking it down, scattering diamonds like unwanted confetti, but not picking up the items. Loudly chewing. Harriet wanted to scream.

She had hated every sound he had made. The way he was chewing, his mouth always slightly open, the way he snored loudly at night, his slow, ragged breathing, and making her wait for him as he walked slowly to the bathroom and blew his nose, a sound that resonated through the entire apartment.

Every day, he made her blood boil by simply being around her. She always knew she needed to leave him, but it wasn't as easy. Every time she tried, something came up: a fabricated illness, a feigned apology, a threat veiled in concern. Now she started to realize that she had Stockholm Syndrome. He made her feel the same way as her mother, like her life wasn't hers to control. Her life was an illusion, a performance for their benefit.

Harriet picked up the amethyst necklace, its smooth surface cool against her palm. She walked to the register, the bells jingling again as she moved.

"Great choice," the salesgirl said, her voice a practiced chirping. Harriet's thoughts raced loudly through her head, a frantic cacophony.

"Sorry?" Her hand hovered nervously over the card reader. She tapped her credit card, still linked to the Monster's account. He would still be following her statements, scrutinizing every purchase, and she wanted him to think she wasn't coming back, that she was moving on.

"I..." she stammered, her throat suddenly dry. "I just... I like the color." She forced a smile, trying to appear nonchalant.

The salesgirl didn't seem to notice her distress, cheerfully bagging the necklace. As Harriet turned away, the amethyst felt heavier in her hand, a symbol of hope in the face of a long and uncertain journey.

"Don't!" Harriet turned around and snapped, feeling Monster's eyes on the back of her neck, a possessive man never leaving her out of sight. Even now, weeks after she'd finally escaped him, the phantom weight of his gaze lingered.

"Oh, I'm so sorry! I thought you were someone else..." she stammered, returning to reality. She looked away from the elderly woman lining up right behind her, mortified by her outburst. *Post-traumatic stress disorder. Breathe.*

She glanced down at the amethyst she was holding, its purple hues shining brightly underneath the overbearing store lights. She still smelled his cologne, too overpowering, a constant, unwelcome reminder as she imagined them walking out of the store together. He was nobody to her now.

A painful memory surfaced. The time they argued in the car. A screaming match fueled by his paranoia and her simmering resentment. She'd gotten out, the finality of the gesture a desperate attempt to regain some control. He must have waited for the door to slam, a childish power play. Instead, she left her car door wide open, forcing him to get out and close it himself, like a taxi driver. It was a small act of rebellion, but she knew it would be enough.

She knew he would get angry, and she was going to get another black eye. Another carefully crafted lie to her co-workers, another wave of shame and self-loathing.

Her phone flashed, pulling her back from the suffocating darkness of the past. *Arden.*

A warmth spread through her chest, a welcome antidote to the chill that had settled deep within her.

'Hey wifey,' he'd texted.

"About to board a plane. I will be flying right past you," Harriet typed, a little smile tugging at the corners of her mouth.

"Drop down to me in a little parachute," he typed back instantly.

The absurdity of the image, the utter lack of logic, and the sheer, unadulterated silliness of it made Harriet's heart feel like it wanted something in a completely irrational way. Right now. The painful and revolting flashbacks of Monster were momentarily banished. Move over, Fear. It's a turn for Love, and Harriet deserves it.

She remembered all their late-night conversations in the past week, fueled by playful banter. She'd asked him a hypothetical question, one that had lingered in her mind long after she'd hit send. Now, he was finally answering her question:

"You have three wishes that I grant you. What are they?"

A thrill shot through her. She already knew what she wanted. She'd replayed this scenario in her head a thousand times.

Arden: "1) Be able to teleport you into my apartment tonight so that when I get home, you are there waiting for me in bed, preferably bent over."

His fingers flew across the keyboard, the words pouring out of him.

"You hear the front door open, and hear my footsteps get louder. You don't move, and you're facing away from the bedroom door, you feel my hands on your hips, and at that point, I tell you to turn your face to look at me. Simultaneously, I drive my hard cock into you."

Her breath caught in her throat. A blush crept up her neck. He was brazen, unrestrained. And it felt incredibly good.

"Your wish is granted," Harriet typed back with fast fingers.

The response was immediate.

"2) would be to allow me to use you almost as a constant vehicle for my cum. Each ejaculation would occur inside your pussy. "

Arden sent a smile emoji.

"You are my personal sperm bank."

"You have one wish left," Harriet typed as everyone had already boarded the plane.

"I'll get to that later," Arden typed, and Harriet put her phone on airplane mode.

On the plane, she couldn't stop thinking about him and all the possibilities. As the plane flew high above the clouds, she thought about his voice, his touch, and all the positions they could be in. She wanted to taste him, smell him, and see if he was real.

Mr. New York, one day, I will drop down to you in a little parachute. She felt an incredible warmth strike through her heart, and inside of her, she already felt his warm cum circulating.

Chapter 15

Sydney Airport, March 2023

Harriet's eyes lingered on the WhatsApp message, the words glowing softly against the screen: *"Drop down to me on a little parachute."*

She'd already read it once, twice, but something about it held her, as though she could draw courage from Arden's playful charm. Lightness, adventure, he seemed to carry both, and somehow pass them to her.

She lifted her gaze to the plane window, clouds drifting beneath her like an endless sea, and warmth spread through her chest. Arden, with his salt-and-pepper hair, that mix of seasoned confidence and boyish arrogance, had brought color back into her life after years muted by shadows.

As the plane edged closer to the city she had fled, memories pressed in, Monster's voice, sharp with control, his demands echoing faintly in her mind. But she looked back at the message, let it anchor her. Arden's words cut through the ghosts, reminding her that this landing wasn't just a return.

The plane touched down smoothly on the runway, and as she stepped out into the balmy evening air, excitement thrummed through her veins. *She was free.*

She imagined spotting Arden waiting near the exit gate, a tall figure exuding confidence, his smile bright enough to rival the city lights surrounding them. Their eyes would meet; hers sparkled with hope and joy, while his held promise and intrigue.

"Hey there," he would call out playfully as he approached, "Did you drop here in a parachute?" She would laugh lightly, feeling lighter than she had in years, like she could float away into this new reality where love and laughter were possible. They would embrace for what would feel like an eternity; it would be a warm cocoon amidst the chaos of their surroundings.

Instead of Arden, or the comforting presence of Anna, she found herself facing Emma Stone, with sharp eyes and a granite jaw, a detective who radiated an aura of quiet competence.

"You were not meant to land yet," Emma stated, her voice devoid of warmth. Harriet's carefully constructed composure crumbled.

"Anna said you spoke, and it was okay?" she questioned, confusion clouding her features. The covert operation, the carefully orchestrated phone call to the man who had shattered her life, was now off the table. The weight of that realization pressed down on her.

Emma's explanation was curt and professional. "We didn't have time to file the paperwork. A court registrar needs to approve it."

The words hung heavy in the air, each syllable a hammer blow to Harriet's hope. The relief she'd felt at the operation's cancellation was swiftly replaced by a chilling dread.

Monster, a predator who had escaped justice for too long, would remain free. The evidence, the meticulously planned phone call that Emma was to record, the proof she needed to see him brought to justice, was not happening. All her planning, all her pain carefully channeled into a plan for retribution, had been for nothing. The thought was a bitter pill to swallow. The anxiety clawed at her, a desperate, suffocating feeling.

"I have a car waiting outside," Emma said, her voice still cold, yet with a hint of something else, maybe pity, maybe understanding. The words felt like a dismissal, a finality. Harriet, feeling utterly defeated, allowed herself to be led away, the weight of her failure pressing down on her.

Her passport felt heavy in her hands, a now-useless prop in the face of a reality far crueler and more unforgiving than the stamped pages inside, getting away from Monster, only having to return.

"What now?"

The fight, it seemed, was far from over, and now, the battle lines had shifted. She knew, with a chilling certainty, that Monster's victory was a reprieve. The hunt was far from over.

"I need to take you somewhere first, to get checked," Emma said, and Harriet's heart sank again, knowing where she needed to go.

Chapter 16

Sydney, April 2023

Harriet sat in the busy clinic, the fluorescent lights and white walls pressing down on her. She hated being here, hated the reason that had brought her to this waiting room. The male nurse asked why she was lining up, and Harriet's short, quiet answer almost made him tear up. He gave the usual sympathetic response: "I'm so sorry that happened to you." She felt numb; she had heard it too many times. He pointed out a few counseling slots.

"I'm okay," she said confidently, as if she walked calmly through a battlefield that had left her scarred but unshakable.

She looked down, thinking about how easily people might assume her trauma came from a stranger, not from the person who was supposed to protect her. A husband who had betrayed her. She scanned the waiting room: trendy, healthy-looking young men in bright clothes, chatting and smiling. *Imagine if this were the 1980s,* she thought. *We'd be sitting here, doomed, bruised, and scared, hiding from judgment and shame.*

Harriet was called in. A younger female doctor with striking blue eyes and dark hair waited in the room. The face mask didn't hide the warmth Harriet sensed in her gaze. She answered questions in more detail than she had planned. The months of putting this off had dulled some of the pain, but it was all there, lingering, waiting to be faced.

"I have no symptoms, but I need to make sure," Harriet said. The doctor nodded. "We'll do it for your peace of mind," she said gently, running through every test.

Needles pricked her arm. Instruments moved inside her body. She felt exposed, raw, but not broken. She was aware of herself in a way she hadn't allowed for years. Trauma had carved her, but it hadn't destroyed her. She felt alive, heart racing, blood rushing. *I'm not empty,* she realized. She could feel the strength in her own body, the capacity to endure, to survive.

When the procedure ended, Harriet sat alone behind the curtain, reflecting. She thought of Arden, of warmth and longing she hadn't allowed herself in years. She realized that life, painful, violent, unrelenting, had also left her with gifts: the ability to feel, to survive, to experience joy in its smallest forms.

"Everything is good," the doctor returned, interrupting her thoughts. Professional, gentle, reassuring. Harriet nodded, letting herself breathe, letting herself exist without fear for a moment. She thought of how the worst experiences of her life had carved her into someone capable of deep emotion, of profound survival. She could feel herself returning to life, slowly.

Later, on the way back to Anna's house, Harriet reflected on the years of abuse at the hands of Monster; the threats, the control, the physical and psychological torment. The black eyes, the manipulation, the forced compliance. She remembered the fear, the numbness, the ways she had survived by becoming invisible. She remembered the police questioning her years ago, the fragmented memories, the concussions, the blackouts. Some of the worst moments were gone, erased by survival itself.

She remembered the breaking point, the moment on the balcony, throwing a suitcase together in a rush, taking only random items. She boarded the plane, leaving sixteen years of hell behind. She drank wine in numbness, watching *American History X* on the plane screen, letting herself go through the motions of survival.

She arrived in the frozen landscape, cold biting through her layers, pain and fear threatening to overwhelm her. She hid in a remote cabin, facing her troubled mother and the ghost of everything she had endured. And then, Arden. Connection. A distraction from the flood of trauma, a small light in a world that had tried to snuff her out.

Could she tell him everything? Could anyone? Some parts might be too heavy, too dark. Yet she felt the possibility of light, of feeling again, as if the worst of life had handed her a gift: the ability to be fully, vividly alive.

Chapter 17

Bondi Beach police station, Sydney, April 2023

Emma's voice was gentle but persistent.

"We are still going to take another statement".

"Harriet, sometimes details slip through the cracks. Sometimes things you didn't think were important…turn out to be crucial. We're just trying to build the clearest picture possible. Can you tell me again about your relationship with him, with examples?"

Harriet took a long pause. She closed her eyes briefly.

"He… he was… charming, in the beginning. He swept me off my feet. You know, love bombing?"

"And later?" Emma asked.

"Later… it was… different. He… he had a temper. He'd get angry over the smallest things. A burnt dinner, a late phone call…traffic."

"Did that anger ever become physical, Harriet?"

Harriet flinched, pulling her arms closer to her body.

Emma waited patiently, giving her space.

"There were…so many incidents. Shoving. Yelling. He… he'd grab my arms. Hold me down, Harriet's voice trailed off.

" Did he ever hit you? We can stop if you need to. But these details matter. Even if they're painful. Think about anything that would help your case."

Harriet swallowed hard and looked up at Emma, her eyes filled with a mixture of fear and anger. She was about to talk, but stopped, lost in the labyrinth of her memories.

"They all started the same way. Like… like I was finally safe. And then… " She shivered, clutching her arms tighter. Emma reached across the table and placed a hand gently on Harriet's arm.

"Take your time, Harriet. We're here to listen. We're here to help. Just tell me what you remember".

Harriet looked at Emma's hand, then back up to her face.

"The memories… they're all a mess. A jumble of yelling, hands, and fear… I can't always separate them. I can't always remember what happened, or when. It's just… a feeling. A constant, horrible feeling".

The fluorescent lights of the interrogation room seemed harsher than usual. Harriet stared at the ceiling, the events of the day, the endless questions, the probing looks, swirling in her mind. She hadn't even cried, not really. Numbness had settled in, a thick, suffocating blanket. How many police statements had she given by now?

"Five statements already," she whispered to the shadows dancing on the wall. Five, beyond all her tears, constructed narratives, designed to protect what little was left of her sanity. But there was more. So much more.

The cracking. That godawful cracking. It had been a decade ago, yet the sound resonated in her bones, a constant, low hum of terror. She remembered lying there, tied to that chair in the garage, the air thick with the metallic tang of gasoline. He had stood over her, a dark silhouette against the dim light, calmly explaining how he would set the house ablaze.

Then, years later, the fragmented images of the accident. The red car, its broken seat belt a symbol of their crumbling lives. His lies. The rain. The blue Tesla was in front of them.

She squeezed her eyes shut, picturing the flashing emergency lights of that Tesla reflecting in the drenched asphalt.

In her mind, Harriet started to compose a scene.

Harriet shivered, the cold rain plastering her hair to her face. "Should have worn a thicker coat," she mumbled, the words catching in her throat. He stood beside the mangled car, a dark figure against the red glow of taillights, his face unreadable.

He didn't offer a hand. Didn't say a word. He just watched as she dragged herself out of the wreckage, the ground slick beneath her.

The memory shifted to a change of scene she remembered.

The cold snip of scissors against her skin. The blurry figure leaning over her. The relief was sharp and desperate as the ambulance doors swung open, revealing the promise of warmth and safety.

Writing. She had wanted to be a writer more than anything. Now, even the simple act of moving her fingers felt heavy, tainted by the events.

She remembered waking in the hospital, the sterile smell of antiseptic filling her nostrils. Her lower body was wrapped in bandages, a terrifying question mark hanging over her future. But she could feel her legs. A wave of gratitude, unexpected and fierce, washed over her.

Then, *the churro shop*. A silly memory, a lifetime ago, when she was a teenager. Crying over a boy, inconsolable. But not now. Now, facing this… this deliberate act of cruelty… she was dry-eyed. Hardened. Changed.

She closed her eyes tightly, biting back the scream that threatened to erupt. The Tesla. That flash of blue. And *him*, deliberately accelerating.

"Just one more thing," she breathed, the words barely audible. One more thing to add to the ever-growing list of his betrayals, his lies, his…

She finally found the strength to open her eyes. "Just one more thing for my statement." Her voice, though still a whisper, held a newfound steel.

Chapter 18

Bondi Beach police station, Sydney, April 2023

The mountain of files on Emma's desk was a grotesque monument to broken promises and brutal betrayals. Each file was a woman, a life fractured by the very person who swore to cherish them. The sheer volume was staggering, a digital tsunami of domestic violence cases all blurring together; Sarah, Maria, Chloe, each story a chilling echo of the others.

What had initially shaken Emma to her core wasn't just the violence itself, but the specific, insidious nature of it. The sexual violence. The cold, calculated violation is perpetrated under the guise of intimacy. Husbands, partners, and lovers, the supposed pillars of their lives, are turning into instruments of pain and degradation.

Aren't they meant to love and care for them? The thought echoed in her mind, a constant, nagging dissonance. It felt like a fundamental violation of the natural order, a perversion of the most sacred bonds.

She stared at the pile, at the epidemic laid bare in her hands. The reports detailed forced intercourse, marital rape, and control through sexual humiliation. The law, she realized with a growing sense of despair, was a broken shield, riddled with loopholes and outdated notions of marital rights. It protected the Monsters, not the victims. The system, rigged against them, allowed perpetrators to walk free, to re-offend, to break another woman.

Today's Monster was Mr. Hanson, nicknamed "Monster" within the precinct. He was a known quantity, a repeat offender with a history of violence against women. His former partner, Harriet, had finally found the courage to speak. Emma had been granted a precious hour to question him before he was released, and not even on bail.

He sat across from her in the sterile interrogation room, a picture of deceptive calm. His military uniform and carefully combed hair were a stark contrast to the bruises and scars Harriet had described. His cold blue eyes, the color of glacial ice, rarely met hers. They darted around the room, calculating and measuring. He was overly confident, a seasoned player of the game. Emma knew at once that he was practiced at manipulation, skilled in exploiting the weaknesses of the system.

"Mr. Hanson, can you explain the injuries your wife sustained?" Emma began, her voice even, professional.

"No comment," he replied, without a flicker of emotion.

Emma pressed on. "Harriet says you forced yourself on her, despite her saying no. She says you've been doing this for years."

He shifted in his chair, a barely perceptible movement of irritation. "She's full of shit." Another question. Another "no comment."

Emma tried a different tactic. She laid out the evidence as clearly as she could: photos of Harriet's bruises, torn clothing, and the doctor's report detailing the trauma.

His response was always the same: "No comment."

Or "She's just trying to get back at me." He was a master of deflection, of playing the victim. He knew that without overwhelming physical evidence or corroborating witnesses, it would be his word against hers. He understood the power imbalances ingrained in the system, the inherent biases that favored the man, the husband, the one with the clean record (on paper, at least). But Hanson did not have a clean record. He had been to prison as a young man at 20 years old. There were several charges in his file, fraud, road rage…Yet the military had stood by him all this time. It made sense, though; they wanted this caliber in their team. Angry and unpredictable, ready to fight if needed.

Emma felt a surge of frustration, a deep, visceral anger. She wanted to scream, to rattle him, to break through his carefully constructed facade. But she knew that wouldn't work. She had to stay calm, to remain professional, to fight fire with cold, hard facts.

"Mr. Hanson," she said, leaning forward, "your pattern of behavior is well documented. We have reports from previous neighbors and officers attending years before, all of whom made allegations of similar abuse. This isn't a one-off incident. This is a pattern of control, of violence, of sexual degradation."

He smirked. "Allegations. Just words. No proof."

His eyes finally met hers, a chilling glint of triumph in their depths. He knew he was winning. He knew the game.

The hour was almost up. Emma had one last card to play. She reached into her folder and pulled out a photograph. It was a picture of Harriet, taken shortly after the assault. Her face was swollen and bruised, her eyes filled with a haunting blend of fear and despair.

Emma slid the photo across the table. "Look at her, Mr. Hanson. Look at what you did." He glanced at the photo, his expression unchanged.

"She's full of shit," he repeated, his voice flat, devoid of any emotion.

The timer on the wall beeped. The interrogation was over. He would be released shortly, free to go home, perhaps to continue his reign of terror on his new partner.

Emma watched him leave, a knot of fury tightening in her chest. She knew this wasn't the end. It was just the beginning. She would find a way, somehow, to break through his defenses, to expose him for the Monster he was. She owed it to Harriet. She owed it to all the women whose stories filled the mountain of files on her desk. The law might not be on their side, but she was. And she wouldn't give up. The epidemic had to stop, one Monster at a time.

Chapter 19

Sydney, May 2023

Emma closed the thick file with a decisive thud, the sound echoing in the sterile interview room. "He won't hurt you again," she said, her gaze meeting Harriet's across the table. It was a practiced phrase, designed to offer comfort, but the hollow look in Harriet's eyes told Emma it was falling short.

Monster, that's what he was in Emma's mind, refused to be questioned. He'd invoked his right to silence, a frustrating but legal brick wall. At least the police had managed to secure a protection order for Harriet. Two years of legal space, however tenuous, between her and the… Monster.

Harriet's last words to the police, before Emma took over, echoed in the room. "He will do this to someone else." The raw fear in her voice had been palpable, a stark contrast to the numb acceptance that now glazed her face.

Emma sighed inwardly. "That is not your problem," she said, her tone deliberately neutral. She knew it sounded cold, but she couldn't afford to internalize every victim's pain. She dealt with Monsters like this every day. She'd crumble if she didn't maintain that distance.

She pushed a card across the table. "You got what most people don't get. You got a protection order for two years. Apply for Victims Support here. They can help you find counseling, housing, anything you need." She handed Harriet the card, its glossy surface reflecting the harsh fluorescent light, eager to finish her Friday shift and head home. The thought of a hot bath and a glass of wine beckoned.

Harriet took the card, her fingers trembling slightly. She looked at Emma, really looked at her, and Emma saw a flicker of something... resentment? Disappointment? It vanished as quickly as it appeared. Harriet mumbled a thank you and rose to leave.

Harriet slammed the heavy door behind her and walked outside. The humid air of the city felt suffocating, clinging to her skin like a shroud. The sounds of traffic and the laughter of passersby seemed discordant and mocking. Was she ever free from him? The protection order was just a piece of paper.

It wouldn't stop the fear that coiled in her stomach, the memory of his voice, the image of his eyes.

She walked, directionless, her feet carrying her through the maze of concrete and steel. The city, usually a source of anonymity and escape, now felt like a prison. Every shadow seemed to hold him, every face seemed to morph into his.

She stopped at a bar, its neon sign a beacon of artificial light in the gathering dusk. *"It's over,"* she whispered to herself, the words a desperate mantra.

She pushed open the door, and the noise and the smell of stale beer washed over her. She needed the numbness, the oblivion, the temporary escape from the reality that gnawed at her.

She ordered a drink, a double vodka, straight. As she swallowed the burning liquid, she closed her eyes. It was a small rebellion, a temporary act of defiance against the fear that threatened to consume her. *"How could Rebecca drink this daily?"* she wondered.

Her phone flashed with a message. It was from Anna.

"Don't forget my housewarming party tonight!"

So, life went on, and it was over with Monster.

But deep down, a chilling voice whispered a different truth. It was far from over. It had just begun. The protection order was a shield, but it was a shield against a ghost she carried inside herself. And that, she knew, was a battle she would have to fight alone.

Chapter 20

Sydney, May 2023

Anna's housewarming had started innocently enough, a few glasses of rosé circulating, followed by a shared joint that loosened tongues and painted smiles on faces. Now, the clock mercilessly ticked towards 2 AM, and the house throbbed with the collective buzz of its occupants. Everyone was high, sentences slurred, bodies bumping against walls for support. Harriet was a walking testament to jet lag and the relentless curiosity of Anna's friends.

Her head swam from the journey and the relentless *"What's it like in the Bondi police station?"* questions from drunk people. She'd been longing for a quiet night, a soft pillow, and the oblivion of sleep. And, in no circumstances did she want to discuss what happened at the police station.

Then, there was Nick. An almost fatherly figure in his demeanor, with a comforting, albeit slightly manipulative, charm. He found Harriet lurking in the back garden, a refuge from the swirling chaos inside. He surveyed the scene with a seasoned eye. *"Let's get out of here,"* he suggested in his voice, a low murmur against the muffled bass. Then, the caveat: *"But have another line before we go."* He produced a small bag from his pocket, presenting it on the garden table like an offering. "It'll help with the jet lag, trust me."

He'd put her on the guest list, he said, and he looked at her, convincing.

Harriet, caught between exhaustion and a flicker of something akin to rebellion, hesitated.

"I'm not sure…"

A girl, a stranger whose name swam somewhere in the hazy recesses of Harriet's memory, yelled, "Go have fun! You deserve it!"

And suddenly, Harriet did.

"Okay," she said, a smile playing on her lips. "Let's go."

They tumbled into a waiting Uber. Nick, emboldened by the shared line, leaned in, attempting a kiss on the backseat. Harriet, however, was not a novice. She gently but firmly rebuffed him. She knew that guys like Nick might try, but they also understood a clear "no." And to his credit, Nick respected it, pulling back without protest.

The club hit Harriet like a tidal wave. It had been years since she'd been in such a place. Suddenly, she felt like she was 18 again, a surge of pure, unadulterated energy coursing through her. The pulsating music vibrated in her bones, urging her to move.

The initial excitement was quickly followed by unwanted attention. Several men, fueled by alcohol and hormones, tried to latch onto her. Nick played the role of protector, effectively keeping them at bay while generously sharing his stash with a growing circle of new "friends" in a dimly lit upstairs room.

They danced for hours, lost in the rhythm and the haze. Then, the inevitable crash. Harriet found herself leaning over a plush velvet couch, emptying her stomach. It was messy, undignified, and yet, somehow liberating. She felt so good being out that even throwing up wasn't a big deal.

A young man, with a genuine concern etched on his face, knelt beside her. "You okay, miss?"

"Sure," she said, wiping her mouth. "I'm fine, just taking a moment." Straightening up, she brushed it off and plunged back into the fray, drawn back to the dance floor by the irresistible beat. Someone bought her a drink. She danced again.

Later, wandering through the labyrinthine club, she couldn't find Nick.

He was probably off with someone, somewhere. Maybe he'd even left.

Harriet leaned against a wall, nursing an empty glass. The initial euphoria had faded, leaving a dull ache in its wake. She felt adrift, alone.

Then, he appeared.

He was tall, undeniably striking, with a physique that spoke of dedication and effortless confidence. And those eyes…they radiated a captivating intensity.

He looked at her. A flicker of recognition, perhaps, or simply attraction. He smiled, a slow, deliberate curl of his lips.

And in the next instant, the empty glass slipped from her hand, shattering silently on the floor as she leaned into him, drawn by an invisible force. Their lips met, a collision of raw energy and unspoken desire. The kiss was passionate and demanding, a promise of something wild and unknown. The night, which had started with rosé and jet lag, was about to take an entirely new direction.

They smiled at each other, and the next minute she was leaning onto him, and they kissed passionately. He asked his friend to buy them drinks. They chatted, leaned onto each other, and finished their drinks. He was a professional athlete, a soccer player. Harriet nearly choked. "Do you want to go…?" they both said at the same time, looking into each other's eyes.

When they opened the door to the apartment, they didn't make it to the bedroom but sat on the couch. Harriet sat on him, and his cock was so hard, and she was dripping wet. "I want you," he said, and Harriet bit his ear whilst she slid up and down his decent-sized cock. "Can you feel how wet I am?" she whispered, and he said to her how much he loved being inside of her.

Next, he was on top of her, and Harriet's legs were on his shoulders. Followed by a shower and Harriet kneeling. She took as much of him as she could of him in her mouth, and she had to admit he had a beautiful cock. Harriet ran her tongue up and down until she started sucking his balls and holding her other hand on his firm, muscular ass. She sucked his balls for a long time, slowly. He looked down at her, and Harriet had long, direct eye contact with him whilst she took one ball at a time in her mouth and finally deep-throated him as far as she could. Harriet was mesmerized by his beautiful, long, dark lashes, and he gasped, *"Wow, this is amazing...you're good at that,"* he mumbled.

She had never seen a boy enjoy it as much. It gave her a huge kick.

He came on her breasts twice, whilst the water ran it all clean. Harriet bent over and grabbed his hard cock. He pushed deep inside of her and kept going until he turned and picked her up and lifted her high. He fucked Harriet up in the air, and she wrapped her smooth legs with water splashing on them around him and held him.

He kept banging her like this forever, and she didn't know where he got all the strength. *"Well, he is an athlete after all",* she thought and smiled ear to ear whilst moaning now louder.

He kept fucking, and her head spun whilst the shower was still running.

She felt amazing. She felt her body, her breasts, and her legs feeling so alive as if she was hit with a bolt of electricity from the sky. They headed back upstairs, and for a moment, they were lying next to each other.

"When you leaned on me in the club, I knew it was going to be good," he said to Harriet and stared at the ceiling. Harriet turned to face away from him, and he held her until she grabbed his cock again and turned on her stomach and put it in her wet, pulsating pussy. She liked how it hit the walls of her vagina from behind, and she squeezed his cock with her muscles. He fingered her from behind, and she was so close. "I can't hold off much longer," he said and got up.

"I thought you were in pain," he said as his cock was a decent size, but they went for it again. He came hard, and Harriet almost came. *Almost.*

They put clothes back on, and she passed out on the couch for a bit, and he was still wired and couldn't sleep. When Harriet headed back to Anna's in the Uber, she didn't feel the aftereffects until the following days. Deliciously sore all over.

Harriet thought she would never see him again unless she put sports on TV, and she might have to watch him play. The strong legs that held her in the shower, and the sexy smile that she couldn't say no to. Maybe she would make herself cum, just watching him, and that's all.

But Harriet ran back to him. She didn't even know why. It wasn't like he was pursuing her, or she was pursuing him that way. Harriet just wanted *something.*

The taxi coughed to a halt outside his beachfront apartment. The glow of the streetlights painted him in an unflattering orange as he waited, a silhouette against the predawn sky. Harriet didn't even offer a greeting, just a nod, her hunger a silent, throbbing thing. Lust, a cheap substitute for the love she'd traded away for now, burned in her throat.

Upstairs, clothes were discarded like shed skins. There was no preamble, no tender exploration. Just a raw, desperate need that he seemed to understand implicitly. He was a willing vessel, and she, a ship adrift in a storm. She sucked him deep, relishing the feel of him, the taste, the animalistic groan that rumbled in his chest. He was a canvas of muscle and athleticism, a stark contrast to 'Monster,' her ex, whose gym-honed physique had become a monument to his self-obsession. This man was different, an athlete, not a showman, whose endurance was a promise whispered in the dark. *He was the perfect rebound.*

They showered together, a brief, perfunctory cleansing before plunging back into the fray. She swallowed his cum, every drop, desperate to fill the hollow ache inside. He paused, catching his breath, before pulling her back into the bed, his body a demanding rhythm against hers.

Then it happened.

A tidal wave crashed through her. Not an orgasm, not pleasure, but a geyser of release, unlike anything she had ever experienced. He was behind her, his hands gripping her hips, when it erupted. A torrent of liquid, like a torrential rain, soaked the sheets and stained the carpet.

Harriet didn't come. She just… squirted. And with each involuntary spasm, a phantom image flickered across her mind: Arden, *'Mr. New York,'* the ghost she couldn't shake.

She remembered a careless boast he'd made, a dismissive anecdote about a past lover who "squirted too much," a cumbersome, messy inconvenience. Has he done this to her? Did his energy somehow manifest at this moment, triggering this unprecedented reaction?

"Mr. New York, how do you do this to me from the other side of the world?" she wanted to scream. *"Just how exactly?"*

The man beneath her, almost a stranger in the bed, was panicking. He stared at the spreading stain on the carpet; his brows furrowed with dismay.

"Is it going to stain?" he asked, his voice laced with a mixture of disgust and bewilderment. "I know girls get a bit wet when they are about to cum, but this is something else." He was completely missing the seismic shift that had just occurred within her.

Harriet felt no shame, only a strange, detached amusement. As she pulled on her clothes, a smile played on her lips. It was a smile directed at Arden, a silent acknowledgment of his lingering power over her.

Did he just pour his life force into her pussy without even touching it? Like a distant muse making her reach a peak no one else could?

She offered a perfunctory apology for the ruined carpet, her mind already miles away, lost in the puzzle of Arden's influence. He was still muttering about stain removers as she walked out, leaving him to grapple with the messy aftermath of a connection he couldn't possibly understand.

Chapter 21

Sydney, May 2023

Harriet's mind still drifted back to Arden. There was something so unique there that she couldn't possibly pinpoint it. The feeling she never had before, a strange mix of comfortable familiarity and intoxicating mystery. It wasn't just physical attraction, though he was undeniably handsome with those disarming brown eyes and that hesitant smile. It was more profound, a connection that tickled the edges of her soul.

He was all the way in New York, though. That was a big problem. Distance. Thousands of miles separated them, an ocean and a continent. But maybe the distance only fueled the attraction? Absence, it seemed, wasn't making her heart grow fonder; it was making it restless, a trapped bird beating its wings against the bars of practicality.

Sydney was the most beautiful city to be in. The vibrant cityscape shimmered under a perpetually sunny sky. The turquoise water of Bondi beckoned with the promise of sun-drenched days. She had everything a girl could want: friends like the effervescent Anna, whose parties were legendary; there could be more fleeting romances with ridiculously attractive people, like the soccer player with the killer abs she just fooled around with. The clubs pulsed with a frenetic energy; a kaleidoscope of light and sound designed to distract and delight.

Yet, dancing under the strobe lights, laughing with Anna over cocktails, even feeling the warm sand between her toes after a morning surf… nothing could erase her yearning for something more. The joy felt fleeting, superficial, replaced too quickly by the hollow echo of emptiness.

Arden. She needed to know what this was, who he was. Something clicked, a spark that ignited in the most unexpected corner of her heart.

Now, weeks later, the spark had turned into a persistent ember, glowing in the darkness of her Sydney life. She tried to ignore it, to bury it beneath layers of sunshine and distraction. But the ember refused to be extinguished.

One evening, as the Sydney sun dipped below the horizon, painting the sky in hues of orange and purple, Harriet sat in Anna's backyard, a glass of wine untouched in her hand. She looked out at the sparkling harbor; the Harbour Bridge was a defiant arc against the darkening sky. She thought of Arden, sitting perhaps in a dimly lit coffee shop in Greenwich Village, surrounded by the clamor of New York City.

A wave of frustration washed over her. She could be living her dream life, now that Monster was gone, the life she'd always imagined. Why couldn't she just be happy? Why was this ghost of a connection a world away haunting her?

Closing her eyes, she took a deep breath. She could ignore it; pretend it didn't exist. She could continue to chase fleeting pleasures, hoping they would eventually fill the void. Or… she could be brave. She could embrace the unknown, face the uncertainty, and see where this… *thing*… with Arden might lead.

With a sudden surge of determination, she grabbed her phone. The glowing screen illuminated her face as she scrolled through her contacts. Finally, she found his name. She had saved him as "husband" when they first spoke. Her thumb hovered over the call button.

Her heart hammered against her ribs. This was insane. Completely and utterly insane. She was about to impulsively call a man she barely knew, who lived on the other side of the world, and… what? Ask him to explain the inexplicable. Ask him if he felt it too.

But something in her refused to back down. The ember within her blazed hotter, fueled by a mix of hope and recklessness. She pressed the button.

The phone rang, each ring echoing in the silent Sydney night. Her palm was slick with sweat. He wouldn't answer. He was probably busy. He'd probably forgotten all about her.

Then, a click. A crackle of static. And a voice, hesitant and slightly sleep-roughened, said, "Hello?"

Harriet swallowed hard. "Arden? It's Harriet."

A beat of silence. Then, "Harriet? Wow. I… I didn't expect to hear from you." His voice. Just hearing his voice sent a shiver down her spine.

"Me neither," she admitted, her voice barely a whisper. "But I needed to…" She paused, searching for the right words. "I needed to know if you… If you felt it too."

Another long silence. The only sound was the distant hum of the city and the pounding of her own heart.

Finally, he spoke. "Felt what, Harriet?" She took a deep breath. "This… connection. This thing between us. Whatever it is."

This time, the silence was different. It was pregnant with anticipation, with unspoken possibilities.

"Harriet," he said, his voice now soft and low. "Believe me, I felt it. I haven't stopped thinking about you."

A wave of relief, so intense it almost knocked her off her feet, washed over her. She wasn't crazy. She wasn't imagining it.

"So, what do we do about it?" she asked, her voice trembling.

Arden's answer, carried across the ocean, was simple, hopeful, and utterly terrifying. "I don't know. But I think we owe it to ourselves to find out."

Chapter 22

New York, May 2023

Harriet felt playful, and she wanted to distract her mind from the other things.

It was the perfect hour to give Arden a call. That afternoon slump hour in the office when you needed a coffee or a nap, preferably both, but had to push through until finishing time. He picked up within a few rings.

"Stand up from your desk," Harriet ordered him.

"Act normal".

"Now, talk quietly and walk over to the bathroom."

She could hear the faint rustle of fabric as he moved. She pictured him, tall and impeccably dressed, his brown eyes probably glinting with mischief. There was a muttered greeting to a passing coworker, then a soft click as he locked the cubicle door.

"OK, now what?" he asked, his voice laced with a barely concealed excitement. "Loosen your tie. Leave your white shirt on."

"Okay…"

"Strip down to your underwear."

She could almost feel his hesitation. "Seriously, Harriet?"

He was holding on to the wall with one arm and juggling his suit trousers off, keeping the phone to his ear.

"I am going to hang up now, but watch the video clip on your phone".

The video message appeared on his phone screen, and he pressed play, the sound muted.

In the video, she was kneeling on the floor pretending to be in front of him, sucking his balls, taking them into her mouth one by one, as he lay on his back on the couch.

She then pretended that she pulled his legs closer and spread them wide apart before her head popped up and down on his hard cock.

She then proceeded to pretend to lick him behind his balls whilst stroking him slowly - and best of all, she pretended to go all in, before the video clip ended.

A text message appeared: "I'm in control, surrender to my dominance. You slut". He was already hard from the anticipation.

"You can't cum" another text message read.

"Not yet".

"Take a photo".

He took a photo from a perfect angle.

He pressed the record to take a few-second video.

"Now, think about my flat tongue up your ass, slowly tasting you."

Another text.

"Now, rolled deep inside you and pulling you closer, and making you squirm. Wet, warm, and tingling."

"Do you want to feel my tongue in you…more and more?"

There was a pause. She knew the struggle he was having now, the pressure building, the need to obey her commands, fighting the need for release.

She waited, her fingers drumming on her desk. Then, the photo arrived. He'd chosen a perfect angle, making his cock look thick and undeniably hard.

The cubicle was quiet, the fluorescent lights buzzing overhead. The only sound was his ragged breathing as he came, a silent explosion of pleasure and obedience.

"Return to your desk".

He cleaned himself up, adjusted his tie, and put the phone in his pocket before opening the door and returning to his desk. Another message appeared on his phone as he placed it next to his laptop.

"Did I say you could cum?" His pulse had quickened instantly. He knew she was teasing, but it was still hot.

He'd cautiously replied, "No, you didn't." "Bad dog. I need you to do something else for me now," Harriet typed back.

Then came the next instruction, the one that had him sweating: "On the way home, take your cock out for me. Outside."

His breath hitched. *Outside?* That was a serious escalation. He'd been hesitant, a little scared of being caught, but the thought of pleasing Harriet, of obeying her command, had overridden his apprehension.

A few hours later, Harriet received a video.

Arden was at the park by the river. He sat on the bench, his zipper open, he pulled his pants a little, and Harriet saw his cock standing rock hard for her. The camera showed the park and the glistening water reflecting the late afternoon sun. He looked utterly vulnerable; the thrill of the exhibition mingled with a palpable fear of discovery.

"Good boy," Harriet typed, a smile playing on her lips.

"Now, go home. And find a black marker pen."

"OK, wifey. I will be home in about 15," he replied, feeling a surge of excitement and anticipation build within him.

"Write wifey…"

"And…send me a photo/video."

"OK, back home," Arden typed.

A few minutes later, a video appeared.

"Wifey" was written across his hard cock in shaky black letters. He looked flushed, his eyes dark with arousal.

"Probably a good angle to show me cuming as well," Arden typed, adding a winking emoji. He was clearly enjoying this.

"Perfect," Harriet smiled, a genuine spark of pleasure lighting her eyes. She hadn't expected him to embrace this so eagerly.

"I was thinking I could cum into a glass just at that angle, show you how much it fills up," he suggested, pushing the boundaries further.

"Would it be possible to have a voice note from you?" he added, his vulnerability returning. "Just saying that you allow me to cum?"

The request surprised her. It was a plea for permission, a final surrendering of control. Harriet paused, considering. This wasn't just about exhibitionism or dominance anymore; it was about trust, about the intimacy of shared fantasy.

She pressed record and lowered her voice.

First, channeling Nigella Lawson, imagining herself slowly stirring a cake dough as she spoke, adopting a linguist's careful articulation. Then, morphing into an older, sexy Italian auntie with a large bust, picturing coming face to face with a tense, eager boy, she purred, *"My sweet boy...you can cum now."* The words were thick with implied indulgence, a promise of unrestrained pleasure.

She sent the voice note.

The silence that followed felt electric. Harriet held her breath, unsure what to expect. She'd opened a door to a new level of intimacy, a raw and vulnerable space where power and pleasure intertwined. And she was just as intrigued as she was apprehensive. *This was going to be interesting.*

Chapter 23

❦

Sydney, June 2023

Harriet stared at her phone, the glow reflecting in her wide, uncertain eyes. The message she'd just typed:

"I think you love me using you as a personal plaything..." – felt impossibly bold, borderline reckless. It hung there, a digital dare, pregnant with vulnerability. For weeks, that unsettling thought had burrowed its way into her mind, feeding on the intoxicating pleasure and equally unsettling power dynamic that defined her and Arden.

Their connection, forged across continents and time zones, was a strange alchemy of shared fantasies and carefully constructed realities. Arden, in the concrete jungle of New York, and Harriet, basking in the sun-drenched shores of Sydney, were an unlikely pair, bound by a digital thread woven with wit, imagination, and a delicious undercurrent of something she couldn't quite name.

The late-night confessions. The dares. The stories they crafted together, stories that blurred the line between fiction and something far more personal.

She'd discovered a part of herself she never knew existed. A playful, sensual woman who reveled in the imagined scenarios, who thrilled at the words he crafted, the images he conjured. He made her feel desired, seen, beautiful. Something she hadn't felt in a long, long time. Before Arden, she had been adrift, lost in the monotonous routine of her non-existent life, her own beauty hidden beneath layers of self-doubt.

His words, sent across the vast expanse of the Pacific Ocean, were a balm to her weary soul. *"You are poetry in motion, Harriet,"* he'd written once, *"a symphony of sun-kissed skin and hidden desires."* She had blushed, reading that, feeling the warmth spread through her like a sunbeam. And that photo she once sent to him, she was in the ocean, her body looking amazing under the hot sun. *"I want to fuck that sexy mermaid",* he texted back.

But lately, a nagging unease had started to creep in. Was she truly seen, or simply a canvas for his own needs, some kind of artistic expression? Was their connection genuine, or merely a performance, meticulously orchestrated for his own amusement? Hence, the message, the risky, agonizingly vulnerable message.

The response pinged back almost instantly. *'I love nothing more,'* it read, stark and unapologetic.

Harriet gasped, a tremor running through her. She re-read the words, each syllable a hammer blow against her carefully constructed defenses. Was he mocking her? Confirming her worst fears? Or was there something else, something deeper, hidden beneath the surface of his provocative statement? She was overthinking.

She stared at her reflection in the phone's dark screen. Who was this woman, this bolder, more daring version of herself that had emerged under Arden's influence? She barely recognized her.

He was the most unique, intriguing man she had ever encountered. His mind was a labyrinth, his words a captivating dance. He saw depths in her that no one else had ever bothered to explore. But could she trust him? Could she trust herself?

The thought of them meeting, of bridging the gap between their online world and the real one, had always been both terrifying and exhilarating. Would the magic dissipate in the cold light of day? Would their carefully crafted personas crumble under the weight of reality?

Another message arrived. *'Tell me what you want, Harriet. Tell me what you need. And I will give it to you.'*

Her heart pounded against her ribs. *What did she want? What did she need?* The answers were a swirling vortex of desire, fear, and uncertainty. She wanted to be seen, truly seen, for the woman she was, not the woman he imagined. She wanted to be loved, not used like she had been by Monster. But she also craved the intoxicating thrill of their game, the liberation she found in his words, the spark of sexuality he had ignited within her.

She typed slowly, carefully choosing her words. *'I want to know who you are, Arden. Beyond the words, beyond the stories. I want to know the real you.'*

The response was delayed this time, the silence stretching between Sydney and New York, thick with anticipation. Finally, a single word appeared.

'Soon.'

Harriet took a deep breath, the salty air of Sydney filling her lungs. Soon. Was it a promise? A threat? Or simply another piece of the puzzle, another layer in the fascinating, frustrating, undeniably captivating game she was playing with Arden, a game that had irrevocably changed her, and that, one way or another, was about to change her life forever. The sun beat down on her skin, but she felt a different kind of fire burning within. A fire fueled not just by desire, but by a newfound sense of self, and a terrifying, exhilarating hope.

That night, as Harriet reached for her journal on the bedside table, she couldn't shake off the sensations that danced along her skin. In her mind's eye, she replayed fragments of the connection with Arden.

With each stroke of her pen, she captured not just physical intimacy but also an emotional awakening.

You not only warm my body up, but my heart that has become so cold. We are lying under the covers, fully naked, and you touch my smooth skin, but I turn away from you. The smell of your skin is like a delicious torment to me. I am lying still, motionless. Not because I am waiting for you to take me from behind, but because I feel something I haven't felt in a long time, if ever. It feels like my skin heats up at your touch. I feel like I am falling. I close my eyes. I feel your hands on my hips, and my heart skips a beat, a salty tear falling down my cheek.

Do I want you to see that? I have so much to give, and I know you have so much to offer. With you, in this moment, I feel everything is so perfect, it's no longer scaring me. I sense the hunger inside of you; it's all for me, the clever, creative, and sensitive girl. I feel like all I ever needed was this. This one fleeting breathtaking moment, you are firmly behind me, spooning me and melting me from ice to water. I feel you getting so hard against my back.

You pull me closer, and I want to hug you until I smell like you, a blended perfume. This delicious torment we have been putting ourselves through, being physically apart, but somehow always so close. And then I feel you slowly entering inside of me, your hand pulling me closer, your smell so divine, my mind floating away. I feel like crying out of longing for you for so long, and all that desire is bottled up. You are real. All those times I had thought how I would give you this ass, you behind me. On the side of the bed, against a kitchen counter, against the wall. Thinking of all the ways. The way you might like it. But you naturally slide inside of me, and our bodies are perfectly aligned. Just me and you. You push in more. I feel all of you inside of me now. You pull out a little bit and go quicker, and you hold me tighter, and I feel all your cock as deep as you can go. Slow and steady, my pussy takes the shape of your cock, and I feel like we both keep falling as you keep going in and out of me, and I keep holding on. Without even knowing, like I am mindless in that moment, I push my hips closer to you so I can take you all in—all of you. You pull me into your hardness, and I want you to stay like this forever. You push a little deeper, and I gasp. Your cock is touching my delicate flesh so deep inside, I feel the heat moving through me.

"Could you stay...just there..." I whisper, holding on to your white sheet, my neck twisting sideways. You push a little bit more, and I feel you tighten up inside of me, and you let go. I am pulsating and cuming so strongly, and all I think is Oh My God... And I feel your cum inside of me, and it's the best feeling there is, you complete me. I am lying still, facing away, no longer tasting salty tears. I think about the past six months, and what I said to you was all wrong. You aren't my distraction at all. You are my wonder. And with that wonder, we both fall asleep peacefully.

Chapter 24

⸴ↀ⸳

S ydney, March 2015

"Please let me go," she begged in her voice, a raw whisper in the stifling air of the living room.

He didn't listen. The dull thud of his military boot connecting with her ribs stole her breath. Pain bloomed, and a sickening heat spread through her torso.

"You went through my phone, you bitch." Another kick, this one harder, sent a fresh wave of agony coursing through her.

"But you are not *Toby Wren!*" Harriet still talked back, defiance flickering in her voice despite the brutal assault. She couldn't help it; the truth clawed at her throat, demanding release.

"You made a fake Instagram account to follow me!" she cried now, the accusation laced with a despair that bordered on madness.

He loomed over her, a dark silhouette against the dim light. "Then what were you doing on Oxford Street?" His voice was low, a dangerous purr that promised more pain.

"I told you, I went to see the parade." The words tumbled out, a desperate plea for him to believe her.

"Who…with?" He gave her a small, taunting shove with his boot, the edge of the sole pressing into her bruised skin.

"No one, I already said this!" Frustration mingled with the pain, a volatile cocktail that fueled her defiance.

"You went with someone, didn't you?" He kicked her again. And again. Each blow stole a little more of her will, grinding it to dust beneath his boot.

The boot landed in Harriet's eye socket, a brutal, blinding impact. Suddenly, she saw nothing but blurry black bat-like figures flitting across her vision. The room spun, and she was lost in a vortex of pain. She was quietly sobbing, a sound barely louder than the rustle of the curtains.

"You lying bitch," the boot landed on her face again, a heavy, crushing weight. She tasted blood, and the metallic tang filled her mouth.

She couldn't remember how long she lay there, a broken heap on the floor. But somehow, driven by an instinct she didn't know she possessed, she got up. She pushed herself to her feet, her body screaming in protest, and ran out the door. She groaned with each step.

No one was shouting her name from behind. He did not care. She kept running, blindly, desperately. Behind the house lay a stretch of dry bushland, a desolate expanse of scrub and withered grass. She plunged into it, ignoring the sharp, dry blades that cut through her legs. Her eyes, swollen and bruised, struggled to focus. Her head throbbed with a relentless, agonizing rhythm. Yet she kept going, driven by a primal need to escape.

Until something was in front of her. A large iguana stood majestically on the path, its scales gleaming in the fading light as if standing guard to stop her.

He was calm and didn't move, like a statue carved from ancient stone. His ancient eyes seemed to hold a knowing wisdom, a silent understanding of her pain.

Harriet froze. The adrenaline that had fueled her escape began to ebb, leaving her weak and trembling. She felt a bone-deep weariness, a surrender that threatened to consume her. Slowly, she turned around.

There were no more tears. The well of despair had run dry, leaving only a hollow ache. She looked back at the house, a dark and silent silhouette against the dying sun.

She had to go back, back to him. The realization settled in her like a cold stone in her stomach. The iguana hadn't stopped her; it had only shown her the truth she had been desperately trying to outrun. There was nowhere else to go. He was her prison, and she, inexplicably, was her own jailer.

Her body ached from his kicks, her face throbbed, and her eyes were swollen shut. She couldn't see where she was going, but she knew she had to keep moving. The last thing she remembered was running into something solid and being knocked down, and now she found herself in an unfamiliar place, surrounded by tall grass and the smell of wet soil. As she struggled to stand up, she felt lost. Until she saw the iguana again.

For a moment, Harriet considered trying to climb over a nearby fence or go around it, but something about the iguana's stillness unnerved her. Instead, she turned around and began to make her way back towards their house. The pain in her body was intense, but she pushed through it, driven by a desperate need to make sense of it all. She needed to get away from him, but something was also taking her back to him. As she drew nearer to the house, she could hear his voice, growing louder with each step. She knew he would be waiting for her. She had to face him and hope for the best.

Harriet steeled herself as she approached the house. She could feel the anger radiating off him from where she stood outside. He was pacing back and forth, his fists clenched tightly at his sides. When he saw her, he stopped and took a menacing step towards her.

"Where the hell do you think you've been?" he spat, his voice dripping with his usual anger. She winced at the sound of his voice, feeling the familiar fear rise within her. But this time, she refused to cower. "I… I went for a walk," she stammered, trying to make her voice sound strong. "I needed some air." He sneered at her response. "A walk? You look like you've been through a war zone." He took another step closer, and she took an involuntary step back. "Tell me the truth, Harriet. Who were you with?" She shook her head, refusing to give him the satisfaction of an answer. "I swear I wasn't with anyone," she said, trying to keep her voice steady. "I just needed some time alone."

He stopped, seemingly lost in thought. "Fine," he said eventually, his tone softening slightly. "Go take a long, hot shower. And when you come out, we'll talk some more."

Harriet didn't trust his sudden change of heart, but she took the opportunity to flee inside and up to the bathroom. She locked the door behind her and collapsed onto the cold tile floor, sobbing in relief. She had escaped for now, but she knew their relationship was far from over. She could *never* get away from him.

Harriet's eyes fluttered open as she woke up to the sound of gentle tapping on the bathroom door. She sat up slowly, wincing at the pain in her body, and tried to compose herself before opening the door. When she did, she found him standing there, looking at her with a mix of concern and curiosity.

"Are you okay?" he asked, his voice softer than she had ever heard it before. She hesitated for a moment, unsure how to answer.

"I'm… I'm fine," she said finally. "What do you want to talk about?" He stepped into the bathroom, closing the door behind him.

"Look, I'm sorry for how I acted earlier," he began. "I was just… I don't know, I guess I lost my temper. It won't happen again." Harriet bit her lip, unsure how to respond. She had seen this side of him so many times.

"It's okay," she said, not quite believing her own words.

"I'm sorry too. I shouldn't have gone through your phone." They stared at each other for a long moment, neither of them quite sure what to say next. And then, out of nowhere, he took a step closer and wrapped his arms around her. She stiffened at first, but then forced herself to relax into his tense, freckled, muscular arms.

Chapter 25

Sydney, June 2023

Harriet was sitting outside in Anna's garden with a glass of Pinot Noir. The wrought iron chair was cool beneath her, a welcome contrast to the late-afternoon warmth that lingered even after the rain. Droplets clung to the leaves of the climbing roses, their sweet fragrance intensified by the damp air. It had been raining hard just an hour ago, a sudden downpour that had sent her scurrying inside. Now, the clouds had parted, leaving a sky scrubbed clean and the air smelling impossibly fresh.

She had picked up a book, titled "Banker's Wife", a flimsy beach read Anna had left behind. Harriet smiled ironically. The life of a banker's wife, all manicured lawns and charity galas in the novel, felt a million miles away from her current reality. But even with the escapist potential, she wasn't able to concentrate. The words on the page swam before her eyes, refusing to coalesce into anything meaningful. Sighing, she put the book down on the small wrought iron table beside her.

She took a sip of wine, the cool liquid a balm against the lump in her throat. The memories were always lurking, waiting for a quiet moment to surface. To distract herself, she pulled out her iPhone and swiped through her notes. It was a chaotic mess, a digital scrapbook of random thoughts, shopping lists, and half-finished poems. Then something caught her eye, a note dated almost a year ago. Instead of picking up the novel, she started to read what she had written when she was still with Monster.

The words on the screen were raw, untainted by the careful editing she employed now. They were desperate, fragmented, almost childlike in their simplicity.

How to Love a Liar

He pulls you into a warm hug, and for one unbearable moment, you almost collapse into him. Tears threaten, but you push them back. Your brain feels tight, locked. You step away. He offers his phone like proof.

"Here, check if you don't believe me."

You refuse. Your shoulders sag as you walk away, drained. You know the truth: he lies. It's what he does.

Years pass, and the lies stretch across everything: school, friends, even the simple details he feeds his family. He weaves entire lives that don't exist, as though deception is oxygen. Lies give him control. The truth is irrelevant. To him, reality is just another story to rewrite. He may even believe the lies are acts of love, but they are nothing more than prisons.

I had no choice but to stop lying to myself. Why should I, when he had already done it for me? I became the woman who could spot betrayal before it arrived. Red flags weren't surprises, they were mile-markers on a road I'd traveled too many times. I devoured books on deception, as well as manuals from FBI agents and interrogators. But I didn't need them. His body language, his rehearsed words, his carefully constructed denials, he was a textbook liar, and I knew it.

Knowing he was hiding things only hardened me. Inside, the cold snowball of suspicion grew heavier, colder, pushing icy air through me every time I neared the truth.

Sometimes I wondered about his family. Did they live in denial, clinging to the version of him he invented? As my therapist suggested, they had taught him to lie, conditioned him to choose illusion over reality.

For him, lying wasn't cruelty; it was survival. His comfort. His control. Truth was dangerous, threatening to unravel the compartments he had built in his mind. So he wove fiction around himself, layer after layer, until even he could no longer see where truth ended and lies began.

But standing beside a liar makes you complicit. I became part of his illusion, part of the false story he fed the world. I stopped asking questions because my sanity mattered more than his explanations. Living in a fog of doubt is suffocating, but the heart clings to love even when the mind is screaming to let go. You learn to mute the alarms, to prioritize survival over clarity.

And yet, I wondered. What would it be like to live with someone honest? To wake without doubt gnawing at my chest? To feel love without suspicion? The thought was almost unbearable in its beauty—a voice of truth, like a torch in the dark, cutting through the shadows of his deception.

When I chose him, I gave up truth for illusion.

Instincts tell their own story. Like a rider on a quiet night, trusting the rhythm of a beloved horse, until a sudden noise, a violent kick, and the rider is thrown, left broken on the ground. Instinct saves and destroys. My life with him was that horse: trust shattered in an instant, control ripped away, leaving me bruised in ways no one could see.

To love a liar is to burn with a fire they cannot feel. To carry a truth they will never face. Liars convince themselves that pain can be justified, that lies can build happiness, that destruction can pass for love. But they don't see the suffering they leave behind. They don't realize how their illusions steal joy from others, strip away dignity, and smother love in shadows.

The truth, for me, became light. A single torch carried through years of heartbreak, leading me out of his darkness.

Written by Harriet — 15/10/2022

Chapter 26

Sydney, June 2023

Harriet was alone at Anna's house. It was mid-morning, and she wandered around, boredom nipping at her heels. She longed to write, to lose herself in the worlds she could create, but her mind was a restless bird, flitting from thought to thought. A flutter in her stomach reminded her that a better life awaited, beyond the Monster's betrayal. Even now, months after finding the picture, he, smiling, with another woman at the airport, a smug grin plastered on his face, anger still simmered within her. She desperately wanted to extinguish it, but it was a tenacious flame, fueled by years of abuse, years of lies.

The washing was piling up in the laundry room, a mundane task that threatened to overwhelm her. She grabbed the bottle of fabric softener, its label promising a gentle embrace for her clothes. She poured the thick, white liquid, watching it drip slowly into the slot. A strange thought flickered through her mind, an unwelcome association. The milky perfection of the softener reminded her, with disturbing clarity, of Arden's… Arden's thick and perfectly colored pure white cum. A blush heated her cheeks, shame mingling with a perverse flicker of longing.

She slammed the lid of the washing machine shut, the click echoing in the small room. She pressed the 'delicate' cycle, watching the green timer illuminate. As the machine began its humming cycle, filling with water, a wave of dizziness washed over her. She slowly bent over, resting her breasts against the cool, vibrating metal. The hum grew louder as the water gushed in, and an insidious fantasy took hold with each pulse. She imagined being filled, like the machine, with the torrent of water, the rhythmic vibrations mirroring a phantom touch. Thoughts of Arden, his perfect cum, flooded her senses.

She reached beneath her tight jogging pants, pushing her knickers aside. Images of Arden, standing behind her, filled her mind. She could almost hear his voice, articulate and carefully measured as if hiding a deeper meaning. She thought of the dangerous beauty of it all. She was soaking wet now, her fingers probing deeper, a gasp escaping her lips, a sharp edge of pain mingling with pleasure. She couldn't take it anymore.

She came, hard and fast, her body shaking, her mind consumed by images of thick, white cum. Her head banged against the washing machine lid. Finally, her breathing slowed, and a sharp pang of emotional longing crashed over her. Was she thinking about Arden too much? Was he controlling her thoughts, her desires?

The green light on the timer flashed. Two minutes.

She felt like he was making her cave in, like she was constantly fighting a losing battle against the magnetic pull of his influence. The incredibly powerful two minutes, and she was still bending over the washing machine, not wanting to let go.

She had forgotten about her anger. And replaced it with sparks and feelings so wild, reluctant to be tamed. *Was Harriet just an independent spirit now?* No, she was connected again, but not to a Monster, but to a place of privilege, a warm glow. Her mind filled with thoughts of lust and love, constant wonder, if she will ever be filled with that purest white cum, all her insides snowed in.

Chapter 27

S ydney/New York, July 2023

The video icon popped up on Harriet's screen and sent a rush of excitement through her. A mischievous smile played on her lips as she answered the call. This was their little secret, their digital rendezvous, a playground for their desires meticulously crafted in the quiet corners of their lives.

The sight was no disappointment. Arden knew how to play this game.

He was in the shower, feeling the hot water rushing down his body, soothing away the sweat, and turning around to face the wall, bending a little bit, and opening up. The steam danced around him, blurring the edges of the camera's view, adding a layer of voyeuristic intrigue.

He splashed water on his hair and faced the camera again. He looked directly at her, a playful glint in his eyes. He knew his power, the way his gaze alone could ignite a fire within her.

He didn't need to flex the muscles in his arms; he just needed to look at her with those intense puppy eyes, and she felt the wetness in her underwear and the sparkles below her belly button. Just the sheer anticipation of what was to come was enough to send shivers down her spine.

Tonight, Harriet was in control. She challenged him. Pushed him to the edge. Teased him until he begged.

"Let's see how well you can submit…." she purred, her voice a low, husky invitation. Arden bit his lip, a visible tremor running through him as he adjusted his position. "Spread those legs wider…" she commanded, reveling in his immediate obedience.

Harriet wanted something special in the back of her mind. Something beyond the usual thrill of the forbidden. She wanted to see how far she could push him, how completely he would surrender.

It was all part of the game, this dance of dominance and submission. She didn't need to test any waters with him, as she knew his resistance would soften. He was eager, such a good boy.

She increased the pace slightly with her commands and felt him getting harder, his breathing becoming shallow and ragged. She could see through the phone his chest heaving, the muscles in his back straining. His heart pounded, the warm water running down and soothing his shoulders even as the heat within him intensified.

She wanted something special, instead of just standard white cum. She worked on him a little longer until his hole pulsed with sensitivity.

"I'm close," he almost asked for permission, knowing he was not allowed yet. The desperation in his voice was a potent aphrodisiac. She turned him like a key until she felt him throbbing, the very air around him thick with anticipation. He tried to maintain control, but she finally told him to lose it.

His chest rose and fell, the rhythm erratic and fast. Every muscle in his body was tense, on the verge of release.

And then, she let him out of his misery and whispered in his ear, "You are allowed to cum now."

"Slowly, pretend you are shooting it all in my hand."

She was full of admiration for his devotion, his willingness to lose himself in the dance she orchestrated. He had given her everything, held nothing back. And in that shared vulnerability, in that exquisite moment of release, they had found something sacred, something uniquely their own.

"Was I good enough?" he asked, his chest rising and falling, his breath catching in his throat, his body trembling with the force of his desire.

She reveled in his absolute surrender.

Tonight, through the glow of the screen, he gave her everything she craved, and even across the distance, his surrender turned her pleasure into something achingly sweet.

Chapter 28

Sydney, August 2023

Life with Monster hadn't vanished with the slamming of the front door. He hadn't been exorcised with the divorce papers. Instead, he had simply mutated, evolving from a snarling beast into a chillingly efficient bureaucrat of torment. He continued his abuse via the financial settlement, weaponizing legal jargon and meticulously crafted loopholes where once he had used fists and cutting words.

Harriet felt like she was drowning in paperwork, each document a lead weight dragging her further into the abyss. After sixteen years of marriage, sixteen years of devotion, selfless giving, she was left with nothing. Homeless, penniless, utterly adrift. He'd kept the car, the furniture, even the chipped teacups that held sentimental value. He'd stripped her bare, leaving her exposed and vulnerable.

So, she'd hired Andrea. A sharp, competent lawyer at Miller & Zarella, a firm reputed for its tenacity. Andrea was a lifeline, a beacon of hope in the swirling storm of her life. But every phone call from Andrea, every update on the case, was a fresh wound.

"He's refusing to disclose his assets, Harriet," Andrea would say, her voice crisp and professional. "We're filing at court, but it could take time."

Time. Harriet felt like she was teetering on the edge of a precipice, and time was the wind threatening to shove her over.

The worst part was the cryptocurrency. He believed he could hide it forever, buried in the digital depths of the internet, a treasure trove only he knew how to access. He'd been secretive about it for years, whispering about investments and future security, always excluding her from the details. Now, it was a tool, another way to exert control, to prolong her suffering.

He was a master of emotional manipulation, and the financial battle was just an extension of that. He demanded Harriet's lawyer supply him with statements of their joint account, even though he already had access to them. It was a power play, a blatant display of his ability to dictate the terms, to keep her dancing to his tune.

"He wants the statements from January 2018 to December 2019," Andrea relayed one afternoon, her voice laced with barely controlled frustration. "Says he needs them for his taxes."

Harriet closed her eyes, the familiar wave of nausea washing over her. Taxes. It was a lie, she knew it. He was just trying to bait her, to force a reaction, to remind her that he still had the upper hand.

"Just… give them to him, Andrea," she said, her voice shaky. "Just… whatever he wants. I can't… I can't do this anymore."

Each phone call, each legal maneuver, set her back on her healing journey. The nightmares, the flashbacks, the crushing weight of betrayal, all intensified with every interaction. It was a never-ending cycle. He was mean. Calculated. He knew exactly what he was doing, and he revelled in it.

Sleeping on Anna's bed, eating instant noodles, scouring job postings that offered little more than minimum wage, this was her reality. He, on the other hand, was probably still living in their house, surrounded by their belongings, revelling in his victory.

One evening, huddled under a blanket that smelled faintly of lavender, she stared out the window at the rain lashing against the glass. The rain mirrored the turmoil within her, the endless stream of accusations and self-doubt. He had taken so much, but he wouldn't take her spirit. She wouldn't let him.

Something shifted within her. The despair was still there, gnawing at the edges, but it was accompanied by a flicker of something else: a quiet, steely resolve.

She knew the road ahead would be long and arduous. She knew the Monster would continue to fight, to claw, to inflict pain. But she also knew, deep down, that she was stronger than he was. She had survived sixteen years of his darkness. *She could survive anything.* She would rebuild her life, brick by painful brick, and she would do it without him. The game wasn't over, not by a long shot. It was only beginning, and this time, she wasn't settling for scraps; she was taking everything that was rightfully hers.

Chapter 29

Sydney, August 2023

Harriet came home to find Nick and Anna perched on the couch, a half-empty bottle of Pinot Noir between them. They were laughing about the absurdities of their dating lives, terrible dates, awkward messages, ridiculous pick-up lines, when Nick, emboldened by the wine, pulled out his phone.

"Look at this, Harriet," Anna giggled, spilling a little wine on the table. The video, a brief, intense moment of pleasure from an unknown woman, caught Harriet off guard. Her pulse quickened, and suddenly, a vivid fantasy of Arden flooded her mind. She imagined a desire so consuming it would shatter all her inhibitions, a thrill far beyond anything Nick and Anna could laugh about. The warmth of the wine spread through her, fanning the flames of her longing.

Harriet sank deeper into the couch, letting her mind drift. The sounds of Nick and Anna laughing, their ridiculous stories, became little more than a faint hum. Every giggle and snort seemed muffled, filtered through the haze of wine and heat building in her chest. Her fingers flexed on the couch cushions as her fantasies grew more vivid. Arden's image dominated her thoughts; she was in control, commanding, and ruthless. In her mind, she was binding him, the Velcro restraints tight against his wrists, his terrified-yet-excited eyes reflecting the stark contrast of fear and thrilling anticipation. She would tease and torment him, a calculated dance between domination and pleasure, pushing him to the brink of unbearable ecstasy. Her imagination painted a scene of complete control, a world where she orchestrated his every gasp, every moan, pushing him to the limits of his physical and emotional endurance. This wasn't about her own pleasure; it was about the power to shape his experience, to mold his every reaction. The scene played out in her mind, the controlled strokes, the deliberate use of her tongue and saliva, all calculated to heighten his arousal and desperation, a symphony of pain and pleasure meticulously orchestrated.

As she sipped the wine, heat pooling low in her belly, Harriet let herself slip fully into the fantasy, imagining every gasp and shiver Arden would give her at her command;

She had a wicked glint in her eye as she was nowhere near finishing.

She ordered him onto the bed.

"Arms out, wide!"

She gave him a quick whip on his legs.

"Listen!"

"Bad boy!"

Another quick whip, and he let out a little moan.

She wasn't going to whip Arden any longer; she was just going to put him in his place, for his own good. For now.

"Don't move your arms."

Harriet moved to the side of the bed and pulled out black heavy-duty Velcro restraints that were already attached to the bed frame on each side.

She carefully pulled the strap tighter over his wrist.

She moved across the bed and decided to climb over him. His cock was still hard, and she was tempted to sit on it and ride him, but again, this wasn't about her pleasure right now. She admired him for a few seconds and strapped his other wrist tight.

"What are you looking at?"

She looked at his eyes, full of excitement and fear.

"What if I cum?" Arden whispered.

"Then there will be a punishment".

"You don't want that now, do you?"

She gave him a look as if she were a warden at the prison, and he was about to be imprisoned for life. His life, and his cock in her hands.

Harriet left his legs free. She needed to place them correctly.

Harriet glanced at something on her bedside, and her plan went out of the window. She decided to improvise to make it all so amazing that he would never forget. He had not seen the little secret Harriet had been storing for him.

"Unclench your jaw!"

"Look up to the ceiling for now and take a deep breath." There was electricity in her voice as she became more spontaneous.

This wasn't her plan at all, but she knew so well what he was yearning for; begging with those brown puppy eyes.

Arden looked helpless, pinned down. Ecstasy was taking over his naked body, his hard cock, and soul as his tongue came forward involuntarily.

As she climbed back on top of him, it felt like moving into a field of a magnet. Arden thought she would be rocking back and forth, mounting him and letting him cum inside of her, her pussy gripping him tightly as he shot his big load of white gold, ready to burst. Harriet looked at him and sensed his wandering mind; maybe he was thinking he would soon be inside her mouth. Fucking her face so hard that her mascara would run down and she would be squirting on the sheets. This wasn't his thing, but she thought she knew exactly what was. It wasn't her sitting on his face, a river of her sweet wetness flowing into his mouth, barely letting him breathe. It wasn't her choking and degrading him, but something even better.

He pushed his legs back and held them for a few seconds. She looked at him and saw how much he was craving it. She gave him all the warmth he craved and held him through all that curiosity and pain that had led to this.

"Keep them like this," She ordered him, and stared at him lying in a perfect sex doll position.

He was staring at the ceiling, but she wanted him to lift his head.

"Look at me, I want to see the fear in your eyes as I use you."

He gasped as she pushed his cheeks apart, exposing his hole, which was clenching tight with nerves. She smoothly slid a finger inside and felt his muscles release beneath her finger.

Then she went into him in one long move, and then, curling her finger, which made him deliciously sore, brushing against his prostate. She knew the pressure would hurt him only for a moment, and she paused, leaving it inside him.

She grabbed his hard cock and started gently stroking it.

"Good boy," she told him, as he looked up at the ceiling again. She started with small strokes, moving in and out. She fucked him with her finger for a while, and he groaned louder, twisting his hands and clenching his fists whilst strapped tightly to the bed. She couldn't help but think of leaning into him with something slightly bigger, filling him with satisfaction and maybe a little more pain. She would never be plunging inches and inches deep into him out of the blue. She would take it slow; he was way too precious.

"Do you like this?" She asked him, as he was too shy to look at her. He was staring at the ceiling, with overwhelming stimulation forming a droplet on the tip of his cock.

"Stop it!" She smacked his cock.

"I need your cum for somewhere else."

He was trying to move as she squeezed him.

She pulled her finger out of him slowly and made sure the straps were not loose.

His body shuddered.

"Open your eyes," she ordered him, and thought about how he might feel. She was creating a little world he couldn't control. Afraid but excited, a little fire was starting to burn inside of him. She put her hands on her hips and stared at him for a minute.

She grabbed his ball, and he was expecting her to squeeze it like before, but she took a clothes peg from the floor and closed it on him. He turned his head and gasped, but she didn't get enough of a reaction from him, so she pulled the peg, slowly at first. Arden was already changing color, so she switched to the other one. She improvised again and tried something. She curled her tongue and lips. She did one quick, sophisticated spit on his balls and another in his tight hole, and he started moaning and gasping louder. He was enjoying her spitting way too much, and it looked like he was about to cum, so Harriet stopped her improvising and moved on to what he was really yearning for. Harriet slid the strap-on dildo over her smooth thighs and spat in her hand. She felt feminine but dominant. And, Arden, on his hands and knees, was ready. As she pushed in, the very first time, his head dropped to the pillow. She felt masculine and felt his submission; she saw all the times she had been in Arden's position. Willingly and unwillingly. The time Monster just took her and saw her like this. When his cold blue eyes stared at her ass as he humiliated her, this time, this moment was going to override that. She was slow and gentle. Arden moaned. She would never hurt him. She would always treat him in the ways she should have been treated. This was the turning point. Arden gasped, and a smile formed on Harriet's face. She was finally free from the torment.

The fantasy reached its crescendo. Harriet's breath hitched as she imagined Arden's surrender for that thing he so badly craved, the complete relinquishment of control to her, his body a canvas upon which she painted a masterpiece of exquisite torment. She would leave him breathless, broken, utterly consumed. The image was so potent that it made her shiver, a thrilling mix of power and submission. With a sigh, Harriet opened her eyes, the afterglow of the fantasy still vivid in her mind. The reality of Nick and Anna's laughter snapped her back, the absurdity of their conversation now oddly comforting. The seed of this new desire had been planted, and Harriet knew, with a certainty that surprised even her, that this wasn't just a fantasy. It was a promise. She wanted to experience this, and she knew Arden was yearning for it.

Chapter 30

New York/ Sydney, September 2023

Arden fidgeted with his phone, the cold morning air nipping at his exposed fingers. He glanced at the bank across the street, a dull, imposing structure against the brightening sky. The coffee shop queue was moving at a glacial pace. He needed his caffeine, and he needed to send this voice note. Taking a deep breath, he pressed record.

"Hello, hello wifey. I am outside at the moment. When I get home, I am going to ask you for permission to get hard."

He cringed, listening back. It sounded insane. But it was the truth, as bizarre as it was. He couldn't record the message at home. Not this morning. The walls felt like they were listening. He couldn't tell Harriet about his… situation. Would she understand? Would she even believe him? Probably not. The 'situation', as he vaguely called it, was a curse. A constant, throbbing reminder that his body was for everyone, he acted…inappropriately. He was a slut. Webcams, strippers, randoms…he couldn't help it.

And last night was one of those nights.

Finally, his coffee was ready. He paid, scalding his tongue on the first sip, and pocketed his phone. Meanwhile, in a car speeding toward the stark, sterile landscape of the police station, Harriet's lips curved into a soft smile as she listened to Arden's voice note. Anna was driving, her brow furrowed with worry. Detective Emma had news. Harriet had spent the last few weeks reliving the nightmare that was her past relationship with Monster, stating grueling statements. Whatever the news was, it didn't feel like her world was ending anymore. Arden's silly, awkward message grounded her. It was a small, bright spot in the darkness. It was…endearing. She thought about him, about the vulnerability he'd shown in his messages, and a warmth spread through her. It was as if she was falling in love with his soul before touching his skin. And, if she could recognize love from afar, if she couldn't hold him, yet still feel deeply, maybe it was time to decide. She wanted to see him in person.

Later that evening, after a surprisingly short and hopefully final meeting with Detective Emma, Harriet found herself staring at her phone.

"When?" Arden had texted.

He was waiting. Eager, it seemed.

Harriet flipped open her diary. Emma didn't need any more statements from her, and frankly, she needed a break from all of this. Anna could have her room back for a bit.

She could just book flights and go. Why not?

A dark cloud momentarily shadowed her thoughts. Monster. He had done exactly that when they were together. Lied, took a flight, cheated, and lied some more. Flown back, lied, and sexually assaulted her. Then gaslit her into thinking it was her fault. She deserved it.

No. She didn't. What she deserved was Love. Not Fear.

Suddenly, a fury, colder and calmer than any she'd felt before, rose within her. A savage protectiveness towards the woman she was becoming. She remembered the dream she'd had last night, where she stood over Monster, a look of pure, unadulterated disdain plastered across her face. And, as Love, I needed to be stronger, more savage.

So, I whispered in Monster's ear, as he was peacefully sleeping next to his new supply. I borrowed Harriet's words: "You can fuck off. And fuck off again to the mountain fuck off, and keep going. Cunt."

Karma is the judge that keeps the balance when humans take advantage. Remember that Monster. And, Harriet, maybe you should book that flight. With a newfound resolve, Harriet opened her laptop. She closed her eyes, took a deep breath, and clicked on the airline website. She wasn't running away from her trauma; she was running towards a possibility. Towards love. Towards a man whose voice made her feel seen, heard, and cherished.

She filled out the booking form, her fingers trembling slightly. "Departure date…" She selected a date only a few days away. This time, she wouldn't be a victim. This time, she would be brave. This time, she would choose love. She clicked confirm.

Chapter 31

New York, September 2023

Arden slumped deeper into his expensive couch, the muted roar of the football game a dull counterpoint to the frantic tap-tap-tap of his fingers on his phone. His thumbs, agile and practiced, flitted between dating apps, each profile a fleeting landscape of potential conquests. He imagined them naked, the act of objectification a flickering spark in his mind, a disquieting light show that reduced women to vessels, empty spaces to be filled. It wasn't the brutal, violent objectification of someone like Monster, a man who wielded power and control like a weapon. But Arden's was a subtler act, a creeping tendril of entitlement disguised as charm, as flirtation, as romance. Between the casual exchanges with nameless girls, he sent a message to Harriet: "So the day is coming." Arden imagined Harriet staring out the airplane window at the swirling clouds, miniature galaxies mirrored in her thoughtful eyes. She would be traveling across continents for Arden, a man she'd met online, a man whose words had initially resonated with a depth she'd found lacking in others. But the casualness of her latest message, the lack of genuine excitement, sparked a flicker of unease. A whisper of doubt, like a rogue comet, threatened to derail his plan. He'd risked everything for this, all those other women out there who thought he was exclusively dating them. It was possible only in New York. This wasn't simply a romantic rendezvous; it was a voyage into the unknown, a foray into a reality that shifted and warped, reflecting Arden's own distorted lens of desire. Would he soon be checking in on the flight tracker when Harriet's plane touched down? Would he soon be canceling dates, giving excuses?

Arden's thoughts, waiting for her, morphed into something else, a potent cocktail of fear and fascination. He realized then that this wasn't just a meeting; it was a step into a new reality, a reality sculpted by their imagination and his own desperate hope, a reality where the lines between love and objectification blurred into something he had never felt before.

She probably wasn't even coming.

Chapter 32

Delta Flight from Sydney to New York, September 2023

"Would you like another glass?" The air hostess offered Harriet more wine. "It is not like you are driving home," she laughed, her eyes crinkling at the corners. Harriet knew she desperately needed sleep. The red-eye flight was already taking its toll, etching shadows beneath her eyes that even the strategically placed concealer couldn't fully erase. But maybe the wine would help. Maybe it would quiet the butterflies in her stomach, the frantic anticipation coiling tighter with each passing mile closer to him. "Yeah, sure." The air hostess stepped back and pulled the cart along to the next passenger. Harriet downed the wine in almost one gulp. She was going to meet him. I, as Love, knew that Arden was easy to fall in love with. He had his quirky side, a fascination with obscure documentaries that he'd enthusiastically recount to anyone who'd listen. His analytical mind dissected every problem with patient precision. But it was his kind, big, golden-brown eyes and his perfectly articulate way of expressing himself that truly captivated her. He made you feel seen, understood, and cherished. Harriet sipped on the second glass of wine and started writing in her notebook, the small tray table vibrating with the plane's hum. "Tall, dark, handsome. Kind, funny, caring," she scribbled. "This guy. The actual man of my dreams. I get to wake up next to this phenomenal human every day, for the rest of my life. And, wherever in the world we are, I know I'll be home, as long as you're there with me. That's what I believe marriage is all about, and honestly, I can't wait. Join me in a toast!" Harriet raised her glass in a silent toast to the empty window seat beside her, a ridiculous grin plastered on her face. She had never felt this way about anyone. With the stars in her eyes and her heart beating fast, she couldn't wait to meet him. It felt destined, as if love had returned in the form of Arden, matching the depth of all she had learned in its absence.

"We know you are not driving anywhere," the air hostess repeated, topping up another passenger's wine. By now, Harriet had polished off the entire miniature bottle. Feeling tipsy and desperately needing a bathroom, she fantasized if Arden was on this flight. It was ridiculous, of course. But the wine was loosening her inhibitions, painting vivid scenarios in her mind. Would he follow her to the bathroom if he were here? Would he be discreet and sneak in when he knew she was done with her quick bladder? Harriet knew what she would do, pull herself up on the sink, her dress up and her knickers on her knees, under the dim lights. The mirror on the wall would complement her features, and her bronze tanned skin would shimmer under the dim lights, her hair platinum blonde now from all the sun and the sea would fall on her rosy cheeks as she gasped loudly. She would pull him straight in, semi-hard or not. They would not be able to waste time. The announcements overhead would go straight past them, and it would be just the two of them, sky high, entering a space together. His cum would circulate in her like he was meant to, and it would be so perfect, just a few seconds of magical life. Letting go of the back of his hair, he would have that release face, where he is between cuming so hard and not being on this planet, and suddenly being dropped back into reality. Harriet, on the other hand, in all her feminine energy, her mind drifting back to the moments of being suicidal, all that darkness spinning into this moment where life shows its absolute best. From bottom to the top. The hum of the airplane engine was a constant, droning lullaby, yet sleep remained elusive. Eleven more hours to go on this flight. Eleven hours to contemplate the implausible, the miraculous turn her life had taken. She stared at the empty wine glass on the tray table, the remnants of its Cabernet contents a dark stain in the bottom. Arden wasn't here. He was a continent away, waiting. She replayed the balcony scene in her mind, the dizzying drop, the suffocating despair, the desperate thought that it was all over. How could she have gotten to that point? Now, high above the clouds, she saw it with a clarity she hadn't possessed on solid ground. Nothing was over. It was the beginning. "Monster," as she now bitterly called him, was a pathetic man who, unable to shine himself, tried to dim her light. He couldn't match her fly; he was just trying to clip her wings so she would fall. The memories surfaced, unbidden and raw: the stinging slap, the dull ache of the black eye, the throbbing pain where his military boots had crushed her spirit, leaving marks more profound than the ones on her face. The lies, the endless, insidious lies. Forgiveness felt like a betrayal of her own suffering. No. She didn't need to forgive Monster. He didn't deserve it. What she needed was to exorcise him, to commit her pain to paper, and to start building a future that was bright and bold, a future where she could finally breathe. Harriet reached for her bag, fumbling for a pen and a notepad. She found them, her fingers trembling slightly. The notepad was open to a page filled with carefully crafted sentences; a pretend bridal speech she had poured her heart into earlier. A bittersweet mile touched her lips. With a decisive stroke, she drew a love heart over it. It was a symbolic act; she still believed in love. Maybe, she thought, you needed to stare into the abyss, to feel the cold finality of a life about to end, to truly move on. And she certainly had felt that. Then he appeared. *Arden.*

The enigma. And, God, she couldn't explain it. Physical attraction from afar? Was this what teenagers felt about celebrities? Was it just charming conversation, a carefully crafted dialogue designed to pull her back from the edge? Or…was it something more? Real love? She didn't know. And that was precisely why she was on this flight, hurtling towards a confrontation with the unknown. She needed to see him, to feel him, to understand how and why he had materialized at that pivotal moment. She needed to see her life reflected in his gaze, to finally make sense of it all. "I am not stupid," she muttered to herself, her fingers gripping the pen tightly. "I am not stupid like Monster's new supply, believing his pathetic lies." "A soccer ball hit me in the corner of my eye." "I tripped and fell." And in telling those lies, she had become a liar, just like the piece of shit who had hit her in the first place. No more. That chapter was closed. Sealed. Done. She started to write, not a bridal speech, but a declaration of independence. A manifesto for a future she could barely imagine but desperately wanted. As the plane soared onward, carving a path through the starry night, Harriet wrote, not about the past, but about the possibility of a future, a future where she finally chose life, not because she was lucky, but because she was strong enough to choose it for herself. And maybe, just maybe, Arden was part of that future. She would find out. The plane landed softly at JFK. On time. Harriet stared at the striking pink sunset through the windows as she stepped out to the arrivals hall. Arden was not waiting for her with the sign that said "wifey," and a bunch of flowers. She didn't want to admit to herself that she was disappointed, and there was undeniable emptiness in that moment he could have been waiting for her. She took a subway to her hotel. All alone. And then she realized that maybe it was better to leave some room to breathe. She tried to put her thoughts aside, but couldn't sleep. She showered, adding conditioner that smelled so velvety and sensual. She knew, as she inhaled the fragrance, that one day she might not be able to use this product any longer. It would forever remind her of this moment, bringing tingling sensations up her spine, the feeling of having a crush, and that dreamy, floaty feeling that something amazing is about to happen. As the delicious fragrance tickled her nose, the poignant memories remained only one night away. Tomorrow night, she was finally meeting her "husband".

Chapter 33

New York, September 2023

The sun dipped low over the Upper West Side, casting a warm, golden hue that danced through the large windows of a quaint restaurant. It was early evening, and the air outside buzzed with the sounds of city life, the distant honking of taxis, laughter from sidewalk cafes, and the rustle of leaves from nearby Central Park. Inside, the atmosphere was intimate yet lively; soft music floated through the room while patrons chatted animatedly at their tables. Harriet sat alone at a small round table near the window, her gaze flickering between her phone and the door. Her patience waned as she sipped on a vibrant watermelon margarita, its bright pink hue contrasting sharply against her delicate Chloe silk Georgette pussy-bow blouse. The fabric clung lightly to her frame, whispering elegance in every movement, but now it felt confining as anxiety crept in with each passing minute. She had flown for more than twenty-four hours and hardly slept; a cocktail of exhaustion and impatience bubbled within her. As Harriet shifted from one drink to another, her thoughts raced back to Arden and why he was late. A figure approached her table. He was tall with tousled hair and an easy smile that spoke of warmth. "Ryan," he said, extending his hand with genuine friendliness. "Manager of this fine establishment," he laughed. "Harriet," she replied, forcing a smile even as disappointment twisted in her stomach. "He is late, isn't he?" Ryan laughed lightly, trying to draw out some levity amidst her growing frustration. She nodded, recounting how they had planned this, how they had promised to meet at this very spot nestled among brownstones and bustling avenues. "And now he's late," she sighed heavily. Ryan shook his head sympathetically, leaning slightly closer as if sharing in her concern. "Where is he coming from?" With a furrowed brow, Harriet showed him the address on her phone, scrolling through WhatsApp messages until she found the last one: "I got you." It had been half an hour since she'd received it.

"Oh, traffic," Ryan mused knowingly, glancing toward the door as if expecting Arden to burst through any moment. "Let me get you another one, on me." There was something comforting about his presence; it eased some of Harriet's tension as he returned with another margarita. She took a quick sip before setting it down almost too forcefully on the table. It dawned on her then that maybe Arden wouldn't show up after all, a realization that settled like a stone in her chest. "Don't worry," Ryan reassured her gently. "I'll check him out when he arrives." His eyes sparkled with kindness as he encouraged her to relax. As Harriet drank fast again, almost staining her blouse with the vibrant liquid, the world outside continued its rhythm. The sky deepened into twilight shades of lavender and indigo while shadows lengthened across the streets. She couldn't help but feel a twinge of hope amidst her worries; perhaps there was still time for surprises. Harriet found herself wandering through her thoughts whilst sipping the margarita. In the heart of this almost anxious atmosphere, waiting for Arden, she recalled the small Sydney yoga studio that stood nestled between palm trees, its windows glowing warmly from within. The faint flicker of candles illuminated the space, casting playful shadows on walls adorned with crystals that sparkled like stars. The scent of sandalwood and lavender filled the air, wrapping around her senses like a comforting embrace as she stepped inside. Harriet had arrived late to Jana's special night, a gathering meant to awaken the goddess within every woman present. Her heart raced slightly as she hopped over cushions strewn across the floor, finally finding her place between two girls with long dark hair and radiant smiles that welcomed her instantly. The energy in the room was palpable; laughter and soft murmurs danced in harmony with gentle music playing in the background. Jana, the tantric healing teacher leading this transformative experience, exuded an aura of calm confidence. She moved gracefully among them, her cheeks flushed as if she were perpetually basking in bliss. Harriet watched her with wide eyes, captivated by how Jana spoke of vulnerability and connection, concepts that felt foreign yet tantalizingly close to what she craved. Tonight was about healing through touch and practice; it was an invitation to shed layers and embrace new feelings. Time blurred as Harriet lost herself in thought, recalling Jana's teachings and how she had imagined touching Arden. Suddenly, everything shifted when she spotted a familiar figure across the room, a face that made her heart jump to her throat. There he was: Arden, approaching this small table beneath a dim light that highlighted his snug blue sweater perfectly, hugging his form. His deep-set eyes sparkled like amber under candlelight, radiating warmth and magnetism that drew her in irresistibly. As he approached her with an effortless grace that made time seem to stand still, their eyes locked in an unspoken connection that sent shivers down her spine.

In this crowded space, it felt as though they were utterly alone. His confident yet gentle smile ignited something deep within her, a longing she had tried to suppress amidst chaotic months filled with uncertainty. She was finally face-to-face with the man who had brought life to her when she was down. Their conversation flowed easily between them; each word exchanged was like a thread weaving them closer together. Laughter spilled from their lips, lightening the mood around them and drawing glances from other diners who couldn't help but smile at their budding connection. Outside, night fully embraced New York; stars twinkled brightly above while sounds faded into whispers around their corner table. Ryan checked on her from behind the bar—a promise fulfilled—and gave a thumbs-up that made warmth blossom in her chest. Arden ordered more drinks effortlessly as they continued to share stories under the low light. With every passing moment spent together,

Harriet felt emotions stirring within, strong feelings rising like tides ready to crash against shores once barren with loneliness. It was Arden's words during their online chats that had kept her afloat through turbulent waters these past nine months; now here he was in flesh and blood before her, a tangible reminder of hope. He picked up her bag and they walked to his car. Harriet felt tired and drunk if she were walking in a dream. She wished she were sober, as she realized she was practically walking into a stranger's car in the middle of New York late at night. What would Ryan's thumbs-up do if something happened to her? She already imagined the news tomorrow, and Ryan from the bar told the news anchor how he served Harriet drinks and was the last to see her with a man in a dark blue sweater. And Ryan would tell the story of how she had flown from Australia to meet a man she spoke to on a dating app. How ridiculous! Was she stupid? Did she think that was safe? What an idiot! People watching the news would laugh. Arden drove his car better than Monster. No speeding, no panic. Harriet felt safe. As they entered the highway, Arden gently touched her knee. Harriet felt her underwear getting wet, her stomach stirring, and all her caution was thrown in the wind. They walked up to his apartment. He was carrying her luggage, showing her around. She had a glass of water. Was the unexpected going to happen, naturally, just like Jana had explained? "Just let go", she almost heard Jana whisper all the way from Sydney. Her Chloe blouse and white bra were on his couch. He was gently touching her. A little too gently, as if he wasn't allowed to touch her. Harriet invited him closer. She didn't say no. "Wait, I won't be long." He walked over to the bathroom. Harriet wandered off to his bedroom. The color combination of his bed coverings looked so inviting: pink and grey, feminine and soft. Safe. All the traveling, the drinks, the excitement, it all hit her at once, and she fell on his bed. Her head on his soft pillow felt like heaven, and within seconds she was asleep.

Arden walked back to the living room, and for a second, he thought she had left. Leaving her bra behind. "Ohhh." He saw her passed out on his bed. He put a blanket over her. A few minutes later, Harriet swung her legs out of bed and sat up cautiously. "It's OK. Sleep." Arden wanted to kiss her forehead for some reason, but thought it might be too much. "You are safe", he reassured her. "Thank you," Harriet pulled the blanket over her head and turned on her side towards the bedroom window. She was finally asleep.

Chapter 34

New York, September 2023

The next morning, Arden's phone woke him, but the call ended before he answered it. *They'll call back if it's important.* He rolled over and glanced at Harriet, still asleep. Arden had to get up. He walked quietly to his office and opened his laptop. Half an hour later, Harriet wandered out of bed and stared at him.

"Working from home is OK." She said and smiled despite her head hurting. Arden was on the phone and motioned to the bathroom. She read his lips. "I won't be long. Have a shower?" Harriet shut the bathroom door and let the warm water run.

"I've got a fucking shitty hangover. Not so romantic," she whispered, trying to steady herself. Finally, she was in New York. With Arden.

His phone rang again. Her chest tightened. *Another girl?* He answered quickly, like it was nothing.

Pieces of last night came back in fragments: Ryan, the bar manager, too much to drink, Arden's hand brushing her knee in the car. The phone rang again. He picked up.

"Call you later," she heard him say, low, private.

In the shower, Harriet pressed her palm to the wall, letting the water run over her. She wanted him there, pressed close, his hands exploring, making

121

her forget. But something was holding him back. It wasn't work. It was something else.

Wrapped in a green towel, she stepped out of the steam, droplets sliding down her skin. The room felt colder than it should have, her pulse pounding in her ears.

Arden was there, phone still in his hand, his expression unreadable.

Her gaze locked on him, sharp and unflinching. The words rose up, burning her throat. *I thought you had some cute blonde waiting here. What the hell is going on?*

She imagined spitting them at him, imagined the way his jaw would tighten, the flicker in his eyes. For a second, the whole scene played out in her head like a reel.

"If I sound cranky, it's because I have the worst hangover," she muttered, watching Arden glance up from his computer.

Hangovers were nothing new, but this time her body wanted something more than water or aspirin. It wanted him. A heat spread through her belly, sharp and urgent, until she could hardly sit still.

She slipped into black underwear, a plain white T-shirt, and jeans, something safe, something that wouldn't betray the images storming her mind. Not the silk dress she longed to wear, not the lace that would have made her feel bold enough to stalk into his office, climb onto his lap, and grind herself against him while his hands held her tight.

The thought alone made her clench, made her ache.

She forced herself onto the bed, trying to steady her thoughts, but her phone buzzed. Anna. *Did you get there safely? About to call Interpol! Let me know you're alive!*

Harriet typed back quickly: *Alive. Don't remember much. Going out later, maybe. Haven't fucked him yet. Perhaps he's gay?* Even her messages sounded fevered, half-crazed.

But Anna was asleep in Australia, and Harriet was here. In his apartment. In his city. And he hadn't touched her.

By two o'clock, he ran out to grab lunch, leaving her restless. Jet lag pulled at her, Netflix blurred on the screen, and when he came back, his body language was all wrong. Nervous. Guarded. He left her smoked salmon bagel on the table.

"I just need to pop out for a bit," he muttered, not meeting her eyes.

Her chest tightened. *Another girl. It has to be.*

She could have been anywhere else, lounging in a bougie marble hotel lobby under glittering chandeliers, one leg crossed, her barefoot dangling, men with dark eyes and smooth accents circling her like moths. She could have been adored. Desired. Wanted.

But she wasn't. She had spent her money, her time, her heart to come here, to Arden. And now he was leaving her alone in his apartment.

Asshole.

Tom Hanks' voice from *A League of Their Own* echoed from the TV: *There's no crying in baseball.*

She had taken a risk coming here. Maybe he didn't like her. Perhaps he wanted her gone. Maybe it wasn't anyone's fault.

But then she remembered his hand on her knee last night. The warmth of it. The certainty of it. That wasn't her imagination. That was real.

Clutching that memory, she changed into a silk dress, sliding it over her skin like armor. It made her feel less like a guest, more like herself. She wasn't going to leave. Not yet. She would stay and see this through, whether it ended in fire or ash.

Even if it shattered her into a thousand pieces.

Maybe then her heart would finally freeze over, cold and impenetrable, like Monster's. His blue eyes had always been detached, glassy, unreadable. Maybe one day hers would look the same.

Maybe that was the only way to survive.

Chapter 35

New York, September 2023

Harriet pulled her laptop from her suitcase, staring at the screen as if it might hold her scattered thoughts together.

I was in your apartment, feeling everything, touching everything. For nine months, you'd been feeding me this illusion, but all it amounted to were the same Ikea plates everyone owns, the fake golden Buddha statues, the cheap fabric draped over a couch. I slid my bare skin across it and cried until my chest ached. Not because you shattered some grand romantic fantasy, it was always fragile, always paper-thin, but because I was an absolute fool for letting it happen. For believing you. For flying twenty-five hours, wrecked with jet lag, tears in my eyes, unable to string a sentence together. For what?

To peel back the layers and expose your lies? To put you out there for all the innocent girls who don't yet know any better? But even they aren't my concern. Life will teach them about men like you in its own brutal way. What I wanted, what I needed, was to understand why I was here at all.

The door clicked open. Arden was back. Harriet's chest tightened, not with longing, not yet, but with pure, unfiltered anger. She stayed on the couch, eyes fixed on him, arms crossed like a shield. His casual stride, the effortless ease with which he moved through his apartment, felt like a knife twisting in her chest. He had left her. Alone.

He leaned against the kitchen counter, golden-brown eyes scanning the room, and for a second, she wondered if he even noticed her. Of course he did. Arden always noticed. But that didn't make it hurt any less.

Harriet's fingers dug into the edge of the couch. Her mind spun. *How dare he expect me to just... exist here, waiting for him, like some pet?*

"I only came here to get pregnant," she spat, words sharp, brittle, slicing through the tense silence. She didn't flinch, didn't waver, though her pulse was hammering in her throat. Let him feel it. Let him know she wasn't here to forgive him, not yet, maybe not ever.

Arden's eyebrows lifted. "I feel... weird," he said, as if that explained anything, as if it excused leaving her to meet someone else. "You just put too much weight on me..." His words stumbled out, trying to reason, trying—and failing—to make it sound okay.

"I said what I said," Harriet shot back, her voice trembling, not with fear, but with fury she barely controlled. *You left me. Alone. For her. And now you expect... what?*

He tried to smirk, half-heartedly teasing. "You sound... fond of something."

Harriet laughed, a bitter, high-pitched bark that sounded nothing like herself. "Fond? Are you joking? " Her hands shook as she gestured wildly toward him. "You're the same as every other man, Arden. Every. Single. One."

He took a step closer, trying to calm her, or maybe to charm her, but Harriet recoiled slightly, anger sparking against the magnetic pull he still had. *Why does he still affect me? How can he make me feel this, this electric pull, when he's clearly lying, abandoning me?*

"You make the ordinary feel... dangerous," she said, but the words were sarcastic, sharp. Dangerous? No. He was reckless. He was selfish. He was *heartbreaking*. And infuriating. She wanted to throw something at him, punch the counter, scream until her lungs burned. Instead, she clenched her fists in her lap, nails digging into her palms.

Arden's eyes softened, and it made her teeth grit. *Soft? Him? Now?* After he had just left me for someone else? She wanted to shake him, knock that effortless cool off his face, make him see how much this hurt.

"You're still here," he murmured, voice low, dangerous in its intimacy.

"Of course I'm still here," Harriet shot back. "Because apparently, I have no other choice. I stay here, fuming, while you do whatever you want. Meet other girls, smile at them, come back like it's all fine. I wonder what you told her? And you want me to… what? Be calm? Be rational?"

Arden didn't answer immediately. He just looked at her, eyes steady, almost challenging. Heat pooled low in her stomach despite herself, anger and desire tangled together in a confusing mess she hated. She hated it, hated him, and yet… she couldn't look away.

"I'm not here because of you," she said finally, voice raw, shaking, almost breaking. "I'm here because I… I have to be. Not because of what I feel. Certainly not because of *you*."

He leaned a fraction closer, and she flinched. Close enough to feel the subtle heat radiating from him, the faint scent she couldn't stop thinking about, cedar, spice, Arden. She wanted to push him away, scream at him to leave, make him feel the weight of his betrayal. But her body betrayed her. The tension, the pull, the magnetic force between them made her knees weak, made her heart race, made her pulse hammer.

"You've changed," he said softly, almost a whisper, but it made her jaw clench.

"No," she said, voice sharp, biting. "I'm the same. You're the one who's changed. Or maybe you never were who I thought you were. Either way… you're a Monster too, Arden. Just like all the rest. And I hate that you can still make me feel…"

She leaned back against the couch, fury rolling through her like a storm, yet beneath it all, confusion festered. Desire, longing, the part of her that still remembered every message, every laugh, every soft moment between them, oceans apart. That part hated her for wanting him. That part hated him for leaving.

And yet, she was still here. Golden-brown eyes fixed on her, challenging, teasing, dangerous. Still Arden. And she… couldn't stop looking.

"Let's fuck."

Harriet's voice cut through the room like a blade, no hesitation, no shame.

She hadn't flown across the world for a man who dangled promises and withheld. Nine months of talk. Nine months of teasing words. And now, here he was, all retreat and excuses.

Not anymore.

Harriet knew her worth. She was more than a body, though her body was fire, her sex a force he couldn't even begin to comprehend. She had a mind that pulsed with ideas, a heart that felt everything too deeply, and a soul that refused to stay small.

Was she about to take his seed, or was Arden about to discover something he had never touched before?

One thing was certain: she hadn't come here for nothing. She had spent too many years being nothing for Monster. That ended now. She was something. She was everything.

And if this burned, if it broke, if it left her shattered, then at least it would become a story. A great story. She still had her hands, after all. Monster hadn't taken those in the car crash, no matter how hard he tried to break and destroy her. She could still write. Not about Arden. Not really. But about a woman. An incredible woman. A powerhouse.

Herself.

Chapter 36

New York, September 2023

I heaved a deep sigh. I'm not a voyeur. I don't like watching people have sex. But this… this was different. I had never seen anything like it. This wasn't just sex; it was experimental, daring, electric. And I couldn't look away.

Arden pushed himself up from the couch, pulling his T-shirt over his head, then dropped onto all fours, eyes dark and mischievous. He wanted her to help him fuck himself. And she did, moving behind him in her floaty orange silk dress, following his utterly crazy idea with curiosity and interest, her hands confident and precise. She guided him, bending his cock slightly toward his ass, adjusting, testing, exploring whether it could work. Every motion was deliberate, intimate, and erotic. My pulse raced at the audacity of it all, the way she followed his lead, the way he arched and moaned, the thrill of their private, experimental choreography.

He disappeared briefly and returned with a bottle of blue Nivea moisturizer. She laughed softly as she spread it on her hands. *This is like sunscreen, it won't work!* I read her lips, catching every teasing inflection. Arden's brief flicker of disappointment only made the tension sharper, more charged.

Then Harriet pushed him down onto the couch and straddled him. Hair falling free, red lipstick catching the light, eyes locked on his, teeth nipping her inner lip, she was in control, fearless, playful. Arden shivered beneath her, taut and ready, and then, he was inside her. Urgent, hot, overwhelming, his release spilling into her silk dress. My chest tightened; I had never seen such raw, unrestrained intimacy. Every detail burned into me, the way she moved, the way he arched, the audacity of it all.

She stepped away, cleaning herself, and he stayed still on the couch. But the image lingered, vivid, electric, impossible to shake. They had created something entirely theirs, experimental, brazen, intimate, and I had been there, watching it all, heart hammering.

Arden felt bad for leaving Harriet alone. He got up and walked over to find her. She was splashing cold water on her face and looking at herself in the mirror. Arden stood in the doorway, watching her.

"Can I take you for dinner?" "What can I do for you?" Harriet shook her head.

"Come." Arden walked to her and took her hand. They walked over to his large white wardrobe. He pulled a couple of collared shirts out.

"Which one do you think I should wear?" Harriet's throat still ached, and her head was throbbing. "And what do you think?" she responded.

"I want you to choose." Arden smiled and grabbed a burgundy one. "This?" "Almost red. Red flag." He tried to make a joke of himself. " No. That one. " Harriet pointed at the darker blue shirt hanging separately next to the official uniforms of the financial district, all the dark blue and black three-piece suits. "That one?" Arden looked surprised. He smiled as he approached her, putting the shirt on.

"You…can do the buttons". Arden looked breathtaking, but Harriet covered her mouth as she buttoned the shirt. She was still angry at him for leaving her alone. She never asked who he met. She decided there and then that whatever he was doing was none of her business. Unconditional Love. "I'd better go get changed too," Harriet said, looking down, still unable to hide her frustration. She picked a green figure-hugging bandage dress that hugged her in a very intimate way. Her breasts peaked perfectly with the low neckline, and her legs looked like a real woman with little flesh moving up and down as she took a step.

She left her hair hanging down, just giving it a quick brush, and added some neutral brown eye shadow that brought up her stunning green eyes. She didn't bother with full make-up as she almost felt like she was resenting Arden, and he did not deserve to see her at her best.

Little did she realize that she looked breathtaking, her fleshier hips moving gracefully in the tight dress.

And as Love, I watched, captivated. This wasn't just about overcoming obstacles; it was two bodies, two souls, exploring desire and trust in ways no one else would dare. She had just guided him through bending himself, hands steady, curiosity sharp, and yet, moments later, they were casually picking out a shirt, every movement intimate, audacious, and charged, even with the fire of her frustration simmering beneath it. The way they moved together, fearless and unrestrained, proved that where desire and hope take root, even amidst the harshest realities, miracles, raw, erotic, and impossible to forget, can bloom.

Chapter 37

New York, September 2023

They drank cocktails, ate dinner in a dimly lit restaurant, and went to a club. Someone passed a key. Cocaine. Harriet was drunk and didn't hesitate. Arden rolled his eyes and followed suit."Hey, I am in New York! The best city in the world!" Harriet laughed and pulled Arden onto the dance floor. It was 5 am by the time they called an Uber. Standing in his kitchen, still a little wasted, they talked about how much fun the club was. Arden threw Harriet a weed gummy; she had never had one before, so she only took a small bite. "Come with me," Arden offered his hand, and soon they were in bed. Naked. Things happened fast, and then slow. Very slow. With a newfound sense of freedom that had washed over her like a warm tide, she let go of all worries about judgment or expectations. It was just them now, two souls intertwined in this sanctuary where vulnerability reigned supreme, just like Jana had taught her. *Let go.* Arden had given her the attention she craved for so long; it was time she returned that affection tenfold. It was something he never expected either. She glanced over at him. The way he looked, both vulnerable and exhilarated, made her stomach flutter. His curly hair was tousled, and his chest rose and fell steadily beneath a layer of sweat glistening under the morning light, peeking through the window. At that moment, she couldn't help but admire him;

"Hey," she whispered, leaning in closer to him.

"You, okay?" Her fingers brushed against his arm gently. Arden turned his head slightly toward her, a lazy smile spreading across his lips. "Just savoring this," he murmured, his voice low and honeyed. The sincerity in his gaze sent warmth blooming throughout her body. She could feel her heart racing again as anticipation coursed through her veins like electricity. She leaned forward to plant a kiss on his forehead, a gesture filled with tenderness, and then let her lips trail downwards ever so slowly. "Harriet…" he breathed, his eyes half-lidded as he surrendered himself to her touch. She took a sip from a glass of icy water resting on the nightstand before burying her face between his soft cheeks. Nothing was awkward about this; it felt undeniably right, like discovering an undiscovered treasure deep within herself that had been waiting for this moment to shine.

"Slow down," he said softly as she explored him with purpose. But she found herself digging deeper into this blissful moment, a mix of rough passion and tender exploration, as they shared breaths laden with unspoken desires. Each soft moan escaped his lips and ignited something primal within her; an intoxicating blend of power and pleasure enveloped them both. As time slowed around them, Harriet marveled at how beautifully imperfect they were together: neither perfect nor broken, but simply existing, wrapped in their world where only they mattered. Harriet submerged into him, leaning her cheek on his soft skin. Her tongue felt like it was touching a glazier; the taste of his skin was like drinking Evian. He buried his face in a pillow and moaned. Harriet barely recognized herself like this, her head buried in him. His body was begging her tongue, and she did not let his legs shake; she was holding them tight. Redness grew on her cheeks, and she pulled her head up. Her fingertip entered him, and she felt him pulsating and pushing back. His curly hair and soft feet. Heart of gold. She was full of adoration for him. Harriet slid her finger in again and stopped. She kneeled and adjusted herself, and all she could think of was how beautiful he was. Inside and outside. "He feels like a feather, so fine," Harriet thought as she felt more and more intoxicated.

He was so melty and moany, still pressing his head on the pillow. She kept going until he turned around, and she pushed his legs back and placed herself on top of him. Harriet felt like she was floating, her head back and forth, he suddenly came inside of her. That was the moment she would never forget; she felt like crying. As she rolled off him, the sunlight spilled over them like liquid gold. She got up and went to the bathroom. Harriet caught sight of herself in the bathroom mirror: flushed cheeks reflecting newfound confidence that bloomed within her spirit like wildflowers breaking through concrete."I can't believe we did that," she thought wistfully while reaching for mouthwash, a symbolic cleansing from remnants of flashbacks of her tongue inside of him, still haunting her mind like shadows on a wall. When Harriet returned from the bathroom, picking up discarded covers from their earlier escapade off the floor, Arden remained still, his body relaxed. She sat on the bed. "Come here," she motioned playfully while biting her lower lip; excitement bubbling within as he approached like an eager puppy drawn by its owner's call. In this sacred space where laughter mingled with sighs and gentle touches ignited flames of passion, they were becoming something more than just lovers; they were healing one another through a connection forged under the golden rays above.

Chapter 38

New York, September 2023

Arden, ever elusive, walked with a brisk, purposeful stride, his gaze fixed on the darkening sky. The city lights flickered like distant stars, and the September leaves whispered beneath their shoes. Harriet's unspoken plea lingered in the crisp autumn air: *Hold my hand.* She watched him, the subtle sway of his hips almost… feminine. *I gave you everything, and you won't even hold my hand,* she thought, swallowing her disappointment.

Arden paused mid-step, eyes narrowing as he took in the view. "Can you believe this place?" he murmured, a dark chuckle slipping past his lips. "With that kind of money? I'd go insane."

They stood before the sprawling mansion of a notoriously reclusive billionaire, its foreboding presence softened by the beauty of its surroundings. Harriet tilted her head, half-amused, half-serious. "Crazy how?" she asked, one brow arched.

Arden shrugged, a roguish smile spreading across his face as he gestured toward the mansion's gilded opulence. "Parties every night. Private jets. Endless possibilities…" He let the pause hang, then added with a mischievous smirk, "Or maybe I would just buy an island."

Harriet laughed softly, but then sobered, her green eyes searching his.

"But would that really make you happy? Would it fill that void inside?"

For a heartbeat, the playful mask slipped. Arden's brown eyes darkened, a flicker of vulnerability breaking through the charm. "Maybe not," he admitted, voice low, almost reluctant. "But it would be fun trying."

As they wandered beneath the grand arches of the estate, Arden finally reached for her hand. The warmth of his fingers against hers was electric, a spark that cut through the extravagance, a reminder that even in the midst of wealth and excess, real connection was the only thing that truly mattered.

Her hand tightened slightly around his, and she let herself hope.

He doesn't love me; he loves getting laid, he loves me inside of him. He loves coming inside of me. But he is holding my hand. At last.

Harriet's heart raced as she nestled closer to Arden; her fingers entwined with his. Today felt different; charged with unspoken words and lingering glances that hinted at something more profound. She heard someone play Erik Satie's nostalgic, gloomy piano piece in the distance, encapsulating her loneliness. But the warmth of his palm against hers was electric, and with every note, she felt an undeniable connection thrumming between them. But then, without warning, Arden pulled his hand away.

Harriet's breath caught in her throat as confusion flickered across her face. "Why did you—?" she began, her voice barely above a whisper, trailing off as she searched his eyes for answers. Arden looked away, momentarily lost in thought as he wrestled with his emotions. There was joy in having her close, yet Fear lurked at the edges of his heart, a Fear of crossing boundaries that had defined their relationship for so long. He could feel the intensity of her gaze on him, and it sent small shivers down his spine. "Harriet," he finally said, his voice steady but soft, "I want this... I want you near me." He paused, taking a deep breath as he turned back to face her fully. "I like you." He stood back a little. "But remember, I told you, I always ruin things." His admission hung between them like a fragile, invisible thread, both beautiful and terrifying. The late afternoon light filtered through the September leaves above them, casting dappled shadows on their faces. Harriet's heart swelled with hope despite the uncertainty hanging in the air. She leaned forward slightly, her eyes searching for clarity. "You're not ruining anything," she replied earnestly. "We can explore this together." Arden's expression softened at her words; there was something undeniably enchanting about Harriet's willingness to embrace the unknown alongside him. The park around them faded into oblivion as they focused solely on one another—their breaths synchronized with the rustling leaves above. As they resumed their tentative hold on each other's hands, warmth flooded back into their touch, a silent promise that spoke louder than any words could convey. They had walked all the way to Central Park, and the sun dipped lower on the horizon, painting the sky in shades of pink and orange, a perfect backdrop for their blossoming *something*.

Chapter 39

New York, September 2023

As twilight descended upon the bustling city, the streets glimmered with a soft, golden hue. Harriet found herself perched on a weathered wooden bench in the heart of Central Park, framed by tall, whispering trees that swayed gently in the cool evening breeze. The sun hung low on the horizon, casting long shadows and igniting the sky with streaks of pink and orange, a picturesque backdrop that contrasted starkly with the tempest brewing within her heart. Harriet's thoughts drifted back to Arden, who had walked off to a nearby cafe to pick up drinks. Arden's charm had ensnared her from that very first "hello, Wifey" they exchanged online, a simple greeting that had spiraled into an intoxicating connection. Yet now, as she sat under a canopy of fading light, doubts clouded her mind like the gathering storm clouds overhead.

"Why do we fall for the wrong ones?" she muttered to herself, her voice barely above a whisper. She absentmindedly traced patterns in the damp wood of the bench, recalling how her heart had never truly belonged to Monster, not like it did to Arden. Even though she was acutely aware of his flirtations with other women and men, how he wrapped his words in silk and spun tales that kept her captivated, she couldn't sever the ties that bound them.

Suddenly, a familiar laughter broke through. Harriet turned to see Arden strolling toward her, his presence commanding yet casual, dressed in a navy-blue shirt that accentuated his lean frame. His dark hair, tousled by the wind, seemed to catch the last rays of sunlight like strands of gold. A smile tugged at his lips as he approached.

"Hey there, Earl Grey for the Lady," he greeted warmly, taking a seat beside her without hesitation and passing her takeaway cup. The world around them faded into obscurity; it was just him and her against the canvas of twilight.

"Hey," she replied softly, trying to mask her inner turmoil beneath a facade of casualness. She studied him, the way his eyes sparkled with mischief and warmth, drawing her closer even as apprehension gnawed at her insides."What are you thinking about?" he asked, tilting his head slightly as if he could read every thought swirling in her mind. "Just… life," she replied evasively, unsure if she could articulate the whirlwind of emotions flooding through her heart. He chuckled lightly, brushing his fingers through his hair. "Life can be complicated." Harriet looked away momentarily to gather herself. "Yeah… especially when it comes to love." Arden's expression shifted subtly; something flickered behind his eyes, a hint of understanding or perhaps guilt? "You're right about that." The unspoken tension hung between them like a delicate thread waiting to snap. She wanted so desperately to confront him about their ambiguous relationship, but found herself entranced by his presence instead. A part of her knew she should walk away before it hurt too much; another part craved every moment spent in this intoxicating limbo. As darkness fell and stars began to twinkle overhead like scattered diamonds against velvet fabric, Harriet felt an undeniable pull towards him, an affection steeped in uncertainty yet laced with hope.

Chapter 40

New York, September 2023

They were back from their walk, and Arden closed his blinds. Arden's heart pounded as he watched Harriet eagerly approach him, her eyes bright and hungry. He had never seen her like this before, so brazen, so uninhibited. Even more than the night before. He couldn't help but feel a mix of fear and excitement as he spread his legs, presenting his lean body to her again. She didn't hesitate for a moment, kneeling between his legs and taking his cock in her mouth. Her warm, wet lips slid over the head, and she began to suck. Arden groaned, his hands finding their way into her hair, urging her to take more. He could feel her teeth graze his sensitive flesh, and it sent a shiver down his spine. She bobbed her head, taking him deeper into her mouth, and he could feel his control slipping away. The room was hot and heavy with desire, and all he could focus on was the sensation of her tongue dancing around the head of his cock. When she finally pulled away, Arden let out a protesting moan. "Harder," he whispered. "Make me beg." Harriet smiled, her eyes twinkling with mischief. She nodded, standing up and reaching for the black crocodile leather collar chain lying on the coffee table. Without another word, she wrapped it around her hand, creating a makeshift whip. Arden's breath hitched as she raised the chain above her head, the tip of it glinting in the dim light. He felt a thrill of anticipation run through him, mixing with the ache in his groin. He knew this was going to hurt, but he also knew he wouldn't be able to stop her. "Do it," he said, his voice barely above a whisper. Without further hesitation, Harriet brought the chain down on his ass cheek, hard. A sharp sting flashed through him, followed by a wave of pleasure. She struck him again, this time on the other cheek, and he arched his back, moaning. She continued to whip him, the sting turning into a burning sensation that he welcomed. He could feel his cock throbbing, leaking pre-cum onto his stomach. "Please," he begged, unable to contain himself any longer. "I want you to lick it," Harriet smirked and, without saying a word, leaned over to lap up the clear fluid from his stomach. She then kissed her way up his chest, teasingly nipping at his nipples before taking his cock into her mouth once more. This time, she bobbed her head faster, sucking harder, and Arden felt himself getting closer to the edge. He couldn't believe how turned on he was by her dominance and how much he loved being at her mercy. As she took him deeper into her mouth, Arden felt his body tense up. He knew he was about to cum.

"I'm close," he warned her, his voice hoarse. Harriet smiled up at him, her green eyes dark with lust. "Then come all over my face," she purred. With that, Arden released his seed, shooting into her mouth. She swallowed every drop, her tongue lapping at the head of his cock until he was finally done. They stayed like that for a moment, catching their breath, before collapsing onto the couch together.

Chapter 41

New York, September 2023

Harriet woke up to Arden staring at her, his face an unreadable mask in the soft morning light. "You know it's Sunday, and I am sorry to do this to you, but I booked you a hotel." "What?" Harriet rubbed her tired eyes, the remnants of sleep clinging to her like a stubborn fog. The words didn't quite register.

"You know we agreed you'd stay until Sunday. It's Sunday." Arden stated, his voice flat, devoid of any warmth. "Fuck your Sunday," Harriet mumbled, still half-asleep and thoroughly disoriented. The reality of his blatant dismissal began to sink in, a cold stone settling in her stomach. "Fine," Arden snapped, turning sharply and stalking towards the bedroom door. The curtness of his reply was like a slap in the face. He bent down quickly, scooped a handful of her underwear from the floor, and unceremoniously chucked them into her half-packed suitcase. "I like you, but I am not in love with you, " she heard him say. Harriet had no time to think, no time to process the dizzying mix of hurt and anger that threatened to overwhelm her. She slammed his door shut with a force that rattled the frame and grabbed her suitcase, stumbling out into the hallway. She needed to get away, needed to breathe air that wasn't saturated with Arden's cold indifference. "What an asshole," she muttered under her breath as she hailed a cab. The

New York cityscape blurred past, a kaleidoscope of indifferent faces and towering buildings. She felt raw and exposed, as if her skin had been peeled away. Did Arden not realize what hell she had been through with Monster? The memories of the volatile relationship, the emotional wreckage, and the constant anxiety were all still so fresh. She had finally clawed her way out, and Arden, with his calm demeanor and seeming understanding, had felt like a safe harbor. Fine, if he wanted to think of them as just sex buddies, she could accept that, maybe. But he could have treated her with a modicum of respect, a sliver of basic human decency. She had flown across the world for him, poured her heart out, and this was the thanks she got. Harriet decided, then and there, that she would not, could not, care about him anymore. He had shown her his true colors, and they were as bleak and unforgiving as a winter sky in the Arctic Circle. She would not waste another second dwelling on his callousness. The cab pulled up to the hotel, a sleek and modern building in Midtown. As she checked in, Harriet felt a flicker of determination ignite within her. She would not let Arden ruin her trip. She would not let him dictate her emotions.

She would have a long, hot shower and wash away the remnants of Arden and his "Sunday." She would get dressed in her best outfit, the one she had packed and almost hadn't worn. She would put on makeup, not to impress anyone, but for herself. She would go out and explore, and she would have the best night of her life in New York City. And so, she did. She dined at a bustling Italian restaurant, laughing with strangers at the next table. She caught a late-night show in a dimly lit club, the music weaving its spell around her. She walked through Times Square, mesmerized by the energy and the lights, feeling a strange sense of liberation. She danced until her feet ached; she drank cocktails with names she couldn't pronounce, and she laughed until tears streamed down her face. For the first time in a long time, Harriet felt truly free. Free from Monster's manipulations, free from Arden's indifference, free to be herself. As the sun began to peek over the horizon, painting the sky in hues of pink and gold, Harriet hailed a cab back to the hotel. She was exhausted but exhilarated. She had turned

Arden's dismissive Sunday into a celebration of her own resilience, her own strength, her own rediscovered joy. He might have thought he could control her narrative, but Harriet had just rewritten it, one electrifying night at a time.

Chapter 42

New York, September 2023

As 'Love' watching everything unfold in New York, shocked me. I had a celestial office, just a comfy armchair nestled among the swirling nebulae and a limitless view of the world below. My job, if you could call it that, was to nudge hearts, to orchestrate those serendipitous encounters, to whisper possibilities into the ears of dreamers. And this time, with Harriet, I thought I had it almost perfectly planned. Arden was a touch arrogant, but undeniably magnetic. Harriet deserved someone who could ignite her soul, someone who would appreciate her fierce loyalty and the quiet strength she carried. She had been burned more than badly before, and I, in my infinite wisdom, thought Arden was the balm she needed. Arden's behavior towards Harriet was so disappointing. He was everything I didn't want him to be. He'd painted her perfect portrait of himself online, capturing the soft glow in her eyes and the curve of her smile. But at the same time, he was living his life in New York, leaving Harriet with whispered promises and a heart full of hope. To his small defense…he didn't think she would fly across the world to see him. He genuinely believed it was a fleeting chat online, a sexy little chapter in his otherwise chaotic existence. He was seeing other people, just living his life in Manhattan, from office, bars to strip clubs, his charm a potent weapon in his arsenal. But she did. Harriet, bless her tenacious spirit, had booked a flight. I didn't even try to send any subtle warnings, a delayed train, a sudden downpour, a misplaced passport, she'd arrived in New York on time, her suitcase bursting with sexy underwear, that green figure-hugging dress, a crocodile collar for him, and the unwavering conviction that their connection was real. Harriet was delusional, in a way, and that was my fault. I had woven such a vibrant tapestry of possibilities in her mind that she couldn't see the threads unraveling. He did say to her she could stay until Sunday. But in her mind, first being disregarded reminded her of Monster; her subconscious would always remind her of that. Then, she was seeing if he was worth staying at all, but it was too late; she was fully taken by his charm or whatever that was he had going on, and wanted to stay until the end. She didn't see what I saw. That he was still a player. He was still not thinking. I was trying to fix things for her, to orchestrate a meeting, to prove that the world, and particularly Arden, was capable of meeting her halfway. Let her find love again. And passion. I wanted her to truly feel again. The reality, of course, could have been far messier. There could have been a moment she would have seen him across the crowded street, his arm draped casually around another woman, the bubble would have well and truly burst.

Harriet, whom I had cherished for so long, would have crumbled. I felt a pang of regret so sharp it echoed through the cosmos. But then, something remarkable happened. I watched as Harriet, for a fleeting second, wanted to lash out. Maybe cry or disappear. But then she straightened her shoulders, took a deep breath, and walked out of his apartment. She didn't confront him, didn't beg for an explanation. She simply walked away. For the rest of her trip, I watched Harriet rediscover herself. She explored the city with a newfound independence. She wandered through the Met, lost in the vibrant colors of the impressionists. She laughed with strangers at a comedy club. She even took a pottery class, her hands kneading the clay with a focused intensity I hadn't seen before. She created Arden's perfect ass into a dog bowl. I laughed so hard. She dined alone in bustling restaurants, savoring the flavors of the city. She danced to live music in dimly lit bars, her laughter echoing through the night. And yes, there were moments of sadness, moments when the image of Arden would flicker in her memory, but those moments grew shorter, less intense, with each passing moment. I was proud of her, though. She had taken a step forward, a giant leap perhaps, and despite Arden's actions, she had the time of her life. Without him. She had found joy in the solitude, strength in the silence, and a vibrant, blossoming future that didn't depend on the whims of a fickle artist. It wasn't the ending I had envisioned, not the perfectly orchestrated romance I had planned. But it was something far more profound. It was Harriet finding love, not in another person, but within herself. As I watched her, a quiet smile spreading across my face in my cosmic armchair, I realized that sometimes, the most beautiful stories are the ones we don't write, the ones that unfold with resilience and grace that even love itself can't predict. Her journey had only begun, and I couldn't wait to see what chapters she would write next, armed with her newfound strength and the dazzling spark of self-love.

Chapter 43

New York, September 2023

Arden's name blinked from the top of Harriet's phone screen. "Coffee?" the message read. "Before you go? I know you're heading out tomorrow." Harriet stared at the illuminated rectangle, her thumb hovering over the keyboard. Her gut twisted with a familiar anxiety. New York had been a revelation. A sanctuary. A place where she could finally hear her thoughts above the din of her complicated life back home. She'd wandered through its chaotic beauty, embraced its solitary energy, and come to a fragile peace with herself. And Arden… Arden was a complication. She replayed their online connection in her mind. Months of witty banter, shared passions, and vulnerable confessions had painted a dazzling picture. But the reality of Arden in person had been… different. Not bad, exactly, but undeniably less vibrant than the digital persona she'd fallen for or perhaps projected upon. The memory of their argument, brittle and sharp, pierced through the hazy contentments cultivated in the city. "I only came to New York to get pregnant!" she'd spat, the venom surprising even herself. An impulsive, cruel jab designed to wound. She hadn't meant it, of course. The fertility idea, without a clinic, had been a footnote in the subconsciousness, a practical consideration, not the driving force behind her journey. She'd just wanted to hurt him. Wanted to puncture the idealized image he seemed to have of her. Now, facing his simple request, she wrestled with conflicting emotions. He had disappointed her; that much was true. Maybe the online fantasy had crumbled under the weight of real-world expectations. But she had disappointed him, too, perhaps. She'd arrived in his city, burdened by her baggage, and unloaded some of it on him. She didn't need him. New York had proven that. She could survive, and thrive even, without the reassurance of a romantic connection, however fleeting. She had been through worse. Far worse. But… a part of her, the stubborn, romantic part, still clung to the possibility, however remote, that there was something real beneath the surface. Was it delusional to still harbor such a thought? Was she caught in a trap of her own making, projecting a fairy tale onto a connection that was, at best, a pleasant acquaintance? Maybe. Probably. Maybe, seeing him one last time, she could finally excise these lingering doubts. Maybe she could assess their connection with a clear head, free from the pressure of expectation, and decide whether a friendship, even a distant one, was worth preserving. And then there was the underlying question that gnawed at her: had she been unfair? Had she expected too much, judged too harshly? Had her own insecurities colored her perception of him?

Finally, she typed a reply: "Okay. Where and when?" The decision was made, and a strange sense of calm settled over her. This would be the final act in their brief New York drama. She would meet him, observe him, and decide. No pressure, no expectations. Just a cup of coffee and a farewell conversation. She would spend her last day in New York with him. Not because she needed him, or because she believed in some grand, romantic destiny now. But because she owed it to herself to see things through to the end, to unravel the threads of her complicated feelings, and to leave the city with a clear conscience. Maybe, just maybe, she could even forgive him, and herself, for the messy reality that had unfolded. And maybe, just maybe, there was still space for something genuine, even if it wasn't the love story she'd briefly, foolishly, fantasized about.

Chapter 44

New York, September 2023

Harriet decided to meet Arden. *Why did she foolishly fall in love?* Maybe the last day together with him would give her some answers before she flew back to Sydney. She'd spent the last few hours dodging his calls, exploring New York, trying to compartmentalize the aching void he'd left simmering in her chest. The city had been a welcome distraction, a kaleidoscope of lights and sounds that temporarily masked the frantic rhythm of her heart. But she couldn't deny the persistent pull, the nagging hope that maybe, just maybe, there was something worth salvaging.

Arden arrived at her hotel, his usually vibrant face paler than usual. "I'm so sorry," he said, his voice a little hoarse. "I'm not feeling too well."

Harriet's brow furrowed. *Was he lying?* Was this some elaborate performance to avoid confronting the mess they'd made of things? Or was he genuinely ill? The thought, traitorously, softened her. Why had he even come? What was this all about anymore?

She had enjoyed New York without him. The freedom of wandering aimlessly, the exhilaration of navigating a new city solo, it had sparked something in her, a realization that she was perfectly capable of being happy on her own. Maybe this sparked something in Arden too, a fear of being irrelevant, of no longer being needed. Or maybe their nights of passion, the whispered secrets and shared laughter, still haunted him somewhat, playing on repeat in the quiet corners of his mind.

"Okay," she said, her voice surprisingly neutral. "We can just… take it easy."

They went for a cocktail at a dimly lit bar, the kind where the bartender knew the intricate history of every obscure liquor. Arden nursed his drink, looking genuinely subdued. Harriet tried to decipher his expression, to catch a glimpse of the truth behind his weary eyes.

Then they went for a walk, the crisp autumn air biting at their cheeks. The city was buzzing, oblivious to the turmoil brewing between them. Finally, they ended up at a Japanese restaurant Arden had chosen. It was a far cry from the delicious and infinitely better Japanese food back in Sydney, a fact that Harriet silently lamented. The rice was slightly overcooked, the fish lacking the vibrant freshness she was accustomed to.

Maroon 5 started playing over the restaurant speakers. Arden, to her surprise, started singing along, his voice slightly off-key but full of unexpected enthusiasm. It was so…*him.* Suddenly, a smile tugged at the corner of Harriet's lips. It was infectious. She laughed.

Maybe she had been too serious about this all. Too serious about whatever their relationship with each other had been or would ever be. Maybe she'd built it up in her mind, romanticizing the stolen moments and ignoring the underlying incompatibility.

But she couldn't shake her feelings about him. The way her heart still fluttered when he looked at her, the way his hand, even slightly clammy with illness, still fit perfectly in hers. She hated herself for feeling this strongly, for allowing him to have this power over her.

The New York skyline looked stunning as they walked back towards her hotel, the twinkling lights reflecting in the Hudson River. A gentle breeze swept through, carrying the scent of exhaust fumes and blooming possibility. Once again.

The revolving doors of the opulent Hotel whirred softly, a stark contrast to the turmoil churning within Harriet. At the front entrance, they said their goodbyes. It felt…insufficient.

"So," Arden began his voice, a low rumble that always managed to soothe her jangled nerves. "I'll see you in the afternoon then, right? I'll swing by and take you to JFK?"

Harriet managed a weak smile.

"I leave work early", he offered.

They stood for a moment longer, suspended in the awkward space between goodbye and leaving. Traffic roared in Manhattan, a cacophony that amplified the unspoken feelings hanging in the air. New York, a city that had promised so much, was now about to be relegated to a memory, a chapter closed.

Finally, he stepped forward. The hug was warm, enveloping, a brief sanctuary in the urban chaos. Harriet breathed in the familiar scent of his cologne, a mix of sandalwood and something vaguely citrusy that always reminded her of summer in Sydney. As they pulled apart, she thought she saw something flicker in his eyes. A sadness? No, that couldn't be. Arden was always so…composed. Stoic, even. It was probably just the harsh sunlight glinting off the buildings.

"You'll be okay?" he asked, his brow furrowed slightly.

"Just tired," she said, and it was partially true. The entire time in New York had been a whirlwind of late nights, and jet lag never left her. But the exhaustion ran deeper, a weariness that came from the constant pressure to succeed, to prove herself.

"Okay," he said, though he didn't seem entirely convinced. "Call me if you need anything."

Harriet nodded, turning towards the revolving doors. As she stepped inside the cool, hushed interior of the hotel, a bitter thought surfaced. *How come Monster had found new love? So easily with all his lies?*

She wasn't a manipulative abuser like Monster, with his ruthlessness and predatory behavior. He'd gotten what he wanted, with a click of his fingers, another woman, someone new to abuse. The "other woman," who had willingly entangled herself with a married man, a cheater, a liar. *Not a catch*, Harriet thought, just another casualty in the ruthless game of his.

She suddenly felt a surge of protectiveness for herself. She hadn't been naive, exactly. But perhaps she had been too willing to believe in the promise of something real. She wasn't that "other woman." She had principles, damn it. She had boundaries.

Harriet paused at the concierge desk. As she waited, she glanced back out at the street. Arden was gone. She raised a hand in a silent farewell to the imaginary man. Her delusions offered a small wave in return, then turned away, determined to focus on the future.

Chapter 45

N ew York, September 2023

The bustling terminals of the airport were alive with the sounds of rolling luggage, distant announcements, and the low hum of anxious conversations. It was late afternoon, the golden hour casting a warm glow through the expansive glass walls, making everything shimmer as if wrapped in a veil of nostalgia. Outside, the sky was painted in the same hues of orange and pink as when she had arrived days earlier, promising a beautiful sunset that would soon fade into twilight over New York.

Midst the chaos, she stood at the edge of the security line, her heart pounding like a drum in her chest.

Harriet's breath caught in her throat as she turned to face Arden one last time. His tall frame seemed to tower over her even more now that they were saying goodbye. The air between them crackled with unspoken words, words that could fill volumes but had no place here.

"What now?" he asked, his voice laced with a mixture of frustration and longing. His eyes searched hers for answers that neither of them had. She swallowed hard, feeling a lump form in her throat.

"I don't know," she whispered, feeling tears prick at the corners of her eyes. She wanted to say something profound, something that would tether them together despite the distance she was about to create. But all that came out was an echo of their shared moments, the laughter over coffee when he finally held her hand during the long walk in Central Park, and the intimate moment she never thought was something she would engage in with anyone. Ever.

Arden took a step back, his shoulders slumping slightly as he turned away from her, moving toward the exit. Each step felt like a dagger to her heart; she wanted to reach out and pull him back into their world, where goodbyes didn't exist. Yet here they were, caught in this painful moment where reality loomed large. As he walked away, Harriet felt time slow down. The sun dipped lower in the sky, casting long shadows across the terminal floor as if urging her to chase after him. But she stood frozen, a statue amidst a sea of movement, her suitcase weighing heavily at her side.

She blinked back tears and fought against an overwhelming wave of despair. "Arden!" she called out suddenly, desperation coloring her voice. He paused but didn't turn around. The air crackled with tension; people around them moved on without noticing their private turmoil. *"I'll always love you,"* she said softly into the growing distance between them, hoping somehow, he would hear it carried on the winds or captured by fate itself. In that moment, everything faded except for their connection, a bond woven through laughter and heartache, but fate had other plans. With one last glance at his retreating figure silhouetted against the sunset glow, Harriet turned toward security.

Chapter 46

New York, September 2023

As Harriet stood at the airline counter, her heart raced with a cocktail of anxiety and disbelief. The fluorescent lights above flickered slightly, casting an unforgiving glare on the screen that declared her ticket nonexistent. "Sorry, it's a ghost ticket," the attendant said with a practiced indifference. "But I will miss my connecting flight!" Harriet's voice trembled as she clutched her carry-on tighter.

"It's okay," the attendant replied blandly. "We'll put you on another flight."

Harriet sat in the crowded departure lounge, her heart thudding rhythmically against her rib cage. The vibrant buzz of travelers filled the air, their laughter and chatter swirling around her like a comforting blanket. Yet, midst this cacophony, she felt achingly alone. She glanced at her phone for what felt like the hundredth time, a silent plea for a message that would never come. The screens overhead flickered with updates on departing flights. Her flight to Los Angeles was delayed once more, but that hardly mattered now; all she could think about was Arden. Over the past nine months, his messages had a way of slipping straight into her heart, always knowing exactly what to say to make her feel seen, wanted, and special.

But today, there was nothing, no text, no call, just a space where his familiar voice should be. Outside, the sun began its slow descent towards the horizon. It cast a warm glow through the large windows that framed Harriet's world, a scene so beautiful it almost hurt to look at it without him by her side. The colors shifted and danced across her face as she leaned back in her chair, feeling both exhilarated and desolate. Around her, couples embraced tightly before parting ways; families laughed as they reunited after long separations; friends shared stories over coffee. Each interaction seemed to amplify Harriet's solitude.

She couldn't shake off the feeling that something was missing, something vital to her happiness. Suddenly, a young couple nearby caught her attention. They were wrapped up in each other's arms, whispering sweet nothings that made Harriet's heart ache with longing. Just then, her phone vibrated against her thigh. With bated breath, she grabbed it, but it was only an automated update about her delayed flight. Disappointment washed over her like a cold wave crashing on a deserted shore. She sighed deeply and looked out at the runway where planes glided effortlessly into the sky. A soft rustle drew her attention back inside the terminal. An elderly couple shuffled past holding hands tightly as if their fingers were woven together by years of love and companionship.

Watching them brought a small smile to Harriet's lips, a reminder that love often transcends distance and time. She closed her eyes momentarily.

"I'll always find my way back to you. Even if it's through my writing."

The thought wrapped around her heart like a warm embrace, filling her with determination rather than despair. As twilight deepened outside and shadows lengthened within the terminal walls, Harriet resolved to wait just a little longer, for both Arden and for love itself.

She was called on her flight, and soon Harriet would be glancing outside at the vibrant Los Angeles skyline silhouetted against the evening sky, where palm trees swayed gently in a warm breeze. She could almost feel the golden hour wrapping around her like a comforting embrace if only she weren't stranded here in this sterile airport.

"You are on the next flight to Los Angeles, but you missed the connecting flight to Sydney." Harriet's stomach plummeted, and not because of the missed connection. One moment, she was reaching for her wallet to pay for her

oat milk latte, the next, a gaping void stared back at her from inside her purse. Empty. Utterly, terrifyingly empty. Her credit cards were gone.

A wave of nausea washed over her, the saccharine sweetness of the latte suddenly cloying. *Maybe, just maybe, she'd left them at the hotel?* But the meticulous order she maintained, the ingrained habit of always, always checking she had them before she left the hotel room, screamed otherwise.

New York City. Nights out. Arden. The pieces clicked into place, forming a jagged, anxiety-ridden puzzle.

She'd been so distracted. So utterly consumed by Arden, by the dizzying highs and disorienting lows of their… whatever-it-was, that she'd been operating on autopilot. The trendy bar in the West Village, the jostling crowds, the clinking glasses, the flashing lights, it was all a blur of perfume, cocktails, and Arden's intoxicating smile.

Arden. Just thinking his name sent a shiver down her spine, a potent mixture of longing and self-reproach. He had a way of making her forget everything, of dissolving her anxieties and painting the world in vibrant, impulsive colors.

And apparently, he'd also made her forget her credit cards.

With trembling fingers, she pulled out her phone and scrolled through her contacts. The automated voice of her bank filled her ear, grating and impersonal. She navigated the labyrinthine menu, her heart hammering against her ribs.

"I need to report my credit cards stolen," she said, her voice barely a whisper.

The next hour was a flurry of bureaucratic jargon, account numbers, and security questions. Each question felt like a fresh sting, a reminder of her carelessness, her preoccupation. Finally, after what felt like an eternity, all three cards were canceled.

She hung up the phone, the weight of the situation settling upon her chest like a leaden cloak. She stared out the window at the airport. The endless stream of people flowed past, each one a potential suspect, a potential threat. Harriet arrived in Los Angeles without credit cards.

At the next check-in counter upon landing, *"Without credit cards, how can I stay in the hotel?"* she pressed to the ground staff, desperation creeping into her tone. *"I can't put it down for incidentals!"*

Just then, a young man stepped up behind her. He was tall and casually dressed in jeans and a fitted black t-shirt that accentuated his easy confidence. His dark hair caught the light as he leaned forward slightly, offering an inviting smile that somehow cut through Harriet's panic. *"I got you,"* he said simply.

Harriet turned to him, surprise flickering across her face. There was something warm in his eyes, a kindness that made her momentarily forget about the chaos surrounding them.

"I'll cover your hotel costs," he continued, his voice steady and sincere midst the noise of announcements blaring overhead and families reuniting with joyous embraces. "Consider it my good deed for today." Her heart fluttered at his unexpected generosity; vulnerability mixed with gratitude swirled within her like a summer storm threatening to break free. "Really? You don't have to do that," she stammered. "Maybe I want to," he replied with a playful grin that sent warmth flooding through Harriet's chest.

"I was on the same flight from New York." "My name is Jesus," he offered his hand. *Jesus to the rescue.*

"Harriet," she smiled at this sudden turn of events, surrounded by strangers yet deeply connected by circumstance.

As they began discussing logistics, the hotel details, and what flight she might catch next time seemed to slow down around them. The chaos of the airport faded into mere background noise; all Harriet could focus on was this unexpected savior standing beside her.

"We should have breakfast together?" he said with a smile as they walked towards the bus taking them to the hotel.

"You're too kind."

It was a bright, sun-kissed morning in Los Angeles, the kind of day that invites adventure. The sky was a crisp blue, punctuated by fluffy white clouds lazily drifting by. As the early rays of sunlight poured into the hotel room, Harriet stirred awake, memories of last night flooding back. She smiled at the thought of Jesus, the charming stranger who had offered his hand with a warm smile and an easy confidence that made her feel better about everything. After a casual breakfast in the hotel's cozy café, where they shared laughter over steaming cups of coffee and buttery croissants, Harriet found herself captivated by Jesus' stories of travel and dreams. They were both bound for different destinations but had been gifted with an entire day before their connecting flights.

"Let's go to Manhattan Beach," Jesus suggested, his eyes sparkling with enthusiasm. Harriet felt a rush of excitement at the idea; she could picture the soft sands and gentle waves beckoning them. "Yes, sure!" she replied, her voice tinged with eagerness. With a swift motion, Jesus pulled out his phone and ordered an Uber. They stepped outside into the warm embrace of the California sun. The air was fragrant with salt and promise, a perfect blend of ocean breeze and summer warmth that wrapped around them like a comforting hug. As they waited for their ride, they exchanged friendly glances. The Uber arrived, its sleek black exterior contrasting beautifully against the vibrant surroundings. As they settled into the back seat, Harriet couldn't help but feel as if this spontaneous adventure might become a cherished memory, a spark in her otherwise up-and-down trip with everything that happened with Arden.

"Have you ever been to Manhattan Beach?" Jesus asked casually, leaning closer as he spoke, his warmth radiating toward her. "No," Harriet admitted, glancing out at the passing palm trees and bustling streets.

"But I've just Googled and it's beautiful." "It is," he assured her with a smile.

"And I think you'll love it." As they drove along the Pacific Coast Highway, sunlight streamed through the window, and the beach loomed ahead, stretching endlessly beneath a flawless sky. As they stepped out of the car onto the golden sand, Harriet felt alive; the waves crashing rhythmically against the shore mirrored her heartbeat as she took in this unexpected journey filled with laughter and warmth from a total stranger.

Chapter 47

Sydney, October 2023

Harriet clutched the crumpled boarding pass, the thin paper in her trembling hand. The *"Ghost Ticket"* had been a metaphor, a cruel one. A trip to hope, a promise of a future that evaporated like morning mist. Just like the ghost ticket, Harriet and Arden's baby would be a ghost. Yet another illusion. He came up on the search, only to disappear. *"Ms., there is nothing there."* Brutal. The words echoed in Harriet's mind, a stark and sterile pronouncement of loss, of something that existed only in her mind.

Tired tears filled her eyes as she boarded the final leg of her flight, the return journey. She requested a glass of Shiraz. The dark red liquid sloshing in the plastic cup reminded her of the blood she had seen staining her underwear, a visceral reminder of the life that wouldn't be.

When she landed back home, she ignored Arden's messages as much as she could. Every vibration of her phone felt like a punch to the gut, a fresh wave of grief crashing over her.

"Do you hate me now?" he typed. "I hope not."

Harriet walked out to the beach, the familiar rhythm of the waves a small comfort. She plunged into the cold water, letting it numb the raw edges of her pain. The sun warmed her empty body, filling it with energy from high above.

"Do you hate me now?"

Harriet repeated the sentence in her mind. *"No, how could I hate you? You brought life to me when I was down."* But as she lifted her arms above the waves, she realized she would have empty arms that hurt the most. You never hold the ghost in your arms.

She felt the absence of her ghost, the grief. But she couldn't tell Arden. She couldn't tell anyone. How could she hate someone willing to give her an entire new life, a baby?

Then, out of the blue, a voice note.

"The miracle baby?" His voice was calm, almost curious.

She let it play out and didn't respond.

The early morning sun painted Anna's room in strokes of gold, turning dust motes into dancing embers. Harriet held the baby close; his tiny form nestled against her chest. Her nose brushed his soft forehead, and she inhaled deeply, breathing in the scent of milk and newborn life. It was a pristine, untainted fragrance, a promise of joy that bloomed in the quiet sanctuary of her arms.

Slowly, the baby boy opened his eyes. They were Arden's eyes, undeniably, impossibly. Golden brown pools, flecked with amber, held a depth that seemed to stretch back into eternity. Looking at them, she felt a pang of something she couldn't quite name, a mixture of love and a fear she couldn't articulate.

"You are everything," she whispered, her voice thick with emotion. She didn't know it, but Harriet played her role as a mother so beautifully in her dream. Each gentle caress, each murmured lullaby, was a testament to a love that felt both ancient and brand new. In this sun-drenched haven, she was simply Harriet, a mother cradling her child, blissfully unaware of the shadows that lurked just beyond the light.

Arden walked quietly to the room, his shoes removed, and his tie left behind on the chair in the hallway. He was a silhouette against the doorway, hesitant, almost reverent. He stared at the bright light filtering through the curtains, a warmth that seemed to radiate from the room itself, from

Harriet. He didn't speak, didn't move, just watched them, an observer in the fragile tableau of mother and child.

And then, the room turned dark. A suffocating darkness extinguished the golden light, leaving behind a bone-chilling cold that seeped into her bones.

Fear crept in, insidious and familiar. It was the same paralyzing fear she had grown to despise, the fear that Monster had cultivated within her. Monster had been so nice, so charming in the beginning, showering her with attention, then subtly, insidiously, violating her boundaries, until she was trapped, a prisoner in his gilded cage.

In the darkness, the baby stopped breathing. His small chest stilled, and his face blossomed into a horrifying shade of blue. Panic clawed at her throat, choking off her scream. Arden was no longer in the room. The silence was deafening, broken only by the frantic thumping of her own terrified heart.

Then, nothing.

She was hanging from the curtains. The rich fabric was twisted and torn, a pathetic testament to a struggle that was now over. Her thyroid bone fractured in three points. Her body was a lifeless weight, swaying gently in the darkness. Blankness. Nothing.

And yet, in the eerie logic of the dream, she drifted, weightless and unreal, like a marionette cut loose.

Her pillow was wet from tears. She woke with a gasp, the cold sweat clinging to her skin. She was at Anna's house, familiar and safe. But the dread lingered, a phantom limb of the nightmare clinging to her.

She lay there, the weight of her past pressing down on her. None of us can run away from our past, of our actions, she thought, the truth settling into her bones like a cold, hard stone. She had chosen to be with an abuser for so long, had allowed him to chip away at her soul, to steal her light. He had robbed her of all her dreams and hopes, leaving her a shell, haunted by the ghosts of what could have been. The golden light of the dream felt impossibly distant now, a cruel reminder of the happiness that had been stolen, perhaps forever.

Chapter 48

Sydney, October 2023

Sydney spring was at its most luminous, with jacaranda blossoms spilling purple across the streets and the scent of jasmine drifting on the breeze.

Harriet stood in Anna's house, in her cluttered room, phone pressed against her ear, the remnants of a half-finished floral arrangement scattered across the table. The cozy room was filled with the lingering fragrance of fresh blooms, a stark contrast to the heaviness hanging in her heart. The soft light filtered through sheer curtains, casting delicate patterns on the wooden floor, yet it did little to lighten the weight of Douglas's words. *"Your mother... has passed away."* His voice was steady, almost too normal, devoid of any emotion that could penetrate Harriet's daze. She blinked slowly, trying to process what she had just heard. The room felt surreal; colors seemed muted as if someone had turned down the saturation of her reality. "Oh," she murmured to herself, memories flooding her mind like a storm. The image of Douglas flickered in her thoughts, his awkward demeanor during their brief encounter at the flower store, his strange fascination with an arrangement that had gone unnoticed by others. *"The weird guy who came to the flower store...and the stalker."* She almost laughed aloud at the absurdity of it all. But laughter felt inappropriate now. Instead, an unsettling silence enveloped her; she was an observer in her own life, watching from a distance as if this moment belonged to someone else entirely. *Why didn't she feel anything?* She thought back to when she faced unimaginable grief after the Monster, a shadow looming over her past that left indelible scars on her soul. *But now?* Nothing. As if sensing her internal struggle, Hope stood beside Harriet, unseen yet profoundly present. It watched with a heavy heart as neglect and absence unfolded before its very essence, a heartbreaking involvement that left Hope feeling helpless. Could it replace what was never truly there? How could it mend the void left by years of detachment? The phone slipped slightly from Harriet's grip as she stared out of her window toward a vibrant Jacaranda tree swaying gently outside, its branches full of life, while she felt utterly numb.

A small bird landed nearby and chirped softly; its song seemed incongruous against her sorrowful silence. *"Harriet?"* Douglas's voice broke through again, pulling her back into reality. "I… I don't know what to say," she finally replied, finding her voice but not quite knowing how to fill it with emotion. "You don't have to say anything," he reassured gently. "Just know that I'm here for you." *A bit weird thing to say from a stalker,* Harriet thought. "I wanted to tell you something when you were visiting here, but you left so abruptly. I wanted to tell you that your mother was sick. She didn't have long to live." "Oh, I am so sorry. I didn't realize. I mean, she wasn't always *nice* to me, so I left…" Harriet swallowed. *Shit, Douglas wasn't a stalker. He needed to just tell her something. In private.* "It's OK. We all knew what she was like. And the drinking." He reassured her. At that moment, Harriet felt a flicker, a tiny spark igniting deep within, a reminder that connection still existed even amid loss and neglect. Maybe love and hope didn't always come from where one expected; perhaps it could be found in unexpected kindness from strangers, too. As she hung up the phone and stared out at the fiery horizon sinking into the afternoon, Harriet realized that while this chapter was marked by grief and abandonment, there remained hope for healing and understanding, a slow journey toward rediscovering love amid all the darkness she had experienced.

Chapter 49

Sydney, October 2023

The silence in her room was a thick blanket, stifling. Harriet stared at the chipped mug in her hands, the lukewarm tea doing nothing to warm her. Outside, the wind howled, mimicking the storm that raged within her. News of her mother's death had arrived three days ago. Three days, and still…nothing. She knew she *should* be feeling something. Sadness, perhaps? Regret? Even anger would be acceptable. But the well was dry. Bone-dry. Her mother, Rebecca. The name tasted like ash in her mouth. Rebecca, who had been more ghost than mother, flitting in and out of Harriet's life like a moth drawn to a flickering bulb. Rebecca had chosen the company of a bottle over the needs of her daughter. Rebecca, whose eyes were always glazed, her words slurred promises that evaporated before sunrise. Then there was her father, the one she should have called Monster. A creature of sudden rages and bruising hands. She remembered the fear, the constant, gnawing fear that had been her companion through childhood. He had died when she was seventeen, a messy car crash involving a truck and a lot of whiskey. Back then, she had felt…relief. The Monster was gone.

The violence was over. Had she grieved? Honestly, she didn't know. She had grieved the *ending* of the terror, not the man himself. Sitting here, in

"

the small room at Anna's house, she had retreated to after leaving the cabin, she felt a similar emptiness regarding Rebecca. The ending. The finality. But not grief. Was it normal? Probably not. People were supposed to mourn their mothers. She imagined friends, colleagues, and even strangers, shedding tears, sharing stories, and celebrating a life. But what life was there to celebrate? A life of addiction, of neglect, of absence? The solicitor's email had mentioned the funeral. It was to be held in the small town where Harriet had grown up, a place she vowed never to return to. Her aunt, Rebecca's sister, expected her to be there. Expected her to…what? Perform grief? Pretend to be the daughter she was never allowed to be? She took a long, slow breath, the scent of pine filling her lungs. Pine reminded her of her childhood. No. She wouldn't go. Staying here, in the quiet solitude of her best friend's house, was her form of…respect. Respect for herself. Respect for the years she had spent trying to understand, trying to connect, only to be met with a wall of indifference. She thought about the countless nights she had stayed awake, listening for Rebecca's stumbling footsteps, hoping she would come in and tuck her in, read her a story, just…be there. The hope had withered long ago, replaced by a cold, hard understanding. Rebecca was not capable of being a mother.

Perhaps, she thought, she had grieved Rebecca a long time ago. Not her death, but the death of the mother she desperately wanted, the mother she deserved. Maybe she had mourned the potential for a loving relationship, a bond that had never been forged. The wind howled again, rattling the windows. Harriet got up and walked to the window, looking out at the swirling wind. The landscape was stark, unforgiving, but beautiful in its own way. She closed her eyes for a moment, picturing Rebecca. Not the Rebecca of the last few years, a gaunt shadow of a woman, but the Rebecca from her earliest memories. A fleeting image of a younger woman, before the alcohol had taken its hold, a woman who had once smiled at her with a genuine warmth. A woman who, for a brief, shining moment, had held her daughter close. That was the memory she would hold onto. Not the pain, not the neglect, but the flicker of love that had once existed. And maybe, just maybe, that was enough. She opened her eyes, the storm outside seeming a little less menacing now. It was okay not to grieve someone you never really knew, despite them being your family. It was okay to choose yourself, to protect yourself. It was okay to simply…be. She walked back to the table, picked up her mug, and took another sip of tea. It was still lukewarm, but the silence in the room no longer felt quite so suffocating. It felt…peaceful. And in that peace, Harriet finally found a small measure of solace. The ending had come, and perhaps, with it, a new beginning.

Chapter 50

Sydney, October 2023

Her eyes welled up, tears blurring the keys, but she kept typing. These were the memories that helped her heal.

The words flowed, imperfect and raw, a torrent of feeling she couldn't contain. *How could she possibly explain it? How could she articulate the bizarre, almost blasphemous truth that had taken root in her soul?*

She was the most honest of them all. That's what made this so excruciating. She couldn't lie, not even to herself. And the truth was… she had found her peace inside someone's ass.

It sounded insane, vulgar even, when put so bluntly. But it wasn't about the act itself, not really. It was about the journey, the almost mystical path that had led her to this precise moment. It was as if the universe itself had conspired, nudging her, directing her with a series of improbable events. Go there, do this, a voice whispered in her heart. And she had obeyed.

And there she was. In his kitchen, a world away from everything familiar, her presence unsettled him; her attitude clashing against his, a charged tension stretching between them. He was a stranger, yet at the same time achingly familiar, like a missing piece of herself she was only now rediscovering.

And then it happened. Naturally. Inevitably. Like breathing, like the sun rising. The unspoken current that had been simmering between them broke the surface.

It wasn't planned. It wasn't rehearsed. Instinct carried her, pure, untamed. Desire took the reins. Harriet sank into him, her tongue teasing, exploring, drawing him into a rhythm that made his body shiver with anticipation. Each touch, each swirl, felt like a promise. She wanted to take him deeper, to claim the place he offered with raw, deliberate submission.

He bent for her slowly, deliberately, baring himself in a way that was both vulnerable and irresistible. The sight of him, strong yet yielding, set her blood racing. His body was perfection, a map she longed to explore with reverence and hunger. And when he revealed himself fully to her, it was like an invitation she could not deny. That place, his most secret self, the place she had already known, called to her again. Healing, temptation, and obsession collided inside her. She couldn't resist

She felt like she had waited years for him. At this moment. For this connection. It was more than just sex; *it was a homecoming.*

His body parts appeared, each curve and contour a signpost on a journey she was meant to undertake. Down, down, down, she followed, hypnotized by the pull, the irresistible urge to lose herself within him.

The place that healed her, the place that inspired her. *Such a taboo.* A source of shame and ridicule, yet for her, it was a sanctuary. It was where she found solace, where she discovered a strength she never knew she possessed. It was a testament to the fact that beauty can be found in the most unexpected places, and that love can bloom in the darkest corners. And as her tears continued to fall, she kept typing, determined to capture the essence of this profound and unconventional truth, no matter how scandalous it might seem to the world.

Chapter 51

New York, October 2023

The scent of rain-slicked asphalt and exhaust fumes hung heavy in the New York air. A scent, I found particularly distasteful. It clung to everything, much like Arden's influence clung to Harriet.

Had Arden completely cursed Harriet?

As Love, I didn't know. I had watched the whole charade unfold from the sidelines, a grim observer of his potential failure. Arden, the quintessential New York player, is a master of fleeting connections and whispered promises. He didn't know what he wanted; that much was clear. He was playing, toying with hearts like poker chips, and Harriet, oh Harriet, had fallen headfirst into his carefully crafted trap.

But Harriet was also fiercely loyal. Blindly, stubbornly, beautifully loyal. And that was the tragedy. She had stayed loyal to the worst person in this world; she had lavished her affection and unwavering support on Monster, a man who deserved none of it.

I shuddered. Monster. Just the name left a bitter taste on my tongue. Whilst he was out there, a whirlwind of cheap thrills and fleeting encounters, Harriet stayed at home, a patient sentinel in a desolate castle. She waited for him, for so many years, clinging to the hope of a redemption that would never come.

She deserved better. She deserved constellations mapped across her skin instead of the shadows cast by Monster's absence. And I, as Love, seemed to have failed her. I had watched her decline, wither under the toxic influence of a man who saw her devotion as weakness.

Then, I made Arden appear. *That swipe right?* A shimmering mirage in the desolate landscape of Harriet's life. Desperate, hoping to salvage the situation, I had perhaps acted rashly. I had nudged, coaxed, and almost shoved Harriet into Arden's arms, thinking this charismatic charmer would somehow save her. I had been so eager to erase Monster's stain, to prove to Fear that he still held sway, that he had overlooked the obvious: Arden was no savior. *Maybe he was simply a different kind of predator.*

And now, Harriet was trapped again, her loyalty re-directed towards a man who saw her as a temporary amusement, a distraction between more enticing conquests. I saw the way Arden looked at her, the casual indifference masked by practiced charm. I knew the games Arden played, the carefully crafted lies, the seductive whispers that promised forever but delivered only fleeting moments.

Harriet needed her freedom. She needed to feel the sun on her face without the weight of expectation, to laugh without the fear of disappointment. She needed to discover who she was, outside the context of her devotion, outside the suffocating walls of her loyalty. She needed to *live*.

I felt a surge of guilt. Maybe I had pushed her into Arden's arms in haste, not for Harriet's benefit, but to save my reputation in front of Fear. Fear, who constantly whispered doubts and anxieties, who challenged my effectiveness, providing the essential energy of Love at every turn. I had been so desperate to prove that I could still orchestrate a happy ending that I had sacrificed Harriet's well-being in the process.

I leaned against a rain-streaked lamppost in melancholic Manhattan. No one could see me, of course.

What could I do now? I couldn't simply erase Arden from her life. I couldn't force her to see the truth. Harriet had to choose her path and break free from the cycle of misplaced loyalty.

My role, I realized, wasn't to orchestrate a perfect romance, but to plant the seeds of self-love, to nurture the dormant strength within her. I had to help her see that her worth wasn't tied to the affections of a man, that her loyalty was a precious gift wasted on those who didn't deserve it. I closed my eyes, focusing my energy, sending a silent prayer into the rain-washed air. I prayed for Harriet to find the courage to choose herself, to embrace her freedom, to finally, truly, live. I had made mistakes, but I wouldn't abandon her now. I would watch, I would wait, and I would be ready to catch her when she finally dared to fall.

Chapter 52

Sydney, October 2023

In Sydney, the sun shone daily, painting the turquoise ocean with shimmering gold. The gentle summer breeze, scented with salt and hibiscus, made Harriet forget the heavy, gritty air of New York, the constant, jarring sirens, and the gnawing disappointment. The sadness. The loss of something she yearned for so badly throbbed less intensely here, diluted by the expanse of the sea and the warmth on her skin.

"That guy is a huge project," Anna had said with an annoyed roll of her eyes, her voice sharp even over the beachside chatter. "Good luck to anyone who takes that on!"

Harriet had just shrugged, pretending disinterest. But she knew, deep down, that she secretly *wanted* that "project." Not in the romantic, relationship-driven way Anna assumed, but in the sense of an actual, challenging project. A multifaceted puzzle to unravel. No one could understand why she was drawn to the complexities of people and saw potential where others saw only trouble, so she didn't bother explaining. She just stirred her cocktail and watched the waves crash.

A message popped up on her phone, momentarily shattering the idyllic stillness.

"You know I think about you."

Then, a second one followed immediately.

"Almost daily."

Her heart lurched, a traitorous flutter in her chest. Harriet didn't know what to reply. She was stuck, paralyzed between the overwhelming urge to talk to him, to hear his voice, to dive back into their messy, tangled world, and the stark realization that she needed to move on. She needed to heal. And… Her mother had passed away. A weight she was still learning to carry. He didn't know.

Eventually, she did respond, but it took her a week. A week was spent wrestling with her emotions, trying to bury the memories that surfaced relentlessly. She wasn't falling asleep with dreams of him underneath her, his legs pushed back just like he wanted, the taste of him still lingering on her lips, a phantom sensation that haunted her waking hours.

She still remembered running her fingers through his curly hair, the way it felt soft and springy beneath her touch. She remembered her index finger gently sliding across the soft hair on his cheek. She couldn't forget his golden, speckled eyes, and the way he took a deep breath, a visible effort to contain himself, to deal with her complexity, her volatile nature, her tendency to be, as he'd once jokingly said, a *"pain in the ass."* Appearing at his apartment, sleep-deprived after a long-haul flight, keeping him awake with her restless energy, yet sprawled out unconscious on his bed on Sunday morning when she left his apartment, abruptly.

She remembered, with a pang of shame, the little, tiny dots of blood on his side of the bed sheets after that one specific time. The time she, perhaps, went too far.

She did go too hard, too deep. In every sense.

Why hadn't she been more attentive, more considerate? Why was she treating him like this? She'd told herself she was being playful, that her intensity was a form of affection. But she forgot to turn around quietly and seductively in his bed instead of jumping on him and riding him.

Just because he was kind, caring, and gentle, she didn't need to be the opposite. She didn't need to test his boundaries or push him to his limits.

The memory surfaced, unbidden, sharp, and clear. He had asked Harriet to whip his cock with a black crocodile leather collar chain, and she went for it. That's the only time a bang of guilt hit Harriet. He seemed so fragile in that moment, vulnerable beneath her.

He *wanted* her to be dominant. He craved the power dynamic, the role reversal that seemed so alien to her own gentle nature.

She understood the theory, intellectually. He was drawn to her strength, her sharp wit, the quiet confidence that she herself often overlooked. He saw a goddess, a queen. He wanted to kneel at her altar, and the idea, frankly, was intoxicating.

But then came the practical application. Dominance, in its purest form, required a ruthlessness Harriet didn't possess. It demanded a level of control that bordered on…meanness. And that, she simply couldn't do. Not to Arden. Not to the man whose laughter bubbled up from his depths like a warm spring, whose eyes crinkled at the corners when he smiled, whose touch was both reverent and playful. She was too deeply, irrevocably in love with every facet of his being to wield power over him in a way that might cause him any type of real pain.

"Playing," however, was a different story.

The memory of that night in his New York bedroom flickered in her mind, a warm ember glowing in the dark. The air was thick with unspoken desires, the low hum of city life filtering through the window. And all that September rain was slashing his windows.

She'd thought she might just nervously agree to a blindfold, her hands trembling as she tied the silk scarf behind his head. But no, it wasn't blindfolds, it was her head inside of him, guided by the unfamiliar weight of command; it had been electric.

She hadn't been cruel, not in the slightest. But she'd teased, she'd tantalized, she'd savored the delicious anticipation that hung heavy in the air. She'd used her voice, low and husky, to issue commands, whispered suggestions that made his breath catch in his throat. She had explored his skin with feather-light touches, relishing the shivers that ran through him. The memory of his surrender, his trust, still sent a shiver down her spine.

She hadn't broken him. She hadn't wanted to. She'd simply…unleashed him. Now, weeks later, the afterglow of that night still lingered.

She could feel the phantom weight of his gaze on her, even though she couldn't see him. She wondered if he thought about it, too. If he, like her, replayed the scene in his mind, savoring the forbidden thrill.

Reaching Anna's house, she fumbled with her keys, the metal cold in her hand. She pictured Arden sitting on the sofa, a book open in his lap, his brow furrowed in concentration. Just the thought of him waiting for her filled her with a warmth that spread through her limbs.

As she pushed open the door, the scent of sandalwood and old books greeted her. He was there, just as she'd imagined, his head tilted as he read. He looked up, his eyes lighting up when he saw her.

"Harriet," he said, his voice a low rumble that resonated deep within her. She dropped her bag by the door, the sound echoing in the sudden silence. She couldn't help the nervous flutter in her stomach.

"Hey," she managed, her voice slightly breathless. She walked towards him, stopping just a few feet away. "I was thinking…"

He closed the book, placing it carefully on the coffee table. His gaze was intense, knowing. He knew exactly what she was thinking.

"About New York?" he asked, a hint of mischief dancing in his eyes.

She nodded, unable to meet his gaze. He stood up, closing the distance between them. He reached out, gently cupping her face in his hands.

"Tell me, "He whispered, his breath warm against her skin. "Tell me what you're thinking."

And in that moment, surrounded by the familiar comfort of Anna's house, she knew she didn't have to be cruel to be dominant. She didn't have to force him into submission. All she had to do was be herself and allow the desires that simmered beneath the surface to finally break free. She just needed to *play*.

Harriet decided to write it all down. The worn leather of the diary felt cool and familiar beneath her fingers.

"I didn't want to cause him any type of pain. When I heard him moaning in bed

when I was behind him, it was the sweetest sound I had ever heard, a low guttural sound that, when I think about it now, makes me feel like you are insanely lucky and screwed at the same time. Knowing you will never have certain experiences again in this lifetime, but you will always have the memory in the back of your head."

She paused, the pen hovering above the page. It was true. That sound, that moment, was etched into her memory, a bittersweet melody that haunted her waking hours. You remember it like having butterflies in your stomach and that little buzz from being intoxicated. She wanted to float on that feeling, on that possibility, of Harriet and Arden. *Together, close.*

She closed her eyes, the memory washing over her. It was the kind of intoxication that made the world shimmer, the air crackle with unspoken promises. She didn't want the butterflies to fly away; she didn't want to stop the buzz. But she knew better than this. She knew eventually that feeling would fade. It always does.

Her pen scratched across the page again. She wrote on the cover of her notebook:

"Every time orange hues of beautiful sunsets fade away, all I think about is you." She could see it, and she could feel it coming. Everything special in this life always fades away and leaves you with an empty heart. The worst pain. Those once-in-a-lifetime feelings.

Harriet sighed, the weight of those words pressing down on her. It wasn't just about him, about this specific, fleeting moment. It was about all the fleeting moments, the ephemeral joys that seemed destined to disappear.

She thought back, searching for echoes of that same potent feeling. When the boy she had a crush on walked past her at school when she was just 13, her body shivered, or when he gave her her first kiss at a party with the tongue, and her friend held her hand, and she felt like walking on sunshine, sly as fuck. Or when a boyfriend at the university smelled so damn good that her nose was permanently stuck on his neck, breathing him in, behind his ear, and below his hairline. She was breathing in the elusive Dolce and Gabbana aftershave that was discontinued years ago. Each memory, a tiny spark of joy, tinged with the knowledge that it couldn't last.

Harriet slammed the book and wanted to just ignore everything and be a child again. It was time to look in the mirror and perhaps realize that the problem was her and not accepting that sometimes we need to absorb these feelings. The mirror reflected a woman who was wise, jaded, and sad. The woman who wanted to feel but was too scared to lose. She replayed the conversation in her mind when he upset her. The words, sharp and accusatory, echoed in her head. "I *only came here to get pregnant, I...*" She couldn't finish the sentence, the disgust and fear choking her. Had she said that? Had she become that desperate, that consumed by the desire to hold onto something fleeting, something that was always destined to fade? Right seed, wrong soil. Or whatever, could it work one day? Could the impossible happen? It was like she wanted to continue to float on the possibility. She knew she could always love him from a distance. Was it painful? Of course. But she wasn't ready to close the chapter. She wasn't ready to write:

The end.

Chapter 53

Sydney, November 2023

Dusky pinks and fiery oranges swirled across the horizon as the sun bowed out, leaving the beach bathed in a soft, lingering glow. The air was thick with the scent of salt and jasmine, a gentle breeze rustling through the palm trees that framed Harriet's new sanctuary. It was late afternoon, and as the waves lapped softly at the shore, they whispered secrets to one another, mirroring the thoughts swirling in Harriet's mind. She stood barefoot on the fine sand, her toes sinking slightly with each step as she walked toward the water's edge. Memories flooded back to her, vivid and intense. She recalled Arden's beautiful, strong neck, how it seemed almost regal in its grace, supporting a head that turned to her with such care and tenderness. His voice, soft yet commanding, echoed in her ears as he gently reprimanded her for pushing too hard when they were lost in their world of passion. "Harriet," he had said, a playful note tingling his tone.

"You're going too hard from behind."

The memory made her smile wistfully; it was a moment etched into her heart forever. With a sudden rush of longing, she knelt at the water's edge, burying her face in her hands. The ocean's rhythm matched her heartbeat as she imagined him there beside her, his energy coursing through every fiber of her being. As she closed her eyes, she could almost feel him there again, the way he would moan softly as she explored every inch of him. Was she tasting him too much? The thought sent shivers down her spine.

He wasn't just a man; he was an experience, an essence that lingered on her tongue long after their encounters faded into memory. The waves grew bolder as if responding to her yearning; they crashed against the shore with more force. Harriet opened her eyes to see the sun dipping further below the horizon, painting the sky in hues of pink and orange, an exquisite backdrop for memories both tender and tumultuous. In that moment of reflection, Harriet understood that these memories were not merely echoes of passion but symbols of love's complexity, joy interwoven with longing. She stood up slowly, brushing off grains of sand from her knees while gazing out at the endless sea before her. She finally admitted it.

There were no words to describe how much she missed him.

Chapter 54

New York, December 2023

Arden leaned against the cool glass of his office building's window, watching as the streets pulsed with energy, people flowing in and out of bars and restaurants like currents in a river. Late afternoon light softened the edges of skyscrapers, and though the streets buzzed with life, there was a quiet, reflective energy beneath it all.

Later, after a long day in the office, inside the bar where he often found himself these days, a dull hum filled the air, a blend of laughter, clinking glasses, and music that felt more like background noise than entertainment. The dim lighting cast shadows across his face; it was a far cry from the vibrant thrill he used to seek.

Tonight, however, he felt detached from the raucous atmosphere. He absently stirred his drink, glancing at the empty stool beside him where conversations once sparked with promise. His thoughts drifted to Harriet, the unexpected whirlwind who had stormed into his life only to vanish just as quickly. Memories of their passionate encounter flickered in his mind like an old film reel: her boldness as she turned their playful banter into something electric, the way she had taken charge that night in his bedroom filled with anticipation.

It was wild and freeing; never had he imagined someone would surprise him so thoroughly. The memory of her laughing eyes made his heart ache. Arden walked out of the bar, his gaze wandered outside to Central Park, bathed in soft evening light, a sanctuary midst urban chaos. He recalled their walk beneath all the trees, brown and yellow leaves falling like whispers of romance carried by the wind. He could almost hear her voice now, playful yet sincere, echoing through time as if she were still there beside him.

"Where are you now?" he whispered to himself, imagining Harriet lounging on a sun-drenched beach in Sydney, her hair dancing with ocean breezes.

Was she thinking of him? Did she recall their fleeting moments filled with unrestrained passion? The thought tugged at his heartstrings, a yearning that felt both exhilarating and painful.

He hailed a cab and carried on his usual route. Ending his day in that half-empty strip club across town where he often sought refuge from monotony, he caught himself staring blankly at dancers who moved mechanically under muted lights. The excitement he once craved felt replaced by something deeper, an understanding that what he truly wanted was connection beyond fleeting encounters and cocktails. Suddenly filled with resolve, Arden pulled out his phone, fingers trembling slightly as they hovered over Harriet's name. What if he reached out? Could he articulate how much her presence had mattered to him? The moment hung heavy in the air around him, a pregnant pause waiting for transformation.

"Message her," the same Russian bouncer Harriet had met during her whirlwind New York trip leaned over Arden's table, a wink punctuating his words.

Arden looked up, caught off guard, a smirk tugging at his lips.

"Even he can see I'm thinking about her," he murmured, a thrill running through him at how obvious it must be.

Chapter 55

New York/Sydney, December 2023

Arden stumbled through the door, the scent of cheap perfume and stale beer clinging to his clothes. The flashing lights of the strip club still danced behind his eyelids. He scrolled his phone with clumsy fingers, typing a blunt message, sharp and raw, the kind that cut straight through distance.

Across the world, in a quiet corner of the Sydney library, Harriet sat surrounded by towers of anatomy books and dusty reference volumes. The sterile text had left her numb, her mind a blank page. She needed something alive, something dangerous, to pull her words into the realm of flesh and heat.

Then his message appeared.

"I can feel myself getting hard," he wrote, crude, unfiltered. Her lips parted, not quite a smile. A blush rose uninvited to her cheeks. She leaned closer to the screen, as though proximity might make the words more real. Her fingers hovered before she replied, shaping his rawness into something sharper, something intoxicating.

"What if I was behind you," she typed, *"my hand brushing over your back, down your hip... squeezing, slow enough that you'd know it wasn't an accident?"*

A pause. Her heartbeat quickened in the silence. Then—

"Damn. That's hot."

She closed her eyes, and the library dissolved. She was no longer surrounded by paper and ink but by Arden's imagined nearness, the tension in his body, the way he might stumble if she pushed him too far.

She felt him in her mind: the heat of his skin, the weight of his presence, the way his body responded to her, his black jeans on the floor, his soft banker's hands on his beautiful cock.

He sent another message, short, urgent. She countered with a description more elaborate, setting the scene, bringing it to life. It became a rhythm, his blunt confessions, her crafted replies. For every crude phrase he sent, she built an entire world around it, drawing him deeper, making him picture not just skin but surrender.

She pictured his head tilting back, the flash of vulnerability in his eyes before it twisted into something else, pleasure, fear, surrender. She wanted to orchestrate him, body and soul, until he no longer knew if the words were hers or his.

The exchange thickened, tension like a wire drawn tighter and tighter. Her hands trembled as she typed, her body betraying her with shivers of anticipation. She could almost hear his breath on the other end, ragged and uneven.

And then, just as she was on the edge of giving him more than words, of spelling out something that would undo them both—

A voice broke the spell.

"We're closing in five minutes," the librarian said softly.

Chapter 56

Sydney, January 2024

The harsh ring of the phone sliced through the relative calm of Harriet's afternoon. She glanced at the caller ID, a knot tightening in her stomach. *"Andrea, from Miller & Zarella."* Harriet took a deep breath after answering the call. *"Oh my God, what now?"* Andrea's voice on the other end was a mix of exasperation and disbelief.

"We had the first hearing. Well, I have to say now I understand what you mean," she said, her voice thick with shock. Harriet braced herself. *Typical Monster, here we go...*

"He interrupted the magistrate. He spoke over her!" Andrea explained, the words tumbling out in a rush. "I have never seen this type of behavior before. He argued with the judge! I was mortified. And the things he was saying! Complete fabrications."

"I did tell you, he is a psychopath," Harriet concluded, a weary sigh escaping her lips. She'd tried to warn Andrea, to prepare her for the irrationality she was about to encounter. But hearing it second-hand, hearing the experienced lawyer, Andrea, reduced to stunned silence, only solidified her own conviction.

The financial settlement from their divorce wasn't moving along. Monster was refusing to disclose, and everything needed to be subpoenaed, even the police records. He was playing a game of cat and mouse, hiding assets behind shell corporations in the Philippines and veiled accounts.

"This will take a long time," Andrea said, her voice regaining some of its professional steel. "He is making this as difficult as possible. We've already subpoenaed his bank accounts, but it's like pulling teeth to get any information. Then there is the cryptocurrency he is hiding…"

"We will subpoena all his exchanges," Harriet interjected, her voice firm despite the exhaustion she felt. "Every single one. He thinks he's being clever, hiding funds in the digital realm, but he's just digging himself a deeper hole."

"He thinks he is smart, but…" Andrea paused, a hint of determination creeping into her tone. "He underestimates us. He thinks because he's delaying and obfuscating, he's winning. But he's not. We need to be methodical."

"We are not going on a fishing expedition here. We are going to do this step by step." Andrea stated, her voice brooking no argument. "We gather the evidence, we build the case, brick by brick. We get him. We will expose everything he is trying to hide." Harriet felt a flicker of hope ignite within her. It was a long and arduous road ahead, but she had a tenacious lawyer on her side, and Andrea finally understood the true nature of the beast they were dealing with.

She imagined Monster, smugly believing he was outsmarting everyone, oblivious to the careful, calculated steps being taken to unravel his web of lies. A slow, satisfied smile crept across Harriet's face. The game was on. And Andrea, from Miller & Zarella, was prepared to win.

Chapter 57

Sydney, February 2024

I watched them, invisible as always, draped across the tapestry of their lives. Again, I couldn't control Arden's urges. He was regular at the strip club, a shimmering beacon beneath the neon lights. He was "out there" for people to admire, to be touched, the webcam, the bars. He was always drawn back to his familiar behavior, a moth to a flame. I, Love, often feel powerless against the complexities of human desires.

And then there was Harriet. He still gave her attention; he was still there for her, in his fractured way. He made her smile, a genuine, bright, sunshine-filtering-through-clouds kind of smile. The longing she had for him was still there, a low hum beneath the surface, but it changed form. It wasn't the desperate, consuming need of before, but something…wiser, sadder, more accepting. She always felt the Universe was playing a trick of some sort, a cosmic prank with profound emotional consequences.

It was just me, and I was sorry, once again. I had no magical powers to make them a traditional couple, to conjure a perfectly packaged love story. This was something so unique, so outside the realm of predictable romance, that not even I, Love, hanging above all the kisses under the mistletoe, package weddings by the cliff tops in Uluwatu or Hawaii, could predict its trajectory.

In Harriet's lonely hours, she logged in to the app again, a digital echo chamber of fleeting connections. She sent a few messages back and forth with a random French guy. Arden had disappeared from the app. She was sure he was still there, lurking in the digital shadows, but she didn't care. A strange sense of liberation bloomed in her chest.

Ironically, as she sipped a red wine, the warmth spreading through her veins, she typed in a new username: Banker's Wife. A playful rebellion against the life she didn't quite have.

She had given her WhatsApp number to the French guy, but she had not even bothered to save his real name. *Mr. Paris.* A phantom figure in her phone, a promise of something…different.

There were messages here and there, sexy snaps and invites from him to come over, each one a tiny spark threatening to ignite a wildfire of impulsive decisions. Harriet was in another world still, a world of quiet dinners and lonely mornings, of Arden's sporadic presence and the persistent hum of discontent.

Until that one Friday night, after months and months had passed, drinking margaritas with Anna and dancing until the morning, she felt she had changed. The weight on her shoulders felt lighter; the resignation in her eyes had faded. She had found a flicker of joy in her own company, in the carefree laughter of her friends.

Harriet took her phone out at the bar, the neon lights reflecting in her eyes, and scrolled through. *Mr. Paris.*

"Oh, bonjour…" She sent him a message, a playful tease sent into the digital void. He replied with a picture.

"I have ropes ready for you." It was a dark joke, laced with a promise of something twisted and exhilarating. A good-looking model guy at the bar smiled at Harriet, his eyes crinkling at the corners.

"Another Margarita?" he asked, his voice a low rumble.

"Sure! Gorgeous necklace, what does it mean?" she asked him, leaning in closer, drawn to his genuine warmth. They leaned on the bar desk, sipping cocktails, the music pulsing around them, and Harriet forgot about Mr.

Paris again. She danced with the Margarita guy, their bodies moving in sync, their laughter echoing in the crowded space. They briefly held hands, their fingers interlacing for a fleeting moment, and smiled, a connection forged in the transient heat of the night.

The night got darker, and the Margaritas made her eyes blurry. The Uber door opened. She stumbled in, alone, the city lights blurring past the window.

The next day, there was a message on the app from Mr. Paris. A reminder of the path she had almost taken, the thrill she had almost chased. And another one on WhatsApp.

Harriet sat on the beach, the pale morning sun doing little to soothe the throbbing in her head. Last night had been a messy blur of tequila shots and questionable decisions, culminating in a very early morning stumble home. Sighing, she pushed her sunglasses up her nose and decided a walk was in order. Anna, thankfully, was awake and game.

They strolled along the shoreline, the rhythmic crash of the waves momentarily silencing the internal drum solo in Harriet's skull. As they passed a brightly colored Mexican restaurant, the aroma of spices and sizzling meat snagged her senses. "Enchilada with extra guacamole," she declared, suddenly craving the comfort food. Anna laughed, knowing better than to argue with a hungry, hungover woman.

Sleepy and now bloated from all the carbohydrates, Harriet walked back home. The familiar sight of their messy house greeted her with a silent, accusatory glare. Dishes were piled high in the sink, a monument to last night's carefree abandon. Clothes lay scattered on the floor, discarded like forgotten dreams. Anna had gone out for the night, the second night in a row, leaving Harriet to wallow in her self-induced stupor.

As she drifted towards an unplanned nap, her phone buzzed again. *"What are you doing?"* popped up on the screen. It was… interesting. At first, she wasn't sure who it was from. An almost forgotten number. A night she wished she could remember more of. *"Oh, I messaged Bonjour last night... before the Margaritas...or was it after?"*

A few deep breaths later, wiping her tired eyes, without even thinking any further, Harriet typed back: *"Come over."*

She lit a candle, the flickering flame casting dancing shadows on the already chaotic room. She stepped over the clothes on the floor, a wave of apathy washing over her.

"Who cares...," she thought, her voice barely a whisper. She realized she hadn't washed her hair since last night. It looked like a mess, so she grabbed a cap and pulled it on, hoping it concealed the worst of it. The door intercom rang, jolting her back to reality.

Maybe she should put on some makeup, she thought. She quickly ran downstairs to the bathroom, splashed some water on her face, and did a quick flick of black eyeliner on her eyelids. It would have to do. She ran to the door and nearly fell to her knees.

He looked gorgeous, with a beaming smile. The classy style was trendy but with a touch of old charm. The wine bottle in his hand glinted in the dim light.

"I'm cold," he smiled, his eyes twinkling with amusement. Harriet's eyes lit up as they walked towards her bedroom, her pulse quickening with each step. Back in her room, she grabbed two glasses and poured the Pinot Noir, the rich red liquid swirling in the candlelight.

"Cheers, or what do you say? Salut?" she offered, slightly breathless. "Santé," he smiled, the French word rolling off his tongue like liquid silk.

He hardly had time to take a sip of wine. Harriet was already on the floor, kneeling. She unbuckled his belt, her fingers trembling slightly. He was semi-hard and stood up straighter as she began to take his balls one by one, sucking them with her eyes closed. She felt the moisture in her eyelashes, her mascara running down her rosy cheeks as he pressed his cock on her face, almost gagging her. She tried not to think of Arden's cock, but she couldn't help but compare. New York and Paris. They were the same size but different. They could both bring up her gag reflexes like this. Mr. Paris was thicker, *like a morning fog over the Seine River*, Mr. New York, thinner but *perfect...*

He said something in French, his smile as warm and inviting as the candlelight flickering across the room. He was nice and polite, speaking in heavily accented English that only added to his charm. This was just a quick transaction, though, a distraction. A fleeting moment, devoid of the deeper feelings, the yearning that gnawed at her when she thought of Arden.

His eyes, the color of rich, dark chocolate, moved over her with an appreciative warmth. He praised her body, her curves, with a genuine, almost innocent admiration. His touch was gentle as he brushed a stray strand of hair from her face. It felt different, clean, almost clinical compared to the familiar, and what Harriet wanted, a little possessive touch from Arden.

They had a nice, interesting chat. Mr. Paris spoke of his travels, his passion for art, and his life in Paris. He was gorgeous, undeniably so. His high cheekbones and the sculpted line of his jaw were even more stunning in the dark candlelight. Yes, he had done modeling, he admitted with a charming shrug, as though it were nothing special. Harriet had to pinch herself; a little thrill of disbelief mixed with a sharp pang of guilt coursed through her.

"Don't think about Arden! Stay in this moment," she mentally commanded herself. She forced a smile, focused on the sound of the French guy's voice, the way his eyes crinkled at the corners when he laughed.

But Arden was there, an insistent hum beneath the surface of the evening. He was there as if he was nudging Harriet with his jealousy despite being 'out there' with other people himself. The thought stung, a bitter pill she couldn't quite swallow. She imagined him, across the world, laughter echoing in his wake, his attention focused on someone else. *Was he thinking of her? Did he feel this same restless, unsettling ache?*

Mr. Paris leaned closer, his hand covering hers on the table. His skin was warm, the gesture intimate. *"You are beautiful, Harriet,"* he murmured, his voice a low rumble. *"And you seem... sad. Is there something on your mind?"*

She met his gaze, a flicker of vulnerability in her eyes. How could she explain the complex web of emotions tangled around her heart? The unrequited longing, the frustration, the lingering hope that Arden might, one day, see her the way she saw him?

"It's complicated," she managed, the word a whisper.

Mr. Paris squeezed her hand gently. "Life is complicated. But sometimes," he added, his eyes twinkling, "a little distraction is all we need."

He raised his glass in a silent toast. Harriet hesitated for a moment, her gaze drifting to the flickering candle flame. Was this distraction what she truly wanted? Or was she simply running, trying to outpace the ghost of Arden that haunted her every thought, every breath?

She took a deep breath, forcing herself to meet his gaze. "Yes," she said, the word barely audible. "A distraction is nice…."

But even as she spoke, she knew. Arden was still there, lurking in the shadows, a constant, unwelcome guest at her table. And no amount of candlelight, French charm, or gentle touches could truly banish him. He was a part of her, woven into the very fabric of her being, and tonight, he was a force she couldn't escape.

" I think you should go now. Au revoir."

Chapter 58

New York/Sydney, March 2024

Harriet stood in front of the full-length mirror in her bedroom, her reflection staring back at her with a mix of curiosity and anticipation. The room was dimly lit, with only the soft glow of a bedside lamp casting long shadows across the walls.

"I want to drag my cock across your tits".

"Unlocking my writer's block, I see," Harriet opened a photo from Arden.

"I was watching a video of a man being plugged and can't get the thought out of my head of you doing this to me," Arden opened.

"I feel honored." Harriet almost laughed. She laughed at herself for feeling this way. She would feel honored because it was what he wanted, and it would almost be the next step in her healing process. Gaping him open in this way, the trust and openness in their connection felt natural.

"I would very gradually increase pressure… " she continued texting back. The text messages, filled with a playful blend of vulnerability and desire, were pushing Harriet beyond her comfort zone in ways she found strangely liberating. The playful dominance and submission in their fantasies reflected not a power struggle, but a deepening mutual respect and a blossoming intimacy that felt both exhilarating and profoundly satisfying. She had never been fascinated by the idea of voyeurism, the thrill of being watched, especially after her experience with the Monster, but tonight was different. Tonight, she was going to watch herself. And, she was going to show Arden what she wanted him to do, following her example. The thought sent a shiver down her spine, a mix of excitement and nervousness that coiled in her stomach. She wore nothing but a silk robe, its deep crimson color contrasting sharply with her pale skin. Her long, wavy hair cascaded over her shoulders, and her green eyes sparkled with determination. On the bed beside her lay her phone, its lens pointed directly at the mirror. She had set it up earlier, ensuring the angle would capture everything she intended to do. The idea had come to her suddenly, a wild thought that had taken from Arden and refused to let go.

Harriet's mind raced as she considered the implications. It wasn't just about the act itself, though that was certainly a part of it. It was about the power of seeing herself in such an intimate, unguarded moment. She had not been in control, neither in her personal nor professional life, but this felt different. This was raw, unfiltered, and completely for Arden's eyes.

She took a deep breath, her fingers trembling slightly as she untied the belt of her robe. It slid off her shoulders, pooling at her feet, leaving her standing naked before the mirror. Her body was a work of art, curves and lines that told the story of a woman who, after years of abuse, started to know her worth. Her breasts were full and perky, her nipples already hardening from the cool air in the room. Her waist was narrow, leading down to hips that flared out, and thighs that were strong and shapely. But it was her ass that drew her gaze, the focal point of tonight's experiment.

Harriet turned slightly, admiring the way the light played over her skin, highlighting the curve of her buttocks. She reached back, running her hands over the smooth, firm flesh, her touch sending sparks of pleasure through her body. She had always loved her ass, the way it felt under her hands, the way it moved when she walked. But tonight, she was going to explore it in a way she never had before.

She glanced at the camera on her phone, its red light blinking softly, a silent observer in the room. *"Here goes nothing,"* she whispered, her voice barely audible. She bent forward, resting her hands on the edge of the bed, her ass raised provocatively. The position felt natural, almost instinctive, as if her body knew exactly what was required of it. She took a moment to adjust, ensuring the camera had a clear view, then reached back, her fingers tracing the curve of her cheeks.

Her touch was light at first, a gentle exploration of the terrain. She parted her cheeks slightly, her fingers brushing against the sensitive skin of her anus. A soft gasp escaped her lips as a jolt of pleasure shot through her. She had played with herself before, of course, but this felt different. This was deliberate, calculated, and yet somehow more primal.

Harriet's fingers circled her entrance, teasing the tight muscle, her breath coming in short, shallow gasps. She watched herself in the mirror, her reflection a study in concentration and desire. Her face was flushed, her lips parted, her eyes half-lidded as she focused on the sensations building within her. She leaned forward slightly, her breasts pressing against the bed, her nipples grazing the cool fabric.

With a slow, deliberate motion, she pressed a finger against her anus, feeling the resistance as the muscle clenched around her. She took her time, letting her body adjust, her breath hitching as she pushed deeper. The mirror showed her every detail, the way her ass stretched to accommodate her finger, the way her lips glistened with arousal. She felt exposed, vulnerable, and yet incredibly powerful.

As her finger slid in, she moaned softly, the sound filling the quiet room. She began to move, her finger sliding in and out, her body responding eagerly to the stimulation. Her other hand joined in, her fingers tracing patterns on her thighs, her hips, her stomach, as if mapping out her desire. She watched herself, mesmerized by the sight of her own pleasure, the way her body moved, the way her face contorted with each thrust.

Harriet's arousal built steadily, her breath coming in ragged gasps as she added a second finger, stretching herself further. Her ass felt full, her muscles clenching and releasing around her fingers in a rhythm that was both natural and intoxicating. She leaned further forward, her weight resting on her elbows, her breasts swaying gently with each movement.

The camera captured it all, the angle perfect as she shifted her position slightly, angling her hips to give herself better access. She was lost in the moment.

And, next, she wanted Arden to submit to her, doing the same with his fingers. She hit the send button with the caption for the video:

"*Eyes on me*"

Chapter 59

New York, March 2024

From my vantage point, high above the swirling chaos of human emotion, I watched Arden. He was making a video for Harriet, a carefully curated slice of vulnerability packaged in a lustrous glow. A surge of something akin to euphoria, almost intoxicating, washed over him, an intoxicating cocktail of submission and exhibitionism.

He fussed with his phone, meticulously adjusting the angle to capture his "best side" in the naked light. He wanted Harriet to see him, truly see him, stripped bare not just of clothing, but of artifice. He imagined her gaze, not just admiring, but commanding, judging. The thought itself sent shivers down his spine. *She would be looking right through him,* he thought, and the idea thrilled him.

"My ass looks so good like this," he told the mirror.

His heart hammered against his ribs, a frantic drumbeat of excitement. The anticipation of showing himself, of being admired and then, perhaps, rewarded with the whispered praise, *"Good boy,"* was almost unbearable. His fingers trembled as he pressed record, his whole body buzzing with a raw, almost electric energy.

Arden was riding a wave, a wave of carefully constructed bliss. And I, Love, knew intimately the ephemeral nature of such things. Waves crash.

The tide recedes. Vulnerability, when offered as a calculated performance, was a fragile thing indeed.

He paused the recording, his brow furrowed. He scrutinized the footage; his eyes narrowed with a critical eye. *Was the lighting flattering enough? Did he hold his jaw at the right angle?* He repeated a take, adjusting his posture, flexing a muscle here, smoothing a crease there. He was clearly in love with something in that room, and it was not the empty space where Harriet was meant to be.

He was clearly in love with himself, which wasn't entirely a bad thing. But the thought settled upon me like a cold weight. I had seen this pattern countless times before. Arden wasn't a narcissist, like Monster, no way.

But was he a performer, playing the role of *"lover"* flawlessly, yet incapable of true connection?

And I, Love, wondered. I, who am supposed to be the very essence of connection, the binding force of the universe, wondered if Arden was at all in love with Harriet. Was she anything more than a mirror reflecting the man he wanted to be; desired, dominant, and ultimately, in control?

The answer, sadly, was a whisper on the wind, a faint echo in the vast chambers of my own being: probably not. He loved the idea of Harriet, the fantasy of her adoration. But the real Harriet, with her own flaws and complexities, her own desires and needs… she was a ghost, a prop in his meticulously crafted performance of love.

The video was sent. The wave had crested. And I, Love, prepared myself for the inevitable crash. The sea of human emotion was a turbulent one, and the tides of self- obsession were often the most destructive. I could only watch, and wait, to see if Arden would ever learn the true meaning of the name I bear or remain forever lost in the reflection of his own desire.

Chapter 60

Sydney, April 2024

Harriet had stared at her phone for a little too long, replaying the video for the fifth time. The low light of her room cast long shadows across her face, mirroring the confusion churning in her gut. It wasn't the content of the video itself that made her feel a certain way, Arden, kneeling, eyes wide and vulnerable. In a position, just for her. It was her overwhelming feeling of elation and excitement triggered by it. She missed the bus and ran to catch the ferry instead. Harriet sat hunched over her notebook at a small table in the corner of the ferry. She had put her phone away; otherwise, she would have been too tempted to watch Arden's video again. She couldn't watch that content in public.

Her fingers trembled slightly as they danced across the page, scribbling down half-formed thoughts that felt as chaotic as the storm outside. With every wave that slammed against the side of the vessel, water splashed onto the windows, distorting her view and mirroring her turbulent emotions. She looked up momentarily from her scribbles to find a pretty girl across from her, completely absorbed in a book whose title made Harriet's stomach twist: *'How Not to Be Addicted to Fuckboys'.*

A cold shiver shot through Harriet's already nauseous belly. She wondered if *"Fuckboy Addiction"* was indeed an emerging medical condition, one that might explain her racing heartbeat and nervous sweats as she struggled with her addiction to Arden.

Was he a fuckboy? She still hadn't forgiven him for leaving her in his apartment that afternoon in New York.

Was he sending videos like the one to her to other people?

A small, but well-known publishing house had given Harriet a chance to write again, but also an ultimatum: deliver or be dropped into obscurity. Anxiety gnawed at her thoughts while she fought to craft something worthwhile amidst metaphors and voices that never seemed to align with his perspective; *the elusive fuckboy who haunted her writing.* As another rogue wave thrashed against them, Harriet glanced back at her notes one last time before surrendering them to fury; the crumpling paper would feel good right now.

"You felt like warm, rosy cheeks..." she recited internally, but even those words failed to soothe her frustration. The ferry rocked violently again; this time, everyone inside lurched sideways as thunder crackled above.

"Good book?" Harriet managed to ask with a strained smile toward the girl who raised an eyebrow in surprise.

"Yeah," she replied casually before returning to her pages. Harriet felt sick, not just from motion sickness but from resentment toward this stranger who was so effortlessly lost in a world of self-help, almost romantic escapism, while she battled demons on paper and within herself. Was it too much to want someone to read her words with that kind of captivated interest? Thoughts raced through her mind like waves crashing upon rocks; she needed Arden for inspiration more than ever, yet here she was drowning in self-doubt. The rain continued its relentless assault on the windows, blurring everything outside into an abstract painting of gray and blue hues. *"Fuck,"* she muttered under her breath without meaning to. "What?" The girl looked up again, curiosity dancing in her bright eyes. "I mean… your book," Harriet stammered quickly, trying to cover up how deep her envy ran. "Is it really good?" "It's alright," said the girl nonchalantly before another wave hit hard enough for everyone aboard to hold their breath. The sea roared like it wanted to swallow them whole, while Harriet's heart raced for reasons beyond nausea alone; was it fear or longing? She couldn't tell anymore as memories swirled around like fish caught in a net. Her past encounters flashed vividly: moments filled with laughter and heartbreak, all centered around Arden, the one she referred to as more than just *a fuckboy* but rather…*a savior in disguise.* In fleeting moments between thunderclaps and crashing waves, Harriet picked up her phone again and began typing furiously from memory; perhaps this would be *the story* after all, a tale not just about heartbreak but rebirth amidst chaos.

Time blurred on that ferry ride; the storm outside and within began to ebb away as clarity dawned upon her: she had something worth writing about after all. Opening her eyes, Harriet looked at the girl again. Still engrossed, unfazed, in her fuckboy self-help guide. At that moment, Harriet almost disliked her. She was jealous of her effortless focus, her self-assuredness, and her ability to seemingly compartmentalize her romantic life into neat, easily digestible chapters from this book that was published by the largest publishing house in the world.

Then, as another wave crashed against the ferry, spraying a fine mist across the window, a flicker of something else, envy, perhaps, or even a grudging admiration, sparked within Harriet's chest. Maybe, just maybe, there was something to be said for taking control, for refusing to be a victim of her own messy emotions. Maybe there was a way to navigate the storm, both within and out there.

Reaching into her bag, Harriet pulled out a fresh notebook. This time, she wouldn't write about Arden. She would write about the storm, about the ferry, about the girl with the book. She would write about the messy, chaotic, unpredictable reality of her own life, videos, *fuckboys, and all.*

Chapter 61

Sydney, May 2024

The world around Harriet fades as she stands at the edge of the water, feeling its cool embrace against her toes. The vast expanse of ocean stretches endlessly before her, mirroring her own boundless longing.

She closes her eyes, allowing herself to be enveloped by the symphony of nature, the whispers of waves echoing her heartbeat.

In this dreamlike state, Arden appears beside her, his silhouette framed by fading sunlight. The air between them crackles with unspoken tension; she can feel it in her bones like electricity waiting to spark. Their eyes lock, and in that instant, time seems to suspend itself.

Why don't you kiss me? she murmurs breathlessly, breaking the silence that hung heavily between them. Her voice is a soft challenge wrapped in desire. He steps closer until their bodies are inches apart. She can feel his warmth radiating toward her like a beacon in the twilight gloom. "Because I want you to want more," he replies, his tone low and teasing. The playful smirk on his lips ignites something deep within her, a yearning that feels both exhilarating and terrifying. With impatience bubbling inside her, she digs her nails lightly into his shoulders.

"I'm tired of wanting," she admits softly.

"Just give in." He tilts his head slightly as if contemplating her request.

Then he arches his back ever so slightly, a movement that sends a shiver down her spine as he leans closer still. Their breaths mingle in the cool evening air; she can taste the saltiness of his skin mixed with a hint of something sweet, like honey dripped on warm toast.

"Then take control," he urges with a sultry whisper that caresses her ear like silk.

A rush of confidence surges through her veins as she steps back for a moment to gauge him fully, his chest rising and falling rapidly under her gaze, flushed cheeks betraying his own desire.

"Turn around," she commands softly but firmly. He obeys without hesitation, turning his back to her and exposing himself completely to whatever may come next. As he arches into her touch, the way she craves him, it feels like they are locked in an intimate dance choreographed by their deepest fantasies.

Her hands glide across his skin possessively as if marking him as hers alone; every caress ignites fire beneath their surface.

"You're mine," she breathes into the wind, feeling powerful yet vulnerable all at once.

With each stroke along his spine and whispered promise against his ear, their surroundings begin to blur, and the ocean fades away until it's just the two of them suspended in this magic bubble where nothing else matters but their connection.

"Now be my good boy," she playfully instructs him, eliciting a low groan from deep within him as he complies willingly, submitting not just physically but emotionally too.

As twilight deepens into the night around them, stars twinkling like diamonds above, their bodies entwined in a passionate embrace that transcends mere dreams; it becomes an exploration of desires long buried beneath layers of reality, a place where love intertwines seamlessly with lust.

Chapter 62

Sydney, May 2024

As Love, I've seen this play out countless times. The slow erosion, the subtle devaluation, the dawning realization that the person they thought they knew was an illusion. I should have intervened with Harriet sooner, yanked her away when Monster first showed his true colors. That crinkled nose, the dismissive, casually cruel *"I don't think I love you anymore,"* a knifing delivered with chilling nonchalance. And it was right after he had sexually assaulted her, most brutally, cementing his ownership before discarding her like a used toy.

Harriet cried silently as he showered, washing away the remnants of their intimacy while her heart shattered into a million pieces. His phone buzzed incessantly with messages from the new supply, oblivious to the silent storm raging in the next room. Harriet, bless her trusting soul, didn't even consider invading his privacy. Her love was a fortress built on faith, a faith he was actively dismantling brick by brick.

At that point, she was blind to his capabilities. He was an illusion, a masterful manipulator who mirrored her desires but harbored only self-serving intentions. He was transactional, a user, a taker, and no matter how much love she poured in, he would always remain emotionally bankrupt. The new supply wouldn't fare any better, a pawn in his twisted game of validation.

Now, a year or so later, Harriet was a woman transformed. She was staying with Anna and finally piecing herself back together. The ache of Monster's betrayal still lingered, but it was fainter, less debilitating. As always, I was there for her.

She was about to head to the shower when a message pinged on her phone. It was from Anna.

Subject: *"You must see this! You can't make this stuff up."* A link to a Facebook video followed.

Harriet's heart clenched. A tremor ran through her fingers as she pressed play.

There he was. Monster. Decked out in an ill-fitting suit, standing under an arch of flowers. *At his wedding.* Declaring his vows to the woman he'd cheated with, the woman who was his new supply.

"I still vividly remember our first date. The first kiss at the Avatar, the long leisurely walk, the pause at the train station."

Harriet choked. Bile burned at the back of her throat. She remembered him messaging her selfies from that train ride, images of his reflection in the window. *He had been on a date!* Even as he whispered sweet nothings into her ear, he was simultaneously courting another. *Whilst married to her.* The audacity of it, the calculated cruelty, stole her breath and crushed her chest.

The video continued, a sickening spectacle of manufactured romance. Then came the vows, the new wife's vows, drenched in naive hope.

"God has blessed me with you," she said, her voice trembling with what Harriet now recognized as the beginnings of a carefully orchestrated deception.

Harriet watched in stunned horror; her breath caught in her throat. Each word spoken, each forced smile exchanged was a testament to his manipulative prowess. This woman, this unsuspecting bride, was now trapped in the same illusion Harriet had so desperately clung to.

This was Monster's pattern. Love was replaced with control, and empathy with disregard. The new supply would one day learn the truth, just as Harriet had. And I, as Love, wasn't so keen to be there to catch her when she fell. Monster had cheated on Harriet before, of course, but this woman was ruthless at heart; she stepped over a marriage, as if Harriet was nothing more than a shadow in her way. The cycle would repeat, a chilling testament to the enduring power of narcissism and the devastating collateral damage it leaves in its wake. Harriet watched in shock, horror, and a strange, burgeoning sense of relief. The relief of being freed from a cage she hadn't even realized she was in.

He went on to describe in detail the night he cheated on his first wife, Harriet, detailing it to the wedding audience. A testament to his unwavering dedication to manipulating the narrative to suit his needs. His words were revolting, a perversion of love and commitment. It was a desperate attempt to shock, to impress. And it was also an admission, laid bare for all to see, of his true nature. She was no longer married to that Monster.

I wanted to shout it from the rooftops. *No one sane acts like this! Harriet, you were not crazy. You were not unlovable. You were a victim of his pathology.* I wanted to tell her how desperately I wanted to protect her, how I wished I had been stronger, more present, to pull her away from the darkness before it consumed her.

I want to tell Harriet how she was devoted to him at home; he was out building a new life in secret. Then he flaunted it in his vows. *Harriet, that is beyond disrespectful.*

He was deceiving the new wife, too, bending the truth, until her love was secured. There is a term for this, Harriet. A predator who preyed on love itself. And, if the new wife had understood that it's always the eyes that give away a person's true soul. His eyes were cold, calculated, and dangerous. As Monster sat in the cinema, Harriet noticed he wasn't paying attention to the movie; he didn't need to because he had already seen it with the other woman. And he was secretive on his phone, messaging her. How many times was he going to watch *Avatar?*

Harriet realized she also needed to cut ties with the version of herself who allowed this to happen right in front of her eyes, this version of her who sat in the cinema, next to "a husband" who had been on the date, behind her back, walking a girl to the train station, kissing her among the treeline walks, and he had the nerve to be sitting next to her watching the same movie they saw together. *Disgusting. What a creep.*

Chapter 63

Sydney, June 2024

Harriet clutched the keys, her knuckles bone white. The housing commission estate loomed, a concrete behemoth casting long shadows. She'd escaped Monster and all his years of abuse, thanks to Anna's unwavering support and the intervention of support services Emma had linked her with, but the assigned apartment felt like a cage before she even stepped inside.

The chipped paint and the graffiti-scarred walls screamed of neglect and despair. She fumbled with the key, her heart hammering a frantic rhythm against her ribs.

As she approached her designated unit, a guttural scream ripped through the air from the apartment next door. A man and woman engaged in a brutal argument; their voices laced with anger and pain. The sound was a chilling echo of her past, a visceral reminder of Monster's rage. Harriet's carefully constructed composure crumbled. The image of Monster's face, twisted with fury, flashed before her eyes. Her hands shook violently; her breath hitched in her throat. She couldn't do this. Not alone. She couldn't bear the constant threat, the ever-present fear that the violence she'd escaped would find her again in this place. Overwhelmed by panic, she fled, tears blurring her vision.

Back at Anna's, she collapsed into Anna's embrace, sobbing uncontrollably. Anna, sensing her distress, gently stroked her hair, murmuring words of comfort. "You can stay here, Harriet," she said softly.

"That was a trigger."

The initial fear and despair slowly gave way to a quiet understanding. Harriet had underestimated the depth of her trauma. Anna's unwavering support became a lifeline, a beacon of hope in the darkness. Though their lives were vastly different, Anna's world was filled with color and creativity, and while Harriet still navigated a landscape of fear and uncertainty, their bond strengthened.

Anna's gentle strength and her unwavering belief in Harriet's resilience proved to be the solace Harriet needed.

In time, the Fear began to subside, replaced by a cautious optimism and a blossoming love that defied the stark contrasts of their pasts and the challenges they faced together. Harriet knew she was safe, truly safe, finally nestled in the warmth of her friend's love.

"I will hand back their keys tomorrow morning," Harriet said firmly. "Yes, stay here as long as you want. You don't belong there." Maybe Anna had been right about Arden, too.

"He isn't going to come save you. No one will. You will save yourself."

Harriet told herself. She would find a better apartment. Peaceful and above all, *safe.* Free from all the triggers from her past. She was now looking forward to the future. She wasn't just going to write about a man. Monster, or Arden. *She was going to write to show her scars so that others could heal. Because no one will save you. You need to save yourself.*

Chapter 64

Sydney, June 2024

Inside the bus, Harriet sat slumped against her seat, her blonde hair cascading over her face like a veil hiding her from the world. She felt invisible, lost within herself among the sea of strangers. She was on the way to take the keys back.

A sudden commotion disrupted her thoughts; she felt nausea, and suddenly she couldn't see anything anymore. She felt herself being lifted off her seat and carried out onto the sidewalk by two concerned passengers, a mother and her daughter. As they lay Harriet gently on the ground, morning sunlight spilled over her pale skin like honey.

The older woman's voice broke through Harriet's foggy mind:

"Take a bite, please." Her accent was rich and warm, infused with genuine care.

"Have you got any water, Mum?" asked the daughter anxiously, scanning their surroundings for help.

"Give it to her first," commanded the mother softly as she opened a bottle and the daughter brought it to Harriet's lips.

The cool water felt refreshing against her mouth; she managed to swallow a few drops before blinking back tears.

"You fainted," whispered the daughter, concern etched across her youthful features as she glanced at Harriet's striking red lips, covered with her favorite Chanel's Red Camellia, now trembling slightly from exhaustion.

"It's okay; we just take the next bus," said the mother, reassuringly, while offering half of her bread to Harriet.

"What's your name? Were you heading to work?" The mother continued with curiosity mixed with empathy as she studied Harriet closely.

"Harriet," she murmured after what felt like an eternity. She hesitated but then added softly, "I was…" Her voice trailed off as the mother noticed her black shoulder bag, with a small white bottle peeking out ominously.

"Did you take these?" The mother noticed and leaned closer with concern deepening in her eyes. Harriet nodded slowly.

"How many?" "I'm not sure… One after another." Salty tears began streaming down her cheeks as memories flooded back, laughter turned to silence, and love turned to pain.

"A boy?" urged the daughter gently despite her mother's disapproving glance. "Relationships are not the end of our story." Harriet couldn't help but crack a fragile smile at this unexpected wisdom from someone so young.

"Right… exactly." She sipped more water as fleeting hope flickered inside her chest. Suddenly, through teary eyes, she thought she spotted him, a figure in black jeans moving through the crowd with an unmistakable gait that stirred something painful yet familiar within her heart.

"Don't do that again," pleads the mother tenderly while placing another piece of bread in Harriet's hand. Their eyes locked in a moment, a silent understanding passing between them.

"I see that unconditional love in your eyes," said the mother softly before embracing both women tightly in an unexpected moment of solace midst of the morning chaos. The mother handed a card to Harriet.

"Here's a number for my psychologist, Amanda. She is amazing." Harriet put the card in her bag and looked like her cheeks were getting some color again as she waved goodbye to the two strangers who gave her a little ordinary love on an ordinary morning.

With gratitude swelling in her heart, Harriet watched as they walked away, their ordinary kindness igniting sparks of color back into her cheeks. As they disappeared into the crowd, Harriet clutched a card handed to her, a lifeline tied up neatly with hope.

"Unconditional love" echoed in her mind like sweet music against urban noise. The slick, expensive paper felt foreign in Harriet's calloused palm. Her fingers, rough from years of worry, traced the embossed lettering. *"Amanda Levine, Ph.D. - Clinical Psychologist."*

The rest of her day was a blur of routine. She dropped the keys off and finished the laundry, the scent of clean linen a small comfort. She picked up groceries, bargain-hunting for the best deals, stretching every dollar until it screamed.

Finally, she arrived at Anna's cramped house. The air inside her room was stale, heavy with the scent of dust and regret.

Taking a deep breath, Harriet retrieved the card from her bag. Her hand trembled slightly as she dialed the number to the therapist. Each ring was a heartbeat; a drumbeat of apprehension mixed with fragile anticipation.

A woman's calm, professional voice answered. "Dr. Levine's office, this is Sarah. How can I help you?"

Harriet swallowed, suddenly unsure of what to say. "Um… hello. My name is Harriet. I… I was given Dr. Levine's number and…" She paused, the words catching in her throat.

"And you'd like to schedule an appointment?" Sarah finished gently. Harriet's breath hitched, a silent surrender to the possibility of change. "Yes," she whispered, her voice barely audible. "Yes, please."

The kindness of strangers, the promise of unconditional love, and the hope for a brighter future are all woven together in the simple act of scheduling a phone call. The ordinary morning had transformed into something extraordinary, a single moment of connection that offered a glimmer of light in Harriet's long-shadowed life.

Chapter 65

Sydney, July 2024

Harriet sat on a plush couch. She lifted her gaze to Amanda, who sat across from her in a supportive posture, her expression calm yet attentive as she had listened to Harriet's long story.

The aroma of freshly brewed green tea lingered in the air as Harriet sipped slowly, trying to find solace in its warmth.

"Your ex-husband was trying to pimp you out to other men," Amanda stated gently, her voice steady yet compassionate. Harriet's heart sank at the words; a lone teardrop escaped her red eyes and rolled down her cheek as she placed the cup down on the glass table between them. Amanda instinctively pushed a box of tissues forward, an offering of comfort that Harriet accepted gratefully.

The therapist continued with conviction, "If you had gone through with it… he would have just used it against you." Harriet's mind flickered back to dark memories, imaginary images of herself curled up on their shared bed, tears soaking into the sheets while his sinister presence loomed over her like a shadowy Monster.

"He would have said: 'I saw you enjoy it,'" she whispered hoarsely. "He would have made it all about me being a slut…" Amanda nodded.

"Harriet, all I can say is that you put boundaries in place and did not do it.

You did the right thing."

A wave of nausea washed over Harriet as she thought about how he had tried to manipulate her for years.

"He will get someone else to do it," she murmured bitterly.

"That size of a door woman has probably already done it." Harriet had shown Amanda a picture of his new supply.

"You can't help her."

The therapist leaned forward slightly, her eyes piercing yet filled with understanding. The room felt heavy as thoughts spiraled through Harriet's mind like storm clouds gathering for rain. She could almost feel his hands on her again, the violation that left scars deeper than skin.

"He is an abuser. Manipulator. He will put her in a weak position where she can't say no." Harriet felt sick thinking about it. How Monster objectified her, and she was nothing but flesh he would have used for his gratification.

"When you woke up with him on top of you…" Amanda's words cut through the haze of recollection like thunder.

"He was raping you. He probably drugged you. He would have done that and had other men use you. It is beyond disgusting."

"Just think about it like this, he didn't get what he wanted from you. It will haunt him forever. He is a cuckold, yes. But more than that, he is an abuser. He tried to violate your boundaries and use you. He *failed*".

"The key to understanding how he, the narcissist, operates is understanding that they aren't human. That person you met in the beginning doesn't exist; it was merely an act."

"We can talk about this as many sessions as you want, but I would rather move on and concentrate on how we can get you better. Start living again".

Harriet nodded.

"These men, they are like a shirt on a hanger, it looks human in shape, but there is nothing inside."

"The nature of narcissists is that they recycle the same patterns with every new victim." She paused to let Harriet absorb this truth before adding gently,

"Even if that new supply possesses qualities you admire, a model's looks or brilliance, they will face abuse too. It's not personal; it's who they are."

Harriet felt tears welling up again, but blinked them away resolutely. She needed strength now more than ever, a sense of closure that had eluded her for so long.

"Let's focus on healing and moving on," Amanda encouraged softly.

Chapter 66

Sydney, July 2024

The water pounded against Harriet's skin, a relentless rhythm echoing the turmoil in her mind. Steam filled the small bathroom, a temporary veil against the cold reality that clung to her like a shroud. Her name was Harriet, and she was a survivor, though for the last year, she couldn't even whisper that word, the weight of shame too heavy on her tongue.

And I, Love, watched her. Bent, raw, trembling, yet still standing. I had never left her side, though she thought I had.

Monster was now her ex-husband, but once, he was the man she thought she loved, the man she thought she would spend her life with. Then, he became exactly what her soul had feared all along: a Monster. It started slowly, insidious cracks appearing in the facade of their perfect life. Then the facade shattered completely. He sexually assaulted her.

She blamed herself, told herself she'd provoked him, that she hadn't been attentive enough, that she was somehow deserving of his violence. It would take years and countless hours of therapy before she could even begin to untangle the twisted knot of guilt he had so expertly tied around her.

But I knew the truth. Love does not excuse violence. Love does not demand humiliation. What he did to her was not me; it was power disguised as intimacy, cruelty dressed as care. He hadn't stopped at rape. He had tried to pimp her out, propositioning other men, suggesting she perform for his amusement. He worked to reduce her to an object, a tool for gratification, stripping her of dignity, of her very self.

Every five years, the idea resurfaced like clockwork, a macabre anniversary of his control. And every five years, she refused, her excuses stacking up like fragile shields. Fifteen years of dodging, deflecting, enduring.

The last time, he cloaked himself in counterfeit tenderness. *"I would love you again if you did it,"* he whispered, dangling hope like poison. *"Our connection might come back."* And in a moment of weakness, of desperate longing for the man she thought he once was, she faltered. He raped her again. She learned that the cruelest betrayals are always delivered by those who hold your heart in their hands.

I burned with her, watching. She thought I had abandoned her, but I had not. I was simply waiting, quietly, for the day she would see me clearly again. She couldn't remember how she managed it, but somehow, she left. Left the Monster. Left the home. Left the ruins of the life she thought she wanted.

Reporting him to the police was excruciating. The interviews. The reliving. The judgment in strangers' eyes. She gave multiple statements, hoping justice would finally be served. She imagined his mugshot plastered across news sites, his name dragged into the light. But it never happened.

Emma urged her to make the call, to coax him into confessing, to anchor the case. She agreed, trembling. It backfired. Justice slipped further away. He moved on seamlessly, slipping into a new life with the woman he had been cheating with all along.

And then came the message. A digital dagger delivered late at night. From *her*. The new woman. The new victim.

I wish you well.

The words echoed in Harriet's chest, hollow and sharp. She stood in the shower, water scorching her skin, still trying to wash away the residue of his touch. She squeezed the empty shampoo bottle upside down, her knuckles white with rage.

I wish you well.

Her lips curled around the phrase, venom seeping into every syllable.

"I wish you well," she whispered.

"I wish you well," she screamed, her cry lost in the roar of water, a primal sound of grief and defiance.

"I wish you well," she hissed again, softer, almost mocking, the irony thick on her tongue.

They weren't words of kindness. Not sympathy. They were a knife. A reminder that she was already erased, replaced, irrelevant. The message carried the unspoken truth:

I have him now. You're in the past. Your pain doesn't matter.

Harriet swallowed hard, bitterness rising. Politeness had never felt so poisonous.

She wished that woman knew the truth, wished she could see the Monster's mask for what it was before he turned on her, too. She wished she could run, could escape, could get free before the jaws closed.

And I, Love, stood watching. I saw Harriet bend beneath the weight of her sorrow, her chest rising and falling like a wounded bird. But I knew what she could not yet imagine. One day, the other woman would choke on those very words. When the lies unraveled and cut her open too, she would learn what Harriet already knew: that what she believed to be a prize was only a curse. And Harriet—my Harriet—wouldn't need to lift a finger. The truth would come for her.

Chapter 67

Sydney, January 2024

The longer Harriet stared at the ocean, grey sky, and the waves, the more complex the scenery became. She sat with her laptop in the corner of the local Starbucks, thinking about Arden. Thinking about the bank statements her lawyer had sent her for a financial settlement from the Monster. He had been in this same Starbucks only weeks earlier. He had found her. *Was he trying to scare her?* Thanks to Arden, she was no longer scared. She felt Arden's presence and his reassuring voice repeating the words *"he is a loser".* She remembered Arden holding chopsticks perfectly and delicately picking up pickles, whilst Harriet couldn't eat what she had ordered.

"Would you like something else if you don't like that?" Arden asked her. Monster would have gotten angry in the same situation, yet Monster would not have ordered her anything. He would have ordered everything from the menu and let Harriet watch him savor all the foods, hungry. Maybe giving her a one piece of sushi with degrading comments. *"That's enough for you. You have put on so much weight".* The tuna sushi sat on the plate as Harriet looked into Arden's deep eyes.

"He is a loser".

Clutching a classic hot chocolate, Harriet continued to stare at the ocean.

It felt as vast as her unconditional love. The soft hum of conversations faded in the background. She had thought the taste of Arden would have diminished with each new pass of the tongue as she took a sip of her drink. She would taste him forever.

In the dim light of the crowded cafe, a message notification appeared on her phone. Harriet continued to stare at the ocean, the waves speaking volumes of sadness.

As she locked eyes with the waves, she locked eyes with her fears. The time she had tried to drown herself.

No matter how much pain she felt, she would not go back into the waves, no longer holding her breath, letting go. *"Give me a reason to stay".* She still gasped as her lungs filled with water.

"Please tell me that you see me." Her last thoughts before everything went black. The water came back out of her lungs as the lifesavers kneeled over her. Once again, she had let the Fear open the gate for all those dark memories of the Monster. "He is unwell." Her psychologist, Amanda, had adjusted her glasses and stated, "he is sick". "It is not your fault".

Now, in the crowded cafe, she grabbed her phone and viewed the message. *No more thinking about Monster and what he caused.*

A message from Arden filled the screen.

It was…a picture. An impressive, artistically lit photo of his cock. So perfect, so sculpted, so undeniably… *there*, that Harriet nearly choked on her hot chocolate. She sputtered, coughed, and then, slowly, a smile crept across her face.

In her eyes, he was built like a Greek god and perpetually radiating a mischievous charm. He was also utterly, gloriously inappropriate.

Laughter bubbled up from her chest, a genuine, unrestrained sound that startled even her. Little did people know that sometimes inappropriate photos were a lifesaver. And Arden knew that the world needed a well-lit penis to remind you that life was more than just spreadsheets and interest rates. She typed a response, a playful glint in her eye. "So hot, now turn around." The reply was immediate: "Patience, Harriet. A connoisseur appreciates the finer details." Harriet shook her head, a smile playing on her lips. Amanda would probably have a thesis written on the therapeutic benefits of unsolicited genitalia. But right now, all she knew was that a single, perfectly lit photo had managed to cut through the fog of despair and remind her that even after the storm, the sun could still shine, albeit with a slightly raunchier glow. Life, she realized, was still worth living, even with the Monster, *such a loser*, lurking in the background. And sometimes, all it took was a well-endowed, artistic nude to remember that.

Chapter 68

Sydney, August 2024

Harriet clutched the phone, the support worker's excited voice a jarring contrast to the quiet dread that had become her constant companion. "We got you an apartment! If you want, that is!" The words hung in the air, heavy with implication. "It's more like a safe house, not permanent but longer term if you're OK with it?" the support worker, linked by Emma, clarified, her tone softening. Harriet was confused. She'd grown accustomed to the temporary nature of her stay at Anna's, the unspoken understanding that it wouldn't last. "You can move in whenever you want." The thought of escape, of finally being safe from Monster, now just a shadowy figure from her past, sent a shiver of both fear and exhilarating relief down her spine. The apartment, she learned, was nestled near the beach. She could almost hear the rhythmic crash of waves in the support worker's voice, a promise of peace. This would be the place where she could write again. Monster would not know where she was.

She missed Anna's garden, the evenings with Pinot Noir, Nick dropping by, and their laughter spilling into the night. But she needed her own space. Within a week, she had moved, trading comfort for solitude. The ocean's roar became the backdrop to her healing. She began quietly, hesitant sketches in her battered notebook, tentative lines of text. Fragments of memory surfaced, slowly threading themselves into stories, each word a small step toward reclaiming herself.

Arden, her first real love in her stories, became more than a memory; he became a presence that lingered in the empty spaces of her life. Her writing turned into a sanctuary, a place where she could face her trauma and transform lingering pain into something lasting, something luminous. One evening, walking along the beach, lost in thought, she imagined him beside her.

This version of imaginary Arden, drawn to Harriet's quiet intensity and the way her eyes seemed to hold the weight of untold stories, learned about her past in small, carefully chosen moments. He didn't pry but offered his unwavering support. Their relationship blossomed slowly, amid shared sunsets and whispered confessions.

He never asked her about Monster but offered his hand to help her build a new life, a life where the echoes of the past were not silenced but woven into the tapestry of a present filled with love and hope. The apartment by the beach became a symbol of resilience, a testament to Harriet's journey, a place where the waves of the ocean gently washed away the shadows of her past, replaced by the warmth of a new love, a love born from resilience and understanding, a love for herself with imaginary characters she dreamed of.

Chapter 69

❧

Sydney, September 2024

Harriet stared at the laptop screen, the glow illuminating the swirling sand-colored paint flecks on her new apartment wall. The ocean, restless, crashed against the shore outside. Her fingers hovered over the keyboard, the cursor blinking mockingly. Arden was her "Mr. Big." The name felt absurd, yet it perfectly captured the overwhelming presence he'd exerted on her life, a digital phantom who'd materialized in New York, a city as vast and unpredictable as the ocean itself. She scrolled through their initial messages; a bizarre courtship conducted entirely in the flickering light of a screen. Had it all been a meticulously crafted illusion? A grand, albeit digitally rendered, seduction? The thought, unsettlingly familiar, wormed its way into the comfortable narrative she'd built around their whirlwind romance. Was she just dickmatized? Did he catfish her with his big dick? Harriet analyzed their initial conversation.

Harriet: "You look like you have good energy."

Arden: "I would say so. But better experienced in person. Some would say..big dick energy?" Harriet: "Yeah, I wouldn't mind, haha."

Arden: "Haha, good good. The big dick part is also true."

Harriet: "I think I found my future husband."

Arden: "Hahah ;) We can work on that."
Harriet: "Yes, please."

The initial thrill of their connection, a heady cocktail of witty banter and undeniable chemistry, had morphed into something more ambiguous. That trip to New York… she still wasn't sure what had been real and what had been projected. Was it the city itself, a kaleidoscope of sensory overload that had distorted her perception? Or was it something more fundamental, something intrinsic to the nature of their relationship? Suddenly, the sound of the ocean outside seemed to ripple with energy.

Harriet blinked, rubbing her eyes, the image dissolving into the familiar, churning sea. Was this the apartment's influence, the old building humming with the strange energies of the tide? Or was it a manifestation of her growing doubt, her subconscious trying to communicate the unsettling truth?

She started typing. She was meant to write about *her* life. But her thoughts were reaching beyond Arden's big dick. It was his being. The moment they shared was still consuming her mind.

His most delicate part tasted like Evian. I felt so safe, finally.

I had never done anything like it in my entire life, never even thought about it. It was something that I considered as not something that the average heterosexual female like me would ever encounter. Until I met my Mr. Big. In every sense.

Before him, intimacy was a battlefield, a minefield of anxieties and forced fake smiles. I was a woman scarred by a marriage to a man who saw me as nothing more than a possession, a trophy to be displayed and used. The divorce was a messy, agonizing affair, a desperate escape from a life that reeked of coercive control and violation. He was a Monster, a predator disguised as a husband, and I carried the invisible wounds of his abuse deep within me. The healing was a slow, arduous process, a journey through therapy, medication, and countless sleepless nights haunted by the ghosts of his cruelty. I had been conditioned to think that as a woman, I was meant to let alpha men take me from behind, be obedient, and just get on with it. There was something wrong with me if I didn't enjoy it. I had never enjoyed sex, and how could I have when I had been nothing but an object?

Then, Mr. Big walked into my life, a gentleman with a heart that mirrored the vastness of his presence. I adored him. His intelligence sparked my creativity. His body was perfect and comforting. His strong neck. His lean legs. The way he looked at me with his brown eyes, I saw nothing but golden speckles. The way he encouraged me was, "Write, you are so talented". The way he appraised my looks, "You look so beautiful. To me, you always look like a flower." The way he adored my breasts and gently touched my back. I felt a shiver down my spine and goosebumps all over me. I realized I had never been in love. I had never felt such an utterly unconditional love in my entire life.

For Mr. Big, I was anything but an object; I was the flower, and he was watering me until I was ready to bloom.

He was a sculptor of my soul, gently chipping away at the walls I had built around my heart. He listened, truly listened, to my stories of pain and fear, offering not judgment but understanding. He celebrated my strengths, nurtured my passions, and whispered words of encouragement that made me believe in myself again. He made me laugh, made me feel seen, made me feel safe.

And then there was the intimacy.

It wasn't a kink or fetish, or I am doing it because I am forced to, he might love me if I do it like it was with my ex-husband. It was different. It was a revelation. It was a tender exploration of bodies and souls, a dance of trust and vulnerability. He never demanded, never pressured, never made me feel like I was obligated to anything. He only asked, "What feels good to you?" And for the first time in my life, I dared to answer honestly.

It was so unexpected.

I was doing it because it felt safe, I was unconditionally allowed to enter my nose inside of him, my tongue, my high cheeks touching his soft skin. I felt alive, I felt sparkles from my spine being transferred into every nerve ending of his most sensitive parts. And when I hesitantly, shyly, tasted the pureness of his skin. It was like a baptism, a cleansing of all the trauma and shame I had carried for so long. It was so pure, it was innocent, it was connection.

It wasn't just the act; it was the intention. I wanted to please him; to give him pleasure, he made me feel beautiful and desired. He wanted to connect with me on a level that transcended the physical, to touch my soul with his touch. He made me understand that sex could be something more than just a transaction, a duty, a source of pain. It could be an expression of love, a celebration of intimacy, a pathway to healing.

In his arms, I realized I had been living a lie. I had been fed how sex should be. I had been conditioned to believe that my desires were wrong, that my body was broken, that I was somehow less of a woman because I couldn't conform to someone else's idea of pleasure. But he shattered those beliefs, one gentle touch, one whispered word, one shared moment of vulnerability at a time.

With Mr. Big, I discovered a new kind of love, a love that embraced my past, honored my present, and empowered my future. A love that tasted like Evian, pure and refreshing, a love that made me feel safe, finally.

A wave of conflicting emotions washed over me. There was a flicker of surprise, then a thread of curiosity, and finally, a soft bloom of affection. The vulnerability in his eyes was undeniable. He wasn't demanding, he wasn't pushing. He was sharing a desire, a part of himself, and entrusting me with its delicate existence. The real intimacy lay in the sharing, the vulnerability, the trust that allowed us to explore the uncharted territories of our desires, together.

When I moved my head from inside of him, I had found the strength to start climbing, inadvertently forging a new me, one who was finally ready to claim her own worth.

She slammed the laptop shut, the silence of the apartment now deafening.

Chapter 70

New York, October 2024

Arden shrugged off the crisp banker's suit as he walked, the fabric a little too constricting after a day of forced smiles and shuffling numbers. The fluorescent hum of the bank faded behind him, replaced by the neon pulse of the city's nightlife. Needing the release of a Negroni, he turned toward the familiar mahogany gleam of "The Vault," the watering hole favored by his cohort of finance bros.

Inside, the air was thick with cigar smoke and the self-assured laughter of men who moved millions with a keystroke. Arden nodded to Mark, Ben, and David, settling into his usual spot at the bar. The conversation, as always, revolved around IPOs, bonuses, and the latest conquests. He participated, of course, throwing in a few choice remarks about a particularly ambitious tech start-up, but his mind felt elsewhere.

The Negronis flowed, each bitter sip temporarily washing away the sterile taste of spreadsheets and boardroom lies. As the night deepened, the inevitable suggestion arose: *"Gentlemen, let's hit the Flamingo."*

Arden didn't resist. The Flamingo, with its promise of fleeting beauty and manufactured intimacy, was a predictable end to these predictable nights. He told himself it was a ritual, a way to unwind, to shed the skin of his professional self.

The Flamingo was a kaleidoscope of flashing lights, throbbing music, and the cloying scent of cheap perfume. He watched the dancers move; their practiced smiles plastered on their faces. He saw their artifice, the desperate need beneath the glossy veneer, and a sliver of something akin to pity flickered within him.

Then he saw her. Her name, according to the small plastic tag pinned to her shimmering dress, was Anya. She was younger than the others, her movements less practiced, her eyes holding a guarded shyness that set her apart. She was from Ukraine, he learned later, her English hesitant, her expression one of tentative hope mixed with an ever-present anxiety.

Something about her vulnerability, so different from the hardened detachment of the other dancers, tugged at him. He found himself drawn to her naivete. He slipped her a bill, more than he usually did, and asked if he could buy her a drink. She nodded, her eyes widening slightly. He tried to engage her in conversation, asking about her life and her dreams. She answered in short, clipped sentences, constantly glancing toward the imposing bouncers stationed near the stage.

He wanted to see her again, outside the confines of this place, where the desperation hung heavy in the air. "Would you ever... would you be free for a coffee sometime?" he asked, the words feeling clumsy and awkward.

Anya looked down, fiddling with the fringe of her dress. He couldn't decipher the emotion in her eyes. Was it fear? Disgust? He wondered if the club had rules about fraternization with the clientele. He imagined them, trapped in some unspoken contract, their freedom as illusory as the glitter dusting their skin.

He liked the strippers, their bodies honed and sculpted, their smiles bought and paid for. They were blank canvases, receptive to his desires. But they lacked the spark, the intellectual fire that burned within Harriet.

Harriet. The thought of her, all the way in Australia, with her messy strawberry blonde hair and her sharp, insightful observations, was a pang in his chest. Harriet, with her complicated past and her fierce independence, had seen through him, dissected his carefully constructed facade, and loved him anyway. Harriet's vulnerability was real, a stark contrast to the carefully curated fragility of the dancers at the Flamingo.

He needed something now. *A touch, a release.* The memory of Harriet's hands on his skin, the way she looked at him with a knowing glint in her eyes, felt like a distant dream. He needed something to fill the void, to silence the gnawing loneliness that Harriet's absence had amplified.

Arden looked at Anya, her eyes wide and uncertain. He saw the flicker of desperation in her gaze, the longing for something more. And a part of him, a small, shameful part, recognized a kindred spirit. He knew, with a chilling certainty, that he could take advantage of her vulnerability. He could offer her a temporary escape, a momentary distraction from the reality of her life. He could, perhaps, even believe he was offering her something more.

But then he looked again and saw not a blank canvas, but a flicker of defiance in her eyes. And for the first time that night, Arden felt a prick of shame. He was not sure who he was ashamed of more, himself or this entire world happening around him. Either way, he was ashamed.

He smiled, a little sadly, and said, "It's okay. Maybe another time."

He left her a generous tip and walked away, the music of the Flamingo suddenly sounding hollow and meaningless. He walked out into the cool night air, the city lights blurring in his vision. The Negronis had lost their edge, and the familiar comfort of the finance bros felt like a suffocating weight. He hailed a cab and gave his address, the quiet solitude of his apartment suddenly seeming less daunting than the empty promises of the Flamingo. He knew he wouldn't sleep well; the image of Anya's wary eyes burned into his mind. And he knew, with a growing sense of unease, that the void inside him wouldn't be filled by fleeting pleasures or manufactured connections. It needed something real, something deeper. *It needed Harriet.*

Chapter 71

Harriet lingered at the balcony door, the warm afternoon sun grazing her bare legs below her denim shorts. A cat darted across the street, vanishing under a parked car, while the smell of sizzling BBQ drifted up from below. Voices grew louder; neighbors were celebrating, laughing. The apartment was decent enough, just a touch of paint away from feeling like home. At least it wasn't the concrete housing commission estate.

She placed her small golden angel Christmas ornament on the glass tray, next to the black Celine candle, the same candle she had lit that very first night she spoke with Arden. The sun still kissed her legs, and she imagined him there, his hands, the memory igniting heat inside her. She shivered. The sun dipped behind a dark cloud, and reality hit: he had never made her cum. She had been so close, riding him, her head rolling back, her body trembling, squeezing, yearning. It would have been perfect if he had lasted just a few seconds longer.

It wasn't just about sex; it was the gift of someone giving her exactly what she asked for, the way life opens up when we offer a fragment of our hearts. She had never felt so alive, so complete, as she had in those moments on top of him.

231

Every song, every scent, every drifting cloud reminded her of him. His puppy eyes, soft and knowing, never judging. Her heart still held hope that one day he would be hers, fully. The golden hoops gleamed in her ears as she brushed her hair down.

A message buzzed from Anna: *"See you soon. If you get there before me, a spicy watermelon margarita for me."* Harriet typed a quick reply, needing any small pleasure to soothe the ache inside her. His words from months ago haunted her: *"I like you, but I am not in love with you."* Every syllable was a twist of the knife. But she knew, he did love her, in his own complicated way. Maybe it would take him time to see how special she was, to recognize the magic that existed only between them.

Later, at the harbor, she fished a piece of watermelon from her margarita. The night was electric, reckless. He was tall, handsome, and suddenly there, standing before her.

"Alex," he offered his hand.

"Get the fuck out of here. How old are you?" Anna laughed, surveying him up and down, before disappearing into the dance floor crowd.

Harriet let Alex take her hand as they walked into the night. She wanted to forget Arden, just for tonight. His eyes darkened with desire as soon as they entered the dimly lit room, and she felt the pull of her body, the heat of anticipation.

They stumbled onto the bed, laughter and urgency mixing. He kissed her passionately, hands exploring, teasing, pressing against her warmth. She gave herself to it, letting it happen, but every groan, every touch reminded her: he wasn't him. He wasn't Arden.

When it was over, she sat up, shivering. "I'm cold," she whispered.

She remembered how her tongue had fit Arden perfectly, like it belonged there, as if their bodies were written to match. It wasn't just skill, it was intimacy, the way two pieces of a puzzle clicked without force. No one else could replicate it.

Alex handed her a black hoodie. She smiled, sliding into it, the oversized fabric soft and comforting. The room was dark, but a sliver of light fell across her arm, and for a fleeting moment, she felt Arden's warmth in that ray of sun, that touch of light she had craved for so long.

On the bus home, Harriet buried her face in the soft fabric of the hoodie, its warmth a small comfort against the night. He knew she would never return it; it was just a fleeting, forgettable one-night stand. She realized, too, that she had left her golden hoops behind, abandoned in the rush to leave.

The night had been meant to make her forget Arden, but all it did was pull him closer into her thoughts, every memory sharper, every longing more insistent.

Chapter 72

Sydney, January 2025

Amanda was visibly sick of hearing about Monster as each counseling session progressed. She gets paid to listen to this, but at times, these women coming to her were like broken records, as harsh as it sounded.

"Yeah, he is *gross.*"

And for the hundred times she repeated to her:

"NO, HE HAS NOT CHANGED. NO, HE HAS NOT CHANGED. NO, HE HAS NOT CHANGED."

Harriet took a tissue. Amanda continued:

"Being discarded is one thing, but to find out that they are very quickly with someone new, it's devastating. They were there the entire time. Classic narcissistic behavior."

"You need to stop looking at social media."

"Harriet, I know what you went through, like all the women who have been through the same. They have a new term, which is "new supplies", and you have been searching desperately for some sort of clue as to when this relationship started, how it all began behind your back, if she is better looking than you, and if they have something you didn't?"

"In your case, definitely not better looking, don't you worry, girl!" Amanda laughed.

"Is Monster happier, and even worse… if Monster had changed?" Harriet asked herself quietly.

"He isn't particularly intelligent or magnetic, but he has that power of persuasion. He can pick up on women's needs and desires, and he can fulfill those. When he wants." Amanda analyzed him.

"And I know what you are thinking, *NO HE HAS NOT CHANGED!*" Amanda laughed again.

"Are you angry because of the new size of the door new supply can't see who he is?" Amanda asked. Harriet stared at the walls. Nodding.

"The one who brought you here. Staring at these walls, the one who liked every hot blonde girl on Instagram. Fire emojis, remember when you told me he said it was because he was trying to get followers, so he added girls from his gym? *Banging, hot dress…*his comments. Remember? The one who *deceived* you.

NO, HE HAS NOT CHANGED.
You are still the same person who pays library overdue fines. He steals books. He is a con man. Still the same, and highly likely he is worse.

He is more cunning and more calculating. He is worse. What she is getting is a pro at lying, cheating, and deceiving. A lot worse."

He kicked me. Head. Military boot. Floor. Knocked out cold. Decisions made over me, without asking. Vasectomy. Another woman. Lies. Manipulation. She fell for it, too. Dark hair. Different. No. He hasn't changed. I know.

And still, no, you're wrong, Harriet. Something feels off, like pieces of me are out there somewhere, where I can't see them. Like a shadow moving in the corners of the world, I don't know. Fear crawls back. Again. Always. Waiting.

"He probably put adverts up of you, Harriet…" Amanda's words shook, a fearful whisper that slammed into Harriet like ice.

"What would he be doing to the other woman?" Harriet asked Amanda.

"She is not your problem," Amanda said, as horrible thoughts circled in Harriet's mind of him love-bombing her, lying to her. It was all Harriet. She was the perpetrator. She was bad. She was the liar. She was the instigator. No matter what Amanda said or explained, Harriet's brain was rejecting again. This is part of Stockholm Syndrome. Trauma bond. I am trying to be greater than anxiety. I am stronger than Harriet's doubt. I am more than Fear. I am trying to give a love story that is bigger than your past pain. Harriet's phone flashed with a message.

"Miss Wifey. Do you want to video?"

YES! YES! YES!!! I jumped around.
"Arden, help me!" Harriet was spiraling *again*.

Chapter 73

Sydney, January 2025

It was again 3 am when Harriet woke up from her dream. This time, she wasn't wiping sweat off her forehead, her heart racing and still hearing Monster's demanding voice.

She felt like everything was different; the tide was turning. Or so she was hoping as she took another sleeping tablet and pulled her blanket up. *Dream.*

Arden was in the dream, touching her shoulder. He felt different. The room was surrounded by older, brown antique furniture, the windows open, with the wind gently blowing in; she couldn't tell which season it was, or which city she was in. She walked around and sat next to the white desk she had had in her childhood. In the middle, it opened upwards, and inside was a mirror and more space. Instead of makeup, she stored her Barbie dolls there. The desk was empty, but it looked new. She walked around the room, and she felt Arden's warmth, a different kind of love. He seemed older, more content. *"Whatever love is",* Harriet looked at herself in the mirror and thought about her overwhelming emotions every time she thought about Arden.

On some level, Harriet was right. I knew she wasn't free from his spell. Maybe now was the time. He had reached that transitional age for a man, and she had healed. Harriet had always found Arden captivating, but it wasn't until she saw him in her dream in a dark brown suit that she realized just how desirable he could be.

Beneath the expensive fabric, his body moved with effortless grace as he arranged her white desk. Her gaze clung to him, heat rising in her cheeks as her eyes traced the way his trousers clung to his hips, leaving little to the imagination.

"Write. Write your story, Harriet," his New York accent slipping into something very proper.

"And will you read what I write?" she asked softly, blinking her eyelashes. "Of course," Arden grabbed a textbook and sat down.

As she began to write, Harriet found it increasingly difficult to focus. Every time Arden leaned over to grab another book or hand her a pen, she could smell his intoxicating scent and feel the heat emanating from his body. She couldn't help but imagine what he might look like without any clothes on. They worked in silence for a while, with only the sound of pens scratching against paper and soft breathing filling the space, but then, Arden leaned back in his chair and sighed heavily, breaking the tension. "This is so frustrating," he muttered under his breath. Harriet looked up from her notes to see him rubbing his forehead, revealing a few strands of sweat-dampened hair. "What is it?" she asked, her voice barely above a whisper. "This chapter," he replied, shaking his head. "I just can't seem to grasp this part." Harriet couldn't help but smile sympathetically. "I know how you feel," she said, trying not to stare at his exposed neck. "Why don't we take a break?" Arden nodded gratefully, and they both stood up from the table. Harriet grabbed her water bottle, and they headed towards the kitchen. As they walked, she couldn't shake the feeling that something was different between them. The air felt charged, electric. When they reached the fridge, Harriet turned to face him, their bodies close enough to touch. She couldn't help but notice the outline of his erection pressing against his trousers. For a split second, she considered reaching out and touching him, but then she remembered where they were, a friend's house, and Anna could walk in any minute. She swallowed hard and turned away, trying to ignore the racing of her heart.

Harriet spent the rest of the break trying to gather her thoughts, but all she could think about was Arden and the way he looked in his suit. She couldn't believe how turned on she was by him. As they headed back to the study room, she found herself wishing they could continue their break for just a little longer. When they sat down again, Harriet couldn't help but feel self-conscious about the way she was sitting, trying to maintain a bit of distance between them. But Arden didn't seem to notice; he was too focused on her first written chapter. They sat in silence for a while longer, with Harriet trying her best not to imagine what was beneath Arden's clothes. Finally, Arden let out a frustrated sigh and stood up again. "I think I need some fresh air," he announced, grabbing his jacket. Harriet nodded, unable to speak, and followed him out of the house. They walked aimlessly for a while, neither of them saying much. The tension between them was palpable, and Harriet could feel her heart pounding in her chest. They ended up at a nearby park, where they sat down on a bench under the stars. The cool night air did nothing to cool Harriet's burning desire for Arden. She could feel his eyes on her, and she knew he was struggling with it too. Without thinking, she reached over and took his hand in hers. His skin was warm and smooth, and she couldn't help but squeeze it gently. "Harriet," he breathed, looking at her with eyes full of longing. She couldn't resist anymore; she leaned in and kissed him passionately, their tongues tangling in a dance of desire. They fell back onto the grass, tearing at each other's clothes as they explored each other's bodies for the first time.

He had finally kissed her. As they lay there, panting and sweaty, Harriet felt a sense of euphoria wash over her that he'd never felt this way about anyone before, and she knew that she couldn't stop now.

Arden's lips trailed down her neck, sending shivers down her spine, and she moaned softly as he whispered her name. But then, they heard footsteps approaching. They both froze, hearts pounding in their chests.

It was Monster, returning from his walk. Harriet quickly scrambled to her feet, tugging at her disheveled clothes. Arden followed suit, his normally confident demeanor replaced by a look of embarrassment. The Monster looked at them curiously. "Having a good time?" he asked, a knowing smirk on his face. Harriet felt her cheeks burn even hotter as she realized they must have looked like they were up to something. "Um, yeah," she stammered, trying to act casual. Monster walked up to her and whispered in her ear:

"Sure, whatever you say. Fat, ugly bitch. Just don't forget about doing what I tell you to do tomorrow." Harriet froze, and he whispered, "I didn't put those ads up of you for *NOTHING*."

"YOU DO AS I SAY."

As he walked away, Harriet couldn't help but feel a mixture of all those feelings of pain from her past life, the numbness, and the tears. She turned to Arden, who was still struggling to button his shirt, unaware of what Monster had said or who he even was. Then she felt relief. This was a nightmare. *WAKE UP!* The Monster is gone.

Chapter 74

Sydney, February 2025

Harriet sat nursing a lukewarm tea, her gaze fixed on the swirling steam. Anna called her and suggested that Harriet speak at one of her women's empowerment events. The idea felt like a physical blow, a jarring reminder of the vulnerability she'd painstakingly rebuilt from.

"It will help other women, and you," Anna insisted, her voice softer now, infused with genuine concern.

"I mean, try it once, you are more confident now since you went to New York and everything". Harriet sighed, the faintest tremor in her voice.

"I am not a public speaker, Anna." Anna's unwavering optimism didn't falter.

"No one is born one; you can become one. With your experience, these women would benefit from hearing how to protect themselves."

Harriet considered the proposition. The New York trip had been her Eat, Pray, and Love moment, not just because of Arden but also a chance to reclaim her life far from the shadow of her abuser, Monster. It had given her a strength she hadn't known she possessed.

Yet, the idea of standing before a room full of strangers, baring her soul, felt terrifying. The memories, the bruises, both physical and emotional, threatened to resurface with the sheer thought. She pictured their faces, their expectant eyes. Would she be able to control the tremble in her voice? Would the pain consume her, drowning out her carefully constructed narrative of survival? The fear was palpable, a cold knot in her stomach. But Anna's words echoed in her mind: *"Help other women."* Perhaps, just perhaps, sharing her story could be a way to finally reclaim her power, to turn her trauma into a source of strength for others.

The next morning, Harriet found herself responding to Anna's email. She agreed. The message was short and to the point, but the weight of the decision hung heavy in the air. It wasn't a sudden burst of courage, but a quiet, deliberate choice. It was a step towards healing, a testament to her newfound strength, and a promise to the women who might one day find solace in her story. This wouldn't erase the past, but it could help to reshape her future, and perhaps, help others find theirs as well. The fear was a constant companion, but it was now overshadowed by a flicker of hope. A quiet determination to face her fears and to speak her truth.

Chapter 75

New York, February 2025

The city never really slept, not even on nights like this. Arden could hear it outside, the faint siren far uptown, the rumble of a late-night delivery truck, the rise and fall of voices spilling from the rooftop bars two blocks over. His apartment was quiet by comparison, the air thick with heaviness.

He sat on the edge of his bed, staring at the garments he had pulled from the drawer earlier. They looked so small, so daring, an unassuming black g-string and a pair of red satin shorts that glowed almost defiantly under the lamplight. He had ordered them weeks ago, the parcel arriving in a plain brown envelope, tucked discreetly into his mailbox. He had carried them upstairs like contraband.

Now they lay before him, waiting. Arden's fingers hesitated. He felt the old tug-of-war—the voice that told him this was ridiculous, dangerous even, and the other voice, quieter but persistent, that told him he was finally moving toward something true.

He stood and slipped into the g-string first. The cool fabric shocked him at first touch, a thin black line that felt like it had no business belonging to him, yet somehow, impossibly, it did. He looked down at himself, both startled and exhilarated.

Next came the red shorts. He slid them up slowly, the satin catching on his skin, hugging his hips, bright and audacious against the muted tones of his apartment. He exhaled, unaware he had been holding his breath, and stepped in front of the mirror propped against the wall.

The man who looked back at him was the same one who walked the streets in pressed shirts and leather shoes, but something was different now. His body language softened, his stance shifted. He tilted his head, running a hand down the fabric, watching how the light rippled across the red sheen.

For a moment, shame tried to creep in, the old lessons, the voices of others. But the mirror was patient. The longer he stared, the more those voices faded, replaced by something else: wonder.

Arden turned sideways, then spun halfway, catching sight of the black strap disappearing beneath the shorts. It was scandalous, it was beautiful, and it was his. He let out a small, startled laugh, the sound echoing strangely in the stillness.

He moved across the room, the satin whispering with every step, the g-string a secret reminder against his skin. He opened the window wider, letting the city air in. Across the street, neon from a late-night deli sign painted his reflection in red and blue. He stood there, lit by the colors of the city, and felt—just for a heartbeat—like he belonged to something bigger.

This was not a disguise. This was not a play. This was reclamation.

Arden raised his chin, squared his shoulders, and let the moment hold him. For the first time in a long time, he didn't feel like he was performing for anyone. He was simply being.

He studied himself, turning left, then right. The shorts clung in ways he hadn't expected, emphasizing lines he'd never considered before. The black strap beneath remained a secret, just barely visible when he moved. A smile flickered across his face, half disbelief, half wonder.

Then, almost without thinking, Arden reached for his phone.

He set it on the dresser, angling it toward the mirror. The small red light blinked, recording. He turned, slowly, letting the camera catch angles he couldn't study otherwise. His back to the mirror now, he glanced over his shoulder, watching as the g-string disappeared beneath the satin, the outline stark and daring.

For a long moment, he just looked, not with vanity, but with curiosity. Who was this version of him, framed by the mirror, captured by the lens? He arched slightly, then shifted his stance, testing how it changed the way the fabric curved and fell. It was as if he were meeting himself anew, documenting proof that this other Arden existed.

Watching the playback later, he knew, would be another kind of discovery, an intimacy with himself that no one else had yet earned the right to see.

As he moved, tilting his body this way and that, a memory rose, unbidden but powerful. Harriet.

He could almost feel her still: the intensity of her devotion, the way she once pulled him past his own guardedness into a space of total surrender. It had startled him then, the rawness of it, how she seemed unafraid of his edges, his defenses. She had buried her face in him without hesitation, as though he were something to be worshipped rather than endured.

The recollection wasn't about the act itself but about what it meant: that someone had once wanted him in his most vulnerable form. He remembered the shock of it, the trust it demanded, and the dizzying realization that he could be both exposed and desired.

Standing there now, in the satin shorts, the camera watching silently, Arden understood why the memory returned. The thread connecting then and now was not lust but liberation. Harriet had given him a glimpse of freedom he hadn't known he craved. Tonight, with the red satin catching the light and the g-string whispering against his skin, he was chasing that same freedom, this time by himself, for himself.

He turned back to the mirror, watching over his shoulder as the lens captured the curve of fabric, the play of shadow and light. For a moment, he let himself imagine Harriet seeing him like this, not with judgment, but with that same fearless acceptance she had once given him.

Arden set the phone down gently on the nightstand, lay back against the sheets, and closed his eyes. Outside, the city moved on without him. Inside, he carried the knowledge that a door had opened, quietly and irrevocably, and that he had finally stepped through.

Chapter 76

S ydney, February 2025

Harriet stood on the podium and put her red notebook away, which she had been nervously clutching with both hands. As the lights shone on her, she glanced at the audience. She started to talk, the champagne still on her tongue, making the words flow.

They all smiled, their faces filled with surprise, admiration, and a mix of emotions. What was she going to say next? She hurried along with her story, skipping the painful parts she wanted to avoid, but they were the necessary evil in her tale.

And as she got to her favorite part of her talk, her eyes lit up.

"Instead of thoughts of revenge, which anyone who has been through what I have been through would have thought was justified, I did something else…" Harriet laughed nervously.

She felt Arden close, even though he was thousands of miles away.

She felt his skin on her cheek, his dim bedroom lights, soft sheets, and his familiar voice, calming and centering her. *Focus.*

"I gave another man pleasure".

She watched the audience and their reaction.

"I made him moan. I made him enjoy it. I stared at the back of his neck, the most beautiful part about him. I wanted to run my fingers through his tanned skin, slowly. My lips and my tongue all over him. When I eventually placed myself on top of him, his soft hands on my ivory shoulders, his words like honey on his tongue I wanted to lick off, *I felt an incredible lightness of being, being a woman, being worthy again.*"

The audience was quiet, their eyes on Harriet.

"See, life brought me this incredible man, a moment with him, a moment that meant more than 16 years of past pain with someone else".

She moved her head, analyzing each face of the audience after what she said.

"There are some good men out there".

Her mind drifted back to the moment with him; she wanted to tell them all about it, and she would tell it without blushing, with such confidence that every girl in this room would love to try. How she gaped him open, how she felt so alive and charged, burying her face inside him. He had been ready for her the moment she ran her index finger near his hole and whispered, *"Be a good boy for me, please"*.

He glanced behind him, and their eyes met for a second. She had never seen such a look in his eyes that spoke volumes of passion and longing. Her hands cradled him at the waist; she positioned him perfectly before making his lips tremble. He was still, remaining graceful and elegant as she rolled her tongue, but she could sense his anticipation as if he were approaching orgasm just thinking about it. She felt tension in his muscles as her tongue went deeper into him. The sound of his moans made her feel incredible. Her breasts were bouncing against the back of his legs as she started moving her tongue faster.

"Slow down", he whispered, wanting to make the moment last.

This is what she wanted to tell everyone, but would she be judged? Where was the line drawn of good taste for them? He tasted so good, she wanted the world to know. She could tell them how she would straddle his lap, lowering herself onto his cock. That is something everyone does.

Or how her pussy would squeeze him so tight he could hardly breathe. That was accepted, but what about her face inside of him, feeling like she was at peace with the world, everything was OK for that moment, she tasted only him and nothing else mattered. She was healing, her perky breasts lowered down, her lips slightly parted, and a moment of genuine happiness filled her entire soul. And that was what she wanted to tell the audience, a group of diverse women, some showing signs of vulnerability, others seemingly strong and self-assured. Harriet cleared her throat, the microphone amplifying the tremor in her voice.

"But I am here to tell you about the man before him."

"It started subtly," she began, her gaze sweeping across the faces in the room.

"Little things. He'd be so charming, showering me with gifts, making me feel like the luckiest woman alive. Then the comments would start, chipping away at my self-esteem, making me doubt myself, my friends, and my family. He'd isolate me, controlling who I spoke to and where I went. He'd monitor my phone, my emails, and even my social media. The violence started slowly too, a push, a shove, a slap… each time escalating, excused as 'accidents or my fault.' She paused, her eyes welling, but her chin remained firm.

"Then came the attempted trafficking. He said, "The connection might come back between us, and maybe he might love me again if I only did what he told me to. He used my vulnerabilities, my fear, and my love for him to exploit me. It was a nightmare I wouldn't wish on my worst enemy."

The women in the room listened intently, some nodding in grim recognition, others visibly shocked. Harriet continued, her voice gaining strength.

"The Monster wasn't some faceless stranger; he was the man who promised me the world. He was the man who had me convinced I was nothing without him. That's the insidious nature of coercive control; it strips away your sense of self, leaving you vulnerable and dependent."

She held up a worn photograph, a picture of a smiling couple, a stark contrast to her current appearance.

"This was me. Happy, unsuspecting. This is what he stole from me, and he almost got away with it. But I escaped." She gestured to the photo again.

"The red flags were all there from the beginning: the jealousy, the possessiveness, the isolation, the constant criticism. If you see those signs, run. Don't underestimate the power of those early warnings; they are your escape route."

Harriet's voice cracked slightly as she concluded, "You are worthy of love, respect, and happiness. You deserve to be free. Don't let anyone convince you otherwise. Your life is valuable, and you are stronger than you think." A hush fell over the room, broken only by the quiet sniffles and the rustling of tissues. The weight of Harriet's story hung heavy in the air, a stark reminder of the insidious nature of abuse and a beacon of hope for those who dared to listen. The women exchanged knowing glances, and a silent pact formed among them; a promise to watch for the red flags, to protect themselves, and to support each other in their journey to freedom.

Chapter 77

Sydney, March 2025

It was one of those mornings, heavy with the promise of rain, a weighty humidity that settled deep into the bones.

The darkened clouds rolled across the sky, blotting out the sun and wrapping the world in a dim embrace. Harriet felt the thunderous tension in the air, a sensation that stirred up memories like leaves whisked away by an autumn wind.

She began her ascent up the familiar staircase, her sneakers squeaking softly against the polished wood, each step echoing her apprehension. The hallway felt narrower than she remembered, the walls seeming to close in around her as if they were whispering cautionary tales.

Past the lonely water cooler, with its sad container of forgotten splashy dreams, and through chairs that stood empty, Harriet arrived at Amanda's office, her sanctuary, yet today, a reminder of so much left unfinished.

As she sank into the plush couch, her fingers grazed the soft, brown blanket adorned with faint patterns, a tactile connection to warmth and safety. Here, she could let the world peel away its harshness.

The rain would undoubtedly find its way to the windows, maybe forming trails like tears, a metaphor she often contemplated.

Today, their conversation took a different turn.

"Have you considered IVF?" Amanda's voice broke through the stillness like a gentle rain on dry soil. She nursed a cup of green tea, steam curling upwards as if seeking escape. The question hung in the air, charged with the remnants of unkind memories and burgeoning hope. Harriet's eyes widened, her breath catching in her throat. The weight of the suggestion echoed like distant thunder; it reverberated through her mind, unsettling yet awakening. "You can travel to one of those beautiful islands…" Amanda continued, a glimmer of mischief in her eyes as she placed the cup down, each movement deliberate and filled with possibility. "Tell that man to meet you there." In this charged silence, Harriet felt the electricity pulse through her, reminiscent of that unforgettable time she first met Arden.

They had shared a moment in Central Park, the kind that made the sky seem bluer and the world somehow pulsate with brighter colors. There was a symphony in the air, and she wondered if Arden had felt it too. Would he remember the warmth that wrapped around them, or was it a moment lost in time, never meant to return?

"There's an entire life behind things, Amanda."

The words slipped out before she could grasp them, laced with reverence.

"Love, too, and I…"

She hesitated, grappling with more than just her feelings.

"I took life by its horns when I went to see him."

"Maybe that island isn't such a bad idea." Amanda leaned forward, her brow slightly furrowed as she pondered Harriet's expression.

"Ever steal anything, Harriet?" Amanda's voice shifted, a playful seriousness weaving through her words.

"Some people steal for pleasure."

She continued, "I think Monster was stealing your time for pleasure, so you couldn't have children."

The harsh reality cut through Harriet like a sharper breeze, a chill that mingled with her warmth, leaving her exposed. It was true, in a grueling way.

"Amputation of limbs is still part of the legal system in some countries for stealing. Maybe there's some misfortune happening to him for stealing your time." Amanda smiled softly, her eyes sparkling with mischief and resolve.

"Life has its way of turning things around. So… go to the islands."

As lightning danced in the distance, Harriet felt an overwhelming swirl of emotions converge. Amanda was always so direct, but her call to action ignited something deep within, a spark that whispered of potential tomorrow.

Just one question remained in her mind.

"How do I bring it up with Arden?"

Chapter 78

❧

Sydney, April 2025

That night, after the appointment with Amanda, Harriet's heart raced as she lay in bed, staring up at the ceiling. Her fingers traced along the lace of her nightgown, the cool fabric doing little to soothe the heat that burned within her. She couldn't deny it any longer; she wanted his cum again. More specifically, she longed to be impregnated by him. It was a taboo thought; she had tried to push away for months, but it had grown into an unyielding desire that consumed her every waking moment.

She wanted him inside her, filling her up with his seed until she was brimming with his white gold. As her mind wandered to thoughts of being inseminated by Arden, Harriet couldn't help but imagine how their lives would change. They would have a child together, a living embodiment of their strange connection, which she wasn't even sure was love in its traditional sense. The idea of carrying his child inside her, feeling it grow and kick, was more arousing than any fantasy she had ever had. Even if it meant IVF, even if it meant she was implanted with a stranger's eggs. It would be his sperm. That was what mattered.

Determined to act on these desires, and after running it through with Amanda, Harriet knew she needed to confront Arden about it. She knew it was a risky move, but she was willing to take that chance. After all, they needed something to reignite their connection. He had been so keen in New York. Why not now? What has changed?

The thought of the conversation terrified her. How would she bring it up? She imagined taking a deep breath before speaking. She practiced in front of the mirror, rehearsing the scene over and over.

"Arden," she began, her voice quivering slightly. "There's something I need to tell you." She imagined him looking up from his newspaper, his eyebrows raised in curiosity. "What is it, wifey?" She swallowed hard, her mouth dry. "I... I want your cum." The words felt clumsy, inadequate for the monumental desire they represented. "For the baby to be created in the lab." The practice runs in the mirror were one thing, but the real conversation felt infinitely more daunting. She knew she couldn't just blurt it out. She needed a softer approach, a way to ease him into the idea. She envisioned him sitting in his usual armchair, the newspaper rustling in his hands. She would sit opposite him, close enough to reach out and touch his hand, but far enough to give him space. She would take a deep breath and sit down opposite him, her heart hammering against her ribs.

"Arden," she would begin, her voice a little steadier than she expected. "Can we talk?"

He would lower the newspaper, his eyebrows drawn together with concern. "Of course, Harriet. What's on your mind?"

She would hesitate, twisting her fingers in her lap. "I've been thinking a lot about... us. And about our future."

He would wait patiently; his eyes fixed on her face. It was the patience that disarmed her, the way he *saw* her when he chose to.

"I know things haven't been... easy lately," she continued, "but New York was amazing, wasn't it? I feel like we were so connected, so... alive." Arden would nod slowly, a flicker of recognition in his eyes. "It was good, Harriet. I enjoyed that a lot."

"I think we need something to reignite that spark," she would say, her voice growing stronger. "Something to bring us closer together." She would pause, gathering her courage. "I went to see a fertility specialist. And we talked about IVF."

Arden's expression wouldn't change, but she could sense his attention sharpening. "I know it's expensive, I know it's not a guarantee," she would rush on, "but I think… I want to try. I want to have a child, Arden. *Our child.*"

Silence would hang in the air, thick and heavy. Finally, Arden would speak, his voice quiet.

"A child? You want a child?"

"Yes," she would say, her voice barely above a whisper. "I want to be a mother. And I want us to be parents together."

She would take a deep breath. This was it. The moment of truth.

"And… and I want it to be with your… with your sperm. I want it to be ours in every way possible."

Arden's eyes would widen in surprise. "What? Are you joking?"

Harriet would lean forward; her gaze locked on his. "No, I'm not," she replied, her voice barely above a whisper. "I want… I want your… contribution. For the baby to be created in the lab." She would hold her breath, waiting for his reaction, the fate of their future hanging in the balance.

Harriet would hold her breath, waiting for his response. Finally, he would set down his paper and turn to face her. "Why now?" he would ask, his voice soft. "I don't know," she would admit. "I just… I've always wanted it. But I never thought you'd agree to IVF." He would run a hand through his hair, looking troubled. "Harriet, we've tried before." Her heart would sink for a moment.

"I understand that," she would say quickly. "But maybe we could try… just once?" Arden would consider her request for a long moment. Then, unexpectedly, he would lean over and kiss her gently on the forehead. "One cycle of IVF. "

"Alright," he would say. "But only this once." Harriet's heart would leap with joy.

They would make love with a fire they'd never known before, their passion reborn in the desire they had just unleashed, and then again, a second time, as if once could never be enough.

Harriet had replayed this conversation in her head a dozen times, each version sounding more absurd than the last. In the end, she'd keep it simple, ask him to meet her on the Island, and let things unfold. Go with the flow.

Choices. Chances. Changes.

She wouldn't just believe in miracles, she would create them.

Chapter 79

Sydney, April 2025

The next morning, Harriet stood at the bus stop, at the edge of the golf course. Among all the manicured greenery behind her, her gaze was lost among the ethereal shapes of the clouds above. She was on her way to sign paperwork at *Miller & Zarella,* the endless battle with the Monster.

She knew exactly what she wanted to do with the money, if it was ever returned to her. To do something good, something different.

The morning sunlight danced around her, illuminating strands of hair that escaped from her loose braid, framing her face like a halo. The bus was late, of course. Typical. Here, in this vast expanse of nature behind her, she felt as if she were floating, adrift in daydreams of a life that could be.

In her daydream, she sat on the soft, impossibly green grass of a perfect spring day. Beside her, Arden sat cross-legged, a small bundle swaddled in a pastel blanket cradled in his arms. Their baby cooed softly, eyes wide with wonder at the world above. Harriet's heart swelled at the sight of the very essence of love embodied in their child. Yes, love. There, she said it. Silently, to herself.

This scene, this perfect family portrait, wasn't just a random fantasy. It was a hope, a possibility, a fragile seed she was trying desperately to nurture. This was the life she secretly wanted. But with Arden… it was complicated.

Yet, an ache lingered within her, a yearning for something more than this idyllic scene. "Do you think they know?" Harriet asked quietly, breaking the gentle hush that enveloped them. She gestured to the clouds as if they were old friends who held secrets just beyond reach. "Do you think they dream too?"

Arden looked up thoughtfully, his golden-brown eyes reflecting both admiration and concern. "Maybe they dream of us," he replied with a half-smile, brushing a finger against their baby's cheek. "Or maybe they're just content to float." The warmth of his voice wrapped around Harriet like a familiar embrace, but an unsettling thought crept into her mind. Would it be better to live up there, lost in her dreams and fantasies, or down here where reality weighed so heavily? Alone or together? That was the question that haunted her. "Sometimes I wonder," she confessed, turning to face him fully now, her voice barely a whisper. "If I'd be happier with my head in the clouds... forgetting everything."

Arden's smile faltered slightly as his eyes searched hers for an answer to a question she failed to voice.

"Harriet?" he asked gently.

She looked away. "Sometimes I wonder what it would be like to forget everything," she murmured. Arden studied her face, his brow tightening. "Sometimes I wonder about you," he said softly. "It's like you're not here, like you're up there." He glanced toward the sky. "Way up there."

Harriet's lips curved faintly. "And what's so wrong with that?" she replied.

But then the roar of the bus interrupted her thoughts, pulling her back to the Sydney bus stop and the reality of the life she was building, one painstaking step at a time. Arden and the baby faded away, leaving only the morning sun and the looming image of the lawyer's office in her mind. She blinked, trying to shake off the lingering scent of baby powder and the phantom weight of Arden's hand in hers.

The bus screeched to a halt, its doors hissing open. She hesitated, one foot on the step, looking back at the golf course. The clouds shifted, their shapes morphing and reforming, offering no answers, only an endless, silent expanse. She took a deep breath and stepped onto the bus, clutching her bag tightly.

The decision wasn't made yet, she realized. She had a feeling that the Monster, even in absentia, still held the key. The settlement wasn't just money; it was freedom. The freedom to choose where her feet and her heart would finally land.

And Arden might just be a fragment of her imagination; a fleeting illusion conjured from years spent battling inner demons alongside the Monster.

Would she be ready to share something so special with an illusion?

Chapter 80

S ydney, April 2025

The Sydney sun rose on a new day, but the light felt bleak, painting the harbor in a dull, metallic sheen. Harriet's heart ached, a raw, pulsating wound. It wasn't just from the calculated betrayals of Monster; it was the terrifying vulnerability that Arden had exposed within her. She was sleepwalking, both literally and through life. She'd woken up moments ago from a nightmare, standing in her living room, screaming. Fragments of the dream clung to her like cobwebs, whispers of fear and accusation.

You won't get kissed, and he won't go down on you because he wants to lie there and be like a woman. Get it? He will never love you. He will just use you.

The voice in the dream, a distorted echo of her anxieties, needled her. It was a cold, calculating voice, the kind that chipped away at your self-worth until there was nothing left.

He is a predator in a financial district suit and a white shirt. You are doing all these things to him, but it won't make him respect you or be loyal to you. It's all words and games. Images flashed through her mind: Arden, detached, almost clinical in his affection; the memory of a fleeting, almost hesitant, boob squeeze whilst she was on top, a moment that now reeked of indifference; the times she'd felt like an afterthought, a convenient placeholder.

Remember when he left you alone in his apartment after you flew across the world to see him? He had already set up the next ones whilst seeing you. The memory of that rainy Friday night in New York stung. She had flown across continents, yearning for connection, only to be handed a remote control and left to the mercies of Netflix while he… what? Prepared his next conquest? *If I don't go now, it will be over.* Arden wanted to tell her. But he said, *"I won't be long."* He hadn't lied, not exactly. He'd been brutally honest because she knew. She could read him. He was going to see someone else. The honesty, somehow, made it worse. It amplified the emptiness, the feeling that she was vying for a prize she would never win.

I like you, but I don't love you.

Those words, stripped bare of pretense, echoed in the pre-dawn silence. They were a branding iron on her soul, searing her with the truth. Did it sound as hurtful as *"I wish you well,"* from Monster's new supply?

"I like you, but I am not in love with you. That's what he said!" she screamed, the words raw and ragged in the quiet apartment. "And you too, whoever you are whispering to me shit, I wish you well, and I wish well to Monster and his new supply because I know he will kill her in the car crash! There is rain, there is darkness, he is driving." Her voice cracked, climbing in pitch. "His driving is dangerous. I've seen it!" Then silence. The echoes died, leaving only the lingering chill of the dream. She looked around, disoriented. The familiar shapes of her living room swam into focus. A half-finished mug of tea sat on the coffee table; a book lay open on the sofa. She had sleepwalked in here, propelled by the turbulent currents of her subconscious. Her heart felt heavy, weighted down by the twin anchors of Monster's past transgressions and Arden's unfulfilled promises. Perhaps sleepwalking was a metaphor. She'd been sleepwalking through relationships, drawn to the familiar comfort of dysfunction, the predictable pain of unrequited love. But here, standing in the stark light of a Sydney morning, with the remnants of her nightmare clinging to her like a second skin, a tiny flicker of defiance ignited. Maybe, just maybe, waking up screaming was the first step to truly waking up.

She walked in circles in the living room until she was exhausted. The carpet blurred beneath her feet, each revolution a silent scream. She needed help. But who could she trust? Who would believe the irrational fear twisting in her gut?

Instead of calling any helplines, writing to friends, or asking Anna, something, a dark, morbid curiosity urged her to sign on to the sex sites she knew Monster had used. Her fingers trembled as she typed, a traitorous part of her wanting to be wrong, wanting to believe this was just paranoia. She tried his email and a random password they had on the home computer for car insurance accounts. It was a long shot, a desperate gamble. It worked. The screen flickered to life, displaying the familiar yet alien interface of the website. Her heart hammered against her ribs; each beat was a frantic drum solo of dread. She scrolled through his profile, her breath catching in her throat. *He had put her up for sale.* And there were so many replies from men. Each message was a hammer blow to her soul. "Beautiful smile," user8906 said, followed by a string of lewd comments. "Willing to travel," another wrote. "How much for the weekend?"

Harriet ran to the bathroom and vomited. The bile burned her throat, a physical manifestation of the sickness consuming her. She retched until her stomach was empty, the metallic tang of blood mingling with the bitter taste of betrayal. It couldn't get any worse than this. Could it? She stumbled back to the living room, the cold seeping into her bones. The replies, the offers, and the blatant disregard for her humanity danced before her tired eyes. That nightmare she had seen about the Monster walking up to her, his eyes vacant, his smile predatory, was telling her about these online advertisements. It was a warning. Sex trafficking. Now that was real. Monster, the man she had married, the man she had built a life with, had been trying to sell her: her body, her life, her very being.

Chapter 81

New York, May 2025

The fluorescent lights of the First National Bank hummed a monotonous tune, a soundtrack to Arden's slowly unraveling sanity. He shuffled papers, the click-clack of the keyboard a dull counterpoint to the cacophony of New York City that seeped in through the double-paned windows. He hated his job. He hated the relentless pressure, the insincere smiles, the constant striving for more, more, more. He hated the screech of brakes, the aggressive honking, the sheer, suffocating density of humanity.

He longed for something else, a quiet he couldn't quite define, a peace he couldn't quite grasp. It felt like a phantom limb, always there, always a nagging reminder of some missing piece. And the closer he got to filling other voids, the further that quiet always seemed.

And then there was Harriet.

Harriet. Just the name conjured a warmth that threatened to melt the icy cynicism that clung to him. Sex, of course, was a significant part of it. But it was more than just the earth-shattering orgasms, the breathless gasps that filled the air. It was the way she looked at him, a complete and utter adoration that both terrified and intoxicated him. Her determination was almost unsettling, a laser focus on her goals, a quiet strength that belied her soft features. And her love… her unconditional love felt like a weight on his chest, a beautiful, overwhelming burden.

He wasn't worthy. He knew it, deep down. He was a mess of contradictions, a twisted knot of desire and self-loathing. He wanted to be a good man, a man worthy of Harriet's love. But the pull of his darker impulses was too strong. He wanted to have his cake and eat it too. He craved the thrill of the casino, the seductive sway of the strippers, the fleeting oblivion of a cocaine binge. He was a typical New York finance bro, a wolf dressed in a bespoke suit, prowling the concrete jungle for his next fleeting fix.

He pulled out his phone, his thumb hovering over Harriet's contact. He'd been on a bender the night before, a blur of blackjack tables and blurry faces. Regret, sharp and bitter, gnawed at him. He needed to hear her voice, needed to feel her presence, even if it was just through a recording.

He pressed the record.

"Hey," he started, his voice sounding rough and strained even to his ears. "I was just thinking about something. Like how I value you coming to New York to see me." He paused, searching for the right words, the words that wouldn't betray the guilt that was eating him alive. "And how you made it all happen. You know, booking the flights, finding the hotel…" He trailed off, the pretense of gratitude feeling hollow and false. He wanted to say more, to express the complex swirl of emotions that threatened to drown him. But the words caught in his throat.

He knew, with a chilling certainty, that he was hurting her. He was taking her love, her dedication, her unwavering faith, and using it to fuel his own selfish desires. He was a black hole, sucking the light out of her sun.

He sighed, the sound heavy with regret. "Thanks," he mumbled, finally hitting send. He knew it was a pathetic offering, a paltry attempt to bridge the chasm he was widening between them.

He stared at the screen, the blue bubble containing his message a stark reminder of his failings. He longed for the quiet he knew Harriet represented, but he was too afraid to relinquish the noise, the chaos, the destructive patterns that had become his crutch.

He was a prisoner of his own making, trapped in a gilded cage of his design. And Harriet, with her love and her light, was slowly fading from view. He had to choose. And he was terrified of the choice he would ultimately make.

Chapter 82

Sydney, May 2025

Harriet lay on the massage table, her eyes closed, naked under the soft blanket. She felt the heat from Jana's hands as she began her work.

It had been so long since the women's circle. She remembered being in a completely new environment, taking it all in with her red cheeks and new emotions. Now, Jana was trying something different on her. She placed her hands above Harriet, and she was instantly transported back in time to Arden's bedroom, with pink and grey cushions scattered across the floor and a soft light filtering through the curtains.

In his bedroom, she was once again floating on top of him, their bodies entwined in an erotic dance. She had never experienced anything like this before. He was inside of her, filling her up.

His touch was gentle yet powerful, and she could feel herself melting into him. As they moved together, she could feel the pain and sadness that had been weighing her down for so long begin to dissipate. It was as if he was absorbing all her negative energy, replacing it with something far more potent.

She opened her eyes to find herself looking down at him, seeing herself through his eyes. His hands were on her hips, guiding her up and down his length. She arched her back, throwing her head back in ecstasy, her long blonde hair creating a bright aura around them. She was confident and in control, squeezing him with her vagina, taking him deeper inside with each thrust. He looked up at her with a mix of awe and desire, his eyes filled with wonder. She saw herself in his gaze, which fueled her passion even more. As they moved together, she felt a connection beyond the physical.

They were two souls united in their shared grief, healing each other through their feelings of Fear, now far away.

Harriet's breath came in ragged gasps as she continued to ride him, her body responding to his every touch. She felt herself changing, transforming under his gaze. The pain in her womb began to fade, replaced by a warmth and fullness she had never experienced before. It was as if he was filling her not only physically but emotionally as well. She looked down at him again, and this time, she saw him looking back at her with love and admiration. He was lost in her, lost in the moment, their souls intertwined. She felt his cock twitch inside her, and with a groan, he came, filling her with his white gold.

It was a powerful moment, and she knew their union had brought them both to a new level of healing. As she collapsed onto him, panting and spent, she felt a sense of peace wash over her. For the first time in a long time, she felt whole. She knew that this wasn't just a physical act but something far deeper.

This time, they had connected on a spiritual level.

The energy healing session was over, and Harriet found herself back in the present, lying on the massage table, naked but under the blanket. She tried to process what had just happened, the intense emotions and sensations that had washed over her. As she sat up, she realized that she felt different. Lighter, more at peace. She looked at Jana, who was gathering her things, and she felt a sudden urge to tell her what she had seen, what she had felt.

"Thank you," she said, her voice barely above a whisper.

"That was…unexpected." She turned, a curious look on her face. "What do you mean?"

She took a deep breath.

"I saw…something magical. I was making love, and it was…"

Her eyes widened in surprise.

She nodded, her cheeks flushing with embarrassment.

"I know it sounds crazy, but I felt like we were healing each other through our… whatever that emotion was." Harriet avoided saying the word, *Love*.

She smiled at her, a warm and understanding smile.

"It's not crazy," she said.

"Sometimes, during energy healings, people can experience things like that. It's a way for the mind to process and release emotions."

She smiled back, feeling a newfound sense of connection to Arden.

"Thank you," she said again.

"You've given me so much more than just a massage today."

She nodded, her eyes softening.

"You're welcome, Harriet."

"Keep these loving emotions within you".

It wasn't just energy; it was something so alive, pulsating with every heartbeat, each thrum stirring deep emotions within her womb, a whirlpool of loss, sadness, and unexpected happiness.

Harriet turned around to face Jana one more time, the healer whose hands had sparked this transformation, and in her memories, the initial bravery of just going for it in New York. She radiated calmness, her brown hair with silver strands cascading like a waterfall over her shoulders, eyes shimmering with wisdom as she smiled softly at Harriet's bewilderment.

"How was it possible to have this kind of out-of-body experience just by your healing energy?" Harriet asked breathlessly, clutching her chest as if trying to contain the emotion from within. Jana chuckled gently, her voice soothing like a balm on Harriet's frazzled nerves. "Healing is more than just a physical act; it's an alchemy of spirit and intention. You opened yourself up to all that embrace," she replied.

"Remember, you came to the circle before you traveled to New York. Now you amplified that connection." As they spoke, Harriet felt drawn back into herself—the memories swirling like autumn leaves caught in a gust of wind when she walked with Arden in Central Park. She thought about

Arden's touch, the way his fingers had danced over her skin as if playing an instrument only she could hear. In that moment of vulnerability and warmth, she had shed layers of grief that had weighed heavily on her heart for far too long. "Embrace it all," Jana encouraged gently.

"Let it flow through you; don't fear what you feel."

Harriet nodded slowly as tears welled in her eyes, not just from sadness but from gratitude for this awakening journey she had embarked upon. She closed her eyes one more time before going home; her womb still felt warm.

And the undeniable pull between Arden still lingered inside of her.

Chapter 83

Sydney, May 2025

Amanda put Harriet on a different medication, *25 mg to start with, if needed, 4 times a night.* She needed to sleep. No more waking up screaming in the living room. She outstretched her arms wide and dreamed as the waves crashed outside her apartment.

Candlelight flickers against his cheeks. The same black Celine candle she lit up a long time ago, when she was in the cabin, still during the storm of survival. She feels the warmth of the candle.

They are in the bathroom, and she has been taking care of Arden, slowly bathing him with a soft sponge. The warm water drips on his back, and the bath foam glistens against his lean, perfect legs.

She runs her fingers over his soft, short beard. She doesn't want to shave him, as she loves him exactly how he is.

She is drying him with a white cotton towel as he sits on the toilet seat. They are both quietly smiling. She glances at his brown eyes, with the familiar gold speckles in his eyes that only she sees, ramping something up deep inside her.

The goosebumps on his skin feel like hot lava bubbling up. With all his being, he lets her close to him. She feels him radiating joy, something she has never felt in him before.

Very few men in this entire world are as lucky as he is to experience a moment like this. Harriet had prepared the makeup. White, the shimmering gold, the midnight black, and the cherry red.

First, she dresses him in the white crispy shirt and slowly does the buttons from top to bottom. He feels the lava bubbling up to his throat, and the soft candlelight in the room starts to feel more like electricity wired straight into his spine. He is carefully observing as she picks up the makeup brush. She brushes him with long strokes of white all over his cheeks and forehead, filling the hollows with gold.

She has him looking like a porcelain doll.

A doll she can play with for a while. It fills up the space inside her, the loss that feels like a song that has been written but never played.

She stands before him in her dark green lacy bra and underwear, lifting the make-up brush and finishing his new look. Smiling. Her all-consuming pain dissipates like a fog off the dark ocean.

He has never felt like this, thoughts bubbling inside him. The makeup brush gently touches his cheeks one last time whilst he is holding back the rocks wanting to break through the Earth's surface. He doesn't want this moment to end. He wants to be her porcelain doll forever. She whispers, "You're so beautiful", and warm cum pulsates overflowing down his shivering leg, glowing as if it were made of fire.

And she knows now. He is not her random desire. He is her divine assignment.

Chapter 84

Sydney, June 2025

As Harriet nestled into a cozy corner of the neighborhood cafe, the delicate tinkling of raindrops danced against the windowpanes. She was still feeling the effects of the energy healing. Some might say it's just nonsense, but it all made so much sense to her. Jana had a gift; there was no doubt about it.

The cafe was alive with chatter, yet it felt intimate as if time had slowed just for her. The warm aroma of freshly brewed coffee mixed with the sweet scent of pastries filled the air, inviting and comforting.

Outside, couples strolled together under their umbrellas, their laughter mingling with the sound of distant accordion music drifting from a nearby street performer. The golden glow of lamplight began to illuminate the streets, casting a magical light that sparkled off the wet pavement.

Harriet gazed out at the scene; despite being one among 8 billion people in the world, she felt inexplicably connected to Arden, a connection that transcended distance and circumstance.

A message from Anna popped up. She wasn't coming.

"Sorry, I'm still stuck in the post office picking up my parcel. The line is to the door!"

As Harriet was people-watching, she imagined if Arden entered the cafe just then, shaking off droplets from his umbrella like a dog coming in from the rain. He would scan the room until his eyes landed on Harriet. A smile crossed his face, one that warmed her heart more than any cup of coffee ever could. She would wave him over, her heart fluttering like butterflies caught in a gentle breeze.

"Sorry, I'm late," he would say breathlessly as he approached her table, his cheeks slightly flushed from the cold outside.

"I got caught up in my thoughts about how we're just two souls adrift in this vast sea of humanity."

Harriet would chuckle softly, brushing a stray hair behind her ear.

"Sometimes it feels overwhelming," she would admit. "But right now? It's just you and me."

He would lean closer, an electric energy pulsing between them as their fingers would brush against one another on the table.

"You know," he would say softly, "in a world with billions of people, I think I'd still find you every time."

The moment would hang in the air like an unspoken promise, deepened by the gentle rhythm of rain tapping against the glass and illuminating their faces with its soft glow.

Outside, life would continue its relentless pace, and people rushed by without noticing, but inside this small sanctuary, they would exist solely for each other.

As Harriet sat alone among the shared laughter and dreams over steaming cups of coffee and flaky croissants of other people, Harriet realized how beautifully intertwined their lives had become despite all odds, a serendipitous connection amid 8 billion souls.

They had matched on the App for a reason. And Monster had pushed her to do it. Something good out of so much bad.

Chapter 85

Sydney, June 2025

As Harriet glanced at her phone screen, her heart fluttered slightly upon seeing Arden's latest photo. He was leaning against his desk, illuminated by the soft glow of late afternoon sunlight filtering through the glass. The crisp white shirt hugged his frame perfectly, accentuating his strong shoulders and confident stance. With his tousled hair and that charming smile, *oh, how he looked so undeniably handsome.*

It was a look that made all those nudes sent in playful banter pale in comparison; there was something about this polished side of him that ignited an alluring spark deep within her.

She could hardly contain herself as she typed out her response, teasingly asking him if he was *"ready to hand in your notice?"* A hint of mischief lacing her words.

Her heart raced at the thought that he might soon be free from his mundane 9-to-5 life. The response came almost instantly: *"I'm about frigging ready to."*

His words were charged with both frustration and excitement, an intoxicating combination that made her smile grow wider.

In a moment of boldness inspired by his playful tone, Harriet decided to send him a picture of herself clad in a snug sports bra and matching leggings. She leaned against her door frame, showcasing her toned figure while maintaining an air of casual confidence. The lighting was soft yet flattering, a perfect contrast to his polished office look.

"How's this for motivation?" she texted along with the image, her heart pounding at the possibility of what could unfold next. Across the world, Arden felt a rush of energy as he stared at her image on his phone screen. The juxtaposition between their worlds, the formal office attire versus her athletic wear, felt electric.

Her confidence radiated through the screen and left him grinning like a fool. He could practically hear her laughter ringing in his ears as he imagined their paths intertwining again. Harriet felt an unshakable sense of excitement about what lay ahead for them both. This moment marked not only a flirtatious exchange but also hinted at their desire for something more, a shared journey toward freedom and passion beyond his daily grind and her troubles.

Her phone buzzed again, pulling her back to the present. It was Arden.

"Consider that some serious fuel," he wrote, followed by a winking emoji. "Heading to the meeting now. After this, I might just draft that resignation letter."

Harriet laughed out loud, picturing him in his suit, imagining the scene when he handed in the letter. The thought of him, finally free, driven by her, was intoxicating.

"Maybe I should start packing," she typed back, knowing she was pushing the boundaries, but unable to resist.

"Packing for what?" he responded immediately. Harriet hesitated for a moment, her fingers hovering over the keyboard. It was time to be bold, to lay it all out on the table.

"For a new adventure," she finally wrote, "wherever you are."

Silence hung heavy in the digital air for what felt like an eternity. *Has she gone too far? Was she being too forward?* Doubts started to creep into her mind, threatening to extinguish the spark of excitement she had been feeling.

Then, another message popped up on her screen.

"Get your passport ready. I'm thinking…an island. Sun, pasta, and maybe a little less office attire."

Harriet's breath hitched in her throat. *He was serious. An Island? With Arden? The thought was almost too good to be true.*

She leaned back against her door frame, a wide, genuine smile spreading across her face. This wasn't just a coincidence, he worded it like that; this was something more. This was a chance to escape the ordinary, to embrace the unknown, to build a life with someone who saw her, truly saw her, and was willing to risk it all.

"Island sounds perfect," she replied, already envisioning the rolling hills, the vineyards, and the warm sun. "Just promise me you'll wear that white shirt at least once."

She also envisioned the baby.

His response was instant: "Only if you bring those leggings."

The world felt wide open, for that moment, and for the first time in a long time, Harriet knew, without a doubt, that she was heading in the right direction.

Chapter 86

S ydney, June 2025

Harriet lay nestled among her plush pillows, her heart heavy yet fluttering with an unspeakable longing. The room was bathed in soft light as she stared at her phone, Arden's voice echoing throughout the room like a cherished melody. She pressed play again.

"I wish wifey were here, cuddling me. Now wouldn't that be something?"

His words wrapped around her like a comforting blanket but also pierced her heart with their bittersweet edge. She smiled softly, lost in memories that washed over her, his laughter, his teasing glances, and those intense moments.

She could almost feel the warmth of his presence beside her; yet reality reminded her that he was miles away, tangled in the lives of others who held pieces of him she could only dream about. With a hand resting lightly on her hips, Harriet inhaled deeply, contemplating whether to record a response. *"Should I tell him?"* she mused internally. The battle within began. And Fear clawed at her thoughts while I tried to whisper sweetly. *"Tell him! Yes! Yes!*

Yes!" But then Fear flooded back in like a cold wave. *"No,"* it warned sternly.

"Remember how he didn't respond right away? How you're left waiting…

on read."

Her heart raced at the thought of Arden being adored by others. Someone else curled up beside him while she remained an unspoken secret tucked away in his heart.

"Others who think they are in a relationship with him," Fear taunted softly. "Others who believe they will have what you can only dream about." A chill ran down her spine as she fought against these thoughts, desperately trying to drown them out with warmth and affection for Arden's memory.

As she lay there, illuminated by that soft golden light filtering through the curtains, Harriet felt utterly alone yet profoundly connected to something larger than herself—a Love that transcended distance and time. Her fingers hovered over the screen as if drawn by an invisible thread connecting them across miles.

Send him a message.

Finally, she exhaled slowly and let go of the phone altogether, letting it rest on her bedside table. A silent acknowledgment that sometimes love meant holding back just as much as it meant reaching out.

Chapter 87

On The Island, July 2025

Harriet clutched the worn map tighter, the salt spray stinging her face. Amanda's words echoed in her ears; a lifeline tossed across the turbulent sea of her grief. *"You deserve this, Harriet. You deserve to know."* Amanda, ever the pragmatist, had pushed her, prodded her, finally forcing her to confront the gaping hole Monster had left in her life.

Monster. Even the name tasted like ash in her mouth. He had been a vortex of chaos, sucking the life and light from everything he touched. He'd taken her family, twisted her reality, and left her drowning in a sea of survivor's guilt. Now, it seemed, he might have even stolen her future.

Arden. The thought of him was a sharp pang, a bittersweet melody in the symphony of her loss. Their time together had been snatched from the jaws of despair, a brief, incandescent flame flickering against the encroaching darkness. She had loved fiercely, desperately trying to build something tangible and hopeful in the midst of the ruins. She had wanted a child, a tiny beacon to push back the shadows, a testament to her love and resilience. But time, that cruel mistress, had been against her.

Her attempt had been frantic, fueled by a desperate hope that bordered on delusion. She had clung to and prayed for a miracle, but their efforts had been in vain.

Had Monster poisoned her, not just with fear, but with something more insidious? Had he somehow stolen her fertility along with everything else?

The ferry shuddered, throwing Harriet against the railing. The Island loomed in the distance, a silhouette against the bruised purple sky. It was a place of whispers and rumors, home to the Embryo world, a cutting-edge fertility clinic shrouded in secrecy and whispered promises. It was her last hope.

She stepped off the ferry onto the weathered dock, the air thick with the scent of brine and something else, something sterile and metallic. The Embryo world was perched on a cliff overlooking the ocean, a gleaming white structure that felt both futuristic and unsettling.

Inside, the air was hushed, filled with the soft hum of machines. Doctors in pristine white coats moved with a quiet efficiency, their faces masked with an almost clinical neutrality. Harriet felt a wave of nausea. *This was it.* This was where she would learn the truth.

The examination was thorough, impersonal, and utterly terrifying. Hours crawled by, filled with probes and scans and questions that stripped her bare, not just physically, but emotionally. The lead doctor, a woman with eyes as cold and blue as the Arctic Sea, finally summoned her to her office.

"Ms. Harriet," she said, her voice devoid of warmth.

"The results are conclusive."

Harriet's breath hitched in her throat. She braced herself, ready for the worst.

"There is no definitive physical reason preventing you from conceiving. Your hormonal levels are…slightly irregular, likely due to trauma, but within manageable parameters. Physically, you can carry a child."

A wave of relief washed over her, so intense it almost knocked her off her feet. She *could* have a baby. There was still hope.

But the doctor wasn't finished. Her lips tightened, and she adjusted her glasses.

"However," she continued, her voice dropping to a near whisper, "there is something else. A… complication."

Harriet's heart pounded. What complication? What new horror awaited her?

"Our preliminary analysis reveals traces of a unique protein signature in your system. A signature we've only seen in individuals exposed to… extreme experimental agents."

Harriet felt a cold dread seep into her bones. Extreme experimental agents? What was she talking about?

"This protein interferes with the egg fertilization process. It doesn't prevent it entirely, but it significantly reduces the chances of a successful pregnancy. Think of it as…a subtle, insidious blockade."

The doctor paused, studying Harriet with clinical curiosity.

"It's…remarkable, Ms. Harriet. This protein signature suggests that you were likely exposed to this agent years ago. It shouldn't still be detectable in your system after this long."

Years ago. Monster. The pieces clicked into place with a sickening thud. He hadn't just taken her family. He hadn't just taken her peace. He had poisoned her, deliberately, meticulously, rendering her dreams of motherhood a cruel, distant possibility.

All the vague memories she had, waking up to Monster on top of her. Amanda suggested he might have been drugging her for years.

The doctor's voice pulled her back to the present. "It's faint, Ms. Harriet, very faint. But with intensive, experimental treatments, we might be able to counteract its effects. It's a long shot, expensive, and not guaranteed."

Harriet looked out the window at the churning ocean. The Monster had stolen so much. He had even stolen the joy of simple, natural conception. He had tainted her body, her soul, with his malevolence. But he wouldn't steal her hope.

She turned back to the doctor; her jaw set with a newfound determination.

"What are my options?" she asked, her voice surprisingly steady. She would fight for this, for the chance to bring something beautiful into a world Monster had tried to destroy. Even if it was a long shot, even if it was expensive, she would fight. She owed it most of all to herself. She would reclaim her stolen future, one painful, expensive, and experimental step at a time.

The humid air clung to Harriet like a second skin as she fiddled with her phone, the screen reflecting the dazzling turquoise water surrounding the small, uninhabited island. Palm trees swayed in a languid rhythm, their shadows dancing on the white sand like playful spirits. This was paradise, a place she'd dreamed of sharing with Arden in her dreams. But dreams had a way of souring, as she knew very well.

Harriet had a message to send, and she knew exactly how to deliver it. Forget flowery prose or scathing emails. She needed a visual punch, a gut-level appeal that would bypass Arden's carefully constructed defenses.

She positioned the phone, angling it just so to capture the incandescent glow of the setting sun on her face. Her smile was radiant, carefully crafted to convey carefree joy, a stark contrast to the turmoil simmering beneath the surface. Then, she adjusted the top of her sundress, drawing it down ever so slightly. The resulting image was undeniably alluring, Harriet, bathed in golden light, her perky breasts subtly accentuated beneath the fabric. It was inviting, suggestive.

This wasn't just a pretty picture. It was a carefully calculated gambit.

Maybe Arden had dismissed her for so long since New York, not for another woman or a man, but for a promotion. A vice president at the monolithic corporation he slaved for. Harriet knew the truth. It was for *his* future, *his* better life. He'd sacrificed meeting her again, traded their what would have been lustful evenings for endless meetings and soulless corporate events. He'd become exactly what he hated.

Now, she was dangling the bait. This island, this life, this version of herself, a happy, untethered woman living out an abandoned dream. The photograph was a question mark hanging in the air: Was this worth throwing away for the sterile comfort of a corner office?

She knew Arden. Knew the fire that still flickered beneath his veneer of corporate ambition. He was a creature of impulse, driven by aesthetics. The island, the turquoise water, and the glistening sand all were appealing. But she knew, deep down, that it was her face, her perky breasts, the *image* of the carefree life she was living, that would truly resonate with him.

She hit send.

Now, she waited. She imagined Arden, hunched over his desk, the harsh fluorescent lights of the office reflecting in his weary eyes. She pictured him seeing the image, the colors exploding on his screen, a vibrant explosion of sunshine and freedom in his drab, corporate world. Would it be enough? Would the promise of paradise, the subtle allure of her body, outweigh the allure of power and prestige?

She closed her eyes, the sound of the waves washing over the shore a gentle lullaby. Maybe this beautiful, selfish selfie would be the catalyst. Maybe it would make Arden question his choices, question his ambition. Maybe, just maybe, it would make him hand in his resignation and meet her here, on this island, where they could start again, carry on where they left off in New York. Or maybe, it would just be a fleeting moment of regret, a pang of longing swallowed by the cold, hard realities of his chosen path.

Only time will tell.

Chapter 88

On the Island/ New York, July 2025

Harriet started questioning her sanity as she stood barefoot on the warm wooden pier. She felt the humidity in her bones as she stared at the most picturesque surroundings at the all-inclusive resort.

Alone.

There were no waves, and a knot formed in her throat; the ocean stood too still and silent.

He wasn't coming.

She had been constantly checking the time and felt wired for weeks leading up to this. No sign of him. She had her head down, looking strained.

Behind the clouds, Fear was beside me, and together we watched on, unable to reach out. Out of our hands, it was all on Arden.

I observed Fear for a moment. No reaction.

A wave of nausea washed over Harriet as images of herself with him crashed through her mind, intimate touches she had imagined, streets she had wandered thinking of him, every song in her AirPods carrying his presence. His hair, the gentleness of his hands, his quirks, and especially his voice, so articulate, precise, each word measured yet full of meaning, haunted her. She had poured him into her poems, made him her everything, the one thing she thought could save her.

And now it was all wrong. Every memory, every fantasy, every longing felt like a cruel trick she had played on herself. She wanted it gone, erased, a fragment of imagination, a dream she could wake from one morning and laugh off. But it clung, relentless, gnawing at her stomach, tightening her chest, echoing through her blood like fire she could not quench. His voice, his presence, his perfection, they were hers, and she had made him hers, and now it was unbearable.

"Miss, miss…" Rajit's gentle voice echoed across the other side of the long wooden pier.

The hope that had kept her alive so far was now simultaneously killing her. In her mind, she expected Rajit to announce a special visitor for her.

"You left your wallet in the reception, Miss Harriet", he hurried with a permanent smile on his kind face.

The ache in her chest made it hard to breathe. Her heart sank, slow and heavy, as though the turquoise sea itself were pulling it under. Each ripple of the tide whispered the truth she had tried not to hear: he wasn't coming. Not today, not ever. Still, she stood there, waiting, as if the ocean might carry him back with the tide.

She knew. What a fool she had been. She stood on the pier alone, swiping a single tear from her cheek with her index finger, pretending Rajit wouldn't notice. Was Arden's attraction to her only ever skin-deep? It was never the forehead kiss kind of love. It was always bread crumbed; she was feeding his ego. All the messages, all the 'attention she deserved', it was nothing but madness. He was a bottom feeder, and she placed him on the pedestal like his love was the King of her. Her fists clenched as she tried to suppress the urge to lash out.

"Miss, your wallet…" Rajit reached out.

She had been so focused on one thing, one thing that should not have been a priority. Ever.

She was now tasting the salty tears, unable to hold back.

Pushing her shoulders back and standing tall, she felt like she was floating in the sea of betrayals and disappointments.

"Look! Behind you!" Rajit's excited voice caught her attention again. A stunning rainbow appeared across the ocean as the speedboat approached the island in the distance.

Harriet felt unsteady on her feet and held her arms wide for balance.

"Miss…are you OK?" Rajit's smile faltered.

"I will be," Harriet replied, holding her wallet and looking at the still ocean. She longed for his presence as the clouds of hazy dreams dispelled across the sky. Harriet had to learn not to keep drowning in missing someone who came to her in waves.

She remembered his cold words, *"You place too much weight on me",* when she cried on his black coach in New York. She remembered looking outside, New York was flooding. Rain slashed his windows. He looked at her with his brown eyes again. And all she saw were tiny bits of gold flying through the vast universe; she adored him so much.

Was there an apology for hurting her?

He took her to an expensive restaurant. And that night, she was on top of him. She felt like floating, between the intense moments of unconditional love, hurt, confusion, and trying to reach him. On top of him, like so many other girls before her and after her.

Goodbye, Mr. New York.

"Excuse me for intruding… were you waiting for someone?" Rajit asked, his voice carrying a trace of shyness.

Harriet didn't answer at first. She kept her gaze fixed on the horizon.

"It's my father's birthday today," Rajit said gently, as though offering her a reason for speaking. "I grew up without him in my life. The sea became my father instead." He smiled faintly, eyes following the same expanse of water.

"My friends were my family, sailing, working here, meeting visitors like you, Harriet. They shaped who I am." His tone held no bitterness.

Harriet finally turned toward him. For a moment, she thought of her mother's lifeless eyes, dulled too often by drink, and wondered if hers looked the same now.

"Yes," she admitted at last. "I was waiting for someone."

"He is not important anymore." It hurt when she said it. "Should have profiled him as an asshole from the beginning." *"Asshole*, hahahaha". Signs could not have been clearer. This initiated a lengthy exchange of looks between them.

"It's just life." Rajit looked at the speedboat getting closer.

"He was just an illusion, a figment of my imagination." Harriet now almost laughed at all her ridiculous hopes, desires, and the irony of it all.

"Abandoning you in such a terrible place? I mean, look where he left you!" Rajit tried to make Harriet laugh. And so, she did. She laughed as the still ocean became wavy again with the approaching speedboat full of laughing tourists.

"Have you ever seen that Steve Martin movie," she asked softly, "where the spotlight hits him and everyone in the restaurant freezes—the conversations, the clinking of glasses—when he announces he's dining alone?"

Rajit shook his head.

"Well," she murmured, "that'll be me tonight, not alone exactly, but painfully, unmistakably lonely."

The waves rose and fell, echoing the hollow ache inside her. She missed him. She missed him in ways that left her breathless and unsteady.

"Just smile," he said. "It fixes everything."

She almost rolled her eyes. As if life were that simple. Soon, women like her would come here and turn from the endless glitter of the sea to the cold blue glow of their phones, searching for something, or someone, that never quite arrived.

Beauty had never been enough. Not her body, not the soft line of her waist. Beauty turned her into an object, the same one Monster once tried to sell, a body for other men to use.

What real men hungered for was something rarer, something that couldn't be faked: a smile that carried life, warmth that couldn't be staged, a pulse that reached deeper than skin. No trick, no manipulation, could conjure that spark.

The spark she once believed would bind Arden to her.

Fear had vanished, or so she thought. She hadn't noticed him standing there moments ago, silently observing. Fear had been watching her doubt, her hesitation.

And then it hit her with a cruel clarity. It was Fear that kept Arden away. Fear that always did this. Fear that, somehow, always found a way to win.

New York, a concrete jungle usually brimming with frenetic energy, felt tonight like a colossal tombstone.

At the airport, Arden slammed his purple United card on the desk, eyes glued to his boarding pass. Her message, timestamped 5:00 a.m., pulsed on the screen like it had a heartbeat of its own.

It wasn't her selfie, but her poem that had claimed him utterly. Every word, every carefully chosen line, traced along his nerves like fire, tugging at him, making his blood drum, his chest tighten. She had made him her muse, turned him inside out with nothing but thought, made him feel alive, exposed, achingly wanted in a way no one ever had. It was maddening, intoxicating.

She had seen him, the part he kept secret, sacred, untouchable, and claimed it as her own. She called it her "happy place," a teasing, forbidden confession that made his pulse spike. The thought of her adoring that most intimate, hidden part of him, worshiping it as her salvation, as her joy, was intoxicating. So taboo, so impossible, it sent a rush through him that he could barely contain. Every line she wrote, every subtle hint, made him burn, made him ache, made him want her in ways he didn't know were possible.

Then the words vanished. Deleted. 11:00 a.m. The flame didn't die; it erupted in memory, relentless and scorching, leaving him raw, trembling, consumed by the thought of her.

Fear hovered at his side at Departures, cold and relentless, pressing into him like a shadow he couldn't shake.

"Yes... you like her. You crave her company. You crave her mind. You crave her lush breasts, the way she sets you ablaze, the way she bends you over, claims you

with nothing but thought."

Then Fear struck again, sharp and unavoidable:

"You love her... as a friend."

Fear pressed closer, relentless, a weight on his chest and shoulders, twisting his mind with cold reason.

Above him, the departure board glared, each minute slipping away like sand through his fingers. The gate was closing. The flight was leaving. Arden felt it pressing on him, every second demanding a choice: step forward or stay in the hollow, meaningless city he was sick of.

And then her memory hit him, sharp and overwhelming: Harriet, claiming him with a confidence that left him trembling, pressing herself against him, taking him in ways that drove him wild. Her tongue against him, pushing him higher, leading him to the most explosive, mind-shattering orgasm he had ever experienced. He had surrendered to her completely, and he had loved it, every second of being consumed, every ache and shiver of pleasure she had drawn from him. He wanted that again, *so badly.*

Chapter 89

JFK Airport, New York, July 2025

"I am here; I am here!" I screamed. The air at the airport was not filled with seashells and salt. It was filled with human odors I didn't particularly like. I chose to breathe to get closer to Arden. I saw his purple card on the desk. He looked down at his phone, and I screamed, *"Can you see me? Can you hear me?"* Arden looked around the counter, trying to catch the attention of the clerk. Harriet is never going to fade from your life like a scar. She will stay because there's more. "She is the most captivating, magical thing that has ever happened to you." I tried to raise my voice.

"Go to the Island." "Go".

Something pushed me from behind, and I hit my face on the hard airport floor with dirty footprints. Something edged closer to my face.

"Fear?"

"This is about you and me." Fear said, its voice a rasping whisper that chilled me to the bone despite the bustling airport terminal.

"You have stepped on my toes far too many times, ruining perfect scare tactics," Fear hissed, its shadowy form solidifying, taking the shape of a gaunt, grinning man.

"You need to leave. Now". He was trying to scare me, but I wasn't easily intimidated. "No, I won't go anywhere." I gathered my courage against his dark shadow, feeling a strange power surge within me, a power linked to my unusual ability to interact with the personified emotions.

Fear lunged, but I anticipated the move. My voice, amplified by an unseen force, echoed through the terminal, silencing the surrounding chatter.

"You are a manifestation of Arden's regret, his fear of facing Harriet's lingering influence. You are a parasite, feeding off his indecision!" Fear recoiled, its form flickering. I focused my energy, channeling the emotional turmoil around Arden, pulling on the threads of his unresolved feelings. The intensity was almost unbearable, but I felt a strange connection to the emotional currents that flowed through the airport, a symphony of anxieties, hopes, and goodbyes. I saw a shimmering, translucent figure materialize beside Fear.

Hope, radiating a gentle warmth. Hope and Fear began to battle it out, a silent war of emotions playing out in the physical realm. I could see Arden's eyes dart nervously, noticing the escalating struggle unfolding in front of him.

Hope pushed back, its light growing stronger until Fear dissipated into nothingness, its dark energy absorbed by the burgeoning hope. Arden, finally looking up, saw me, the remnants of the emotional battle, and the purple credit card still on the desk. He looked at the card, then at me, a flicker of understanding dawning on his face.

The Island, it seemed, held a power even greater than Fear; a power he was finally ready to face. He picked up the card, a ghost of a smile gracing his lips. He was going to the Island. And I, the unlikely messenger between a man and his emotions, knew my work was finally done.

Chapter 90

Countryside NSW, July 2025

Monster's new marriage was based on lies. Just like everything in his life.

"The other woman," who became Monster's second wife, had complained about continuing headaches. She felt like he was dismissing, minimizing, and invalidating her feelings. He was committed to misunderstanding her; he shamed her when she was trying to speak her heart and mind. She tried to express her emotions and tell him about her head hurting so much.

Monster was driving his new wife to the hospital, the same woman who gushed, *"My love, God blessed me with you."* She had known he was married. She chose to believe his lies, to swallow his manipulation, until her loyalty became unshakable. When Harriet, trembling with panic and grief, warned her of the truth, the woman dismissed her with a single, polished cruelty: *"I wish you well."*

Now, she was lying on the side of the road, her dark hair covered in clumps of sticky, dry blood. A yellow pole had gone straight through her throat; glass shattered everywhere. Another car was only inches away from her. She was taking her last breaths, blood spattering through the hole in her throat up towards the night sky.

The Monster sat by the side of the road. Alive and well. Barely a scratch on him. He had carefully rearranged the scene and made it look like she was the one driving.

The same old blame-shifting, framing, and organizing, followed by calculated answers ready for the police and ambulance arriving shortly. He cleared his throat and let out the most ridiculous, forced fake laugh. The one Harriet knew very well.

He looked down at her, feeling both exhilarated and empty. He knew he had to leave her here, on this empty road. He would find another woman soon enough.

He couldn't decide if he had just made the greatest mistake of his life or tasted the greatest pleasure he would ever know. She had been so obedient, swallowing every lie without a flicker of doubt. With Harriet, it was different. He hadn't needed to shove her off the balcony to push her toward death; his words and actions, his calculated cruelty, had worked like strings in a puppet master's hands. He had tried to kill her on the road, too, but even then, she had slipped from his grasp.

"Oh well", he thought, the adrenaline still pulsed, like a sweet, sickening hum beneath his skin. He meticulously cleaned himself, the glint of his smirk mirroring the chilling satisfaction in his eyes as he looked at himself in the shattered side mirror of the tangled car.

The police were baffled, as there were no leads or witnesses, just Monster's lies, which he believed himself. He knew he would forget her, and she would not haunt him for the rest of his days, just like Harriet, just another one disregarded without a second thought.

His laughter broke the stillness, a forced, hollow sound that danced in the air, masking the gravity of the situation, reminding him of the emptiness that filled his life.

Chapter 91

∾⟡⟡∾

On the Island, July 2025

Harriet's green irises burned with an unspoken yearning. No more just hoping for a voice note, and hearing his soft-spoken, captivating words, which instantly made her body warm, like she was sitting in the sauna in her solitude, meditatively staring at the steaming rocks. She pinched herself. No more voice notes, sometimes with a mangled, a mishmash of low voice and interference.

She was observing and admiring his cock again, in the secret chambers of her mind. Never did she think that a vein straining against the skin in a very particular spot would look so seductive, perfectly aligned, and stopping halfway through his decent-sized beauty. Her eyes grew larger, measuring, inch by inch. There was still a long way to go towards the tip, the skin getting smoother, the color changing to a shade of pink only he possessed. And the hair. She loved all that hair, positioned on his body in the perfect spots like a map. She would love to run her tongue along and learn every single curve.

Arden was a world she could explore, every curve a continent she longed to know. Harriet wanted to trace him with her fingertips, feel the rise and fall of him beneath her hands, map the landscape of him with lips and hands alike. He was endless, hers to wander, and she would lose herself in him forever, discovering new places in the contours of his body, in the warmth of his skin, in the quiet power of his presence.

Her eyes lit up with an ocean-green spark, and, like the sharp bite of lemon on her tongue, she vividly remembered how he tasted; her thoughts so fiery she should have been clutching a shot of tequila instead of her lukewarm morning latte. She wasn't in the middle of a Sydney Starbucks, lost in a daydream of him, where the soft hum of conversations drifted into the background, distant and muffled, as though the world itself had paused while he filled every corner of her mind.

She was trying to contain her thoughts, which were growing wilder by the second, as she remembered how he trembled. She bit her lip, glanced at the ocean through the large windows, and, like the tide receding from the shore, flowed back towards the shore again, bringing forth the same feeling she had then and now. As she savored all those little details that burrowed somewhere deep inside of her, a question surfaced: was he deliberately leaving her wanting more? Just like she wanted her readers to turn pages until their fingers were sore, she got it. She was the same.

He was in the bathroom, the door open. An upside-down shampoo bottle caught her eye. Was he like everyone else, squeezing the last dregs of life out of things until there was absolutely nothing left? Was that how he approached her, too? Savoring, consuming, until she was an empty vessel? Just like Monster had done to her and gotten away with it. The thought stung more than she expected. Maybe she was overthinking.

Then the shower glass door opened. He emerged, a towel slung low around his hips, leaving a tantalizing glimpse of the very terrain she'd been mentally mapping just moments before. The steam followed him, wrapping him in a hazy glow. He ran a hand through his damp hair, and droplets of water scattered like diamonds.

"Hey," he said, his voice a low rumble. "Sorry, it took longer than I thought. The hot water was… therapeutic."

His eyes met hers, and that familiar heat flared within her. But this time, it was tempered with a new awareness, a slight hesitation. She saw a question in his gaze, a subtle testing of the waters.

Harriet took a deep breath, the scent of his soap filling her lungs. "Everything okay?" he asked, stepping closer.

Against all odds, Arden had come to the island, proof that some bonds refuse to be broken. Just when Harriet had surrendered to hopelessness, he appeared before her, saying *"Hey, wifey"* as if it were nothing, as if the impossible had simply bent to life's strange magic.

She nodded slowly, but the question lingered in the air, unspoken. Was everything okay? Maybe it would be. Maybe it wouldn't. But for the first time, she wasn't just swept away by the tide. She was standing on the shore, observing, considering, ready to choose her course.

"I was just thinking about my writing, it has been all over the place," she said, her voice surprisingly steady. "Trying to figure out the next chapter."

He smiled, a slow, knowing curve of his lips. "And what's the chapter about?"

Harriet met his gaze, her green irises gleaming with a newfound determination. "It's about wanting," she said, "and what you do when you finally get it."

Chapter 92

❦

Sydney, August 2025

Harriet clutched the phone so tightly that her knuckles ached. Outside, the late winter wind howled, mimicking the tempest that had raged inside her for the better part of two years. Andrea's words, crisp and professional, cut through the storm, each syllable a tiny shard of hope piercing the dense fog of despair.

"It's Andrea, from Miller & Zarella." The familiar voice, normally a source of dread associated with endless paperwork and soul-crushing depositions, now resonated with a fragile promise. "We had the hearing. The judge wondered where you were, but with all the police reports that we subpoenaed, it made perfect sense that you could not face him."

Harriet swallowed, the lump in her throat as big as a fist. The police report. A stark, unflinching record of the escalating abuse, the calculated cruelty, the erosion of her very being. She had lived them, endured them, but seeing them laid bare in black and white had been almost as devastating.

"We managed to track down his cryptocurrency," Andrea continued, her tone shifting, gaining momentum. "Several funds were spread over several exchanges. He even had one under his former last name."

Harriet felt a flicker of something akin to triumph. He thought he was so clever, so untouchable, hiding his assets in the murky world of digital currency, *the arrogant bastard.*

"He had been transferring huge amounts to an account in the Philippines. We may never recover that," Andrea's voice dipped in a moment of somber acknowledgment. "But I discovered something, he did something to his new wife, not sure what exactly, these types of abusers never change – " Andrea paused, a low, guttural sound escaping her lips. Andrea muttered, "His Filipino wife is already gone. Karma's just waiting for him next."

A shiver ran down Harriet's spine. "You can pay someone to get rid of him…for a dollar over there." There was a chilling satisfaction in Andrea's words, a dark justice whispered across the miles. It wasn't revenge she craved, not exactly. Still, the thought of him facing consequences, of him experiencing even a fraction of the fear and helplessness she had endured, was undeniably…cathartic.

Andrea cleared her throat, snapping Harriet back to the present. "We are going into negotiations now, and suggesting 65% for you, Harriet. Light at the end of the tunnel. You won't be left with nothing, like he thought."

Sixty-five percent. The number hung in the air, almost unreal. He had systematically bled her dry, financially and emotionally, leaving her feeling hollowed out and worthless. The thought of starting over, economically secure, was a dizzying prospect.

Tears welled in Harriet's eyes, blurring her vision. Not tears of joy, not yet. They were tears of exhaustion, of relief, of cautious optimism battling against years of ingrained fear.

"Thank you, Andrea," she managed to croak, her voice thick with emotion. "Thank you for everything."

"You're welcome, Harriet," Andrea said softly. "You deserve this. We'll keep you updated on the negotiations. *Just…try to breathe.*"

Harriet hung up the phone and walked to the window. The sky was a bruised purple, but a sliver of the setting sun managed to break through the clouds, painting the horizon with a fleeting band of gold.

She closed her eyes, took a deep breath, and let the fragile warmth bathe her face. It wasn't just the money. It was the validation, the acknowledgment of what she had suffered, the knowledge that she was not alone, that someone had fought for her, and believed in her.

The healing would take time, a long and arduous journey. But for the first time in a long time, Harriet felt a flicker of hope, a fragile ember glowing in the darkness. She might be scarred, she might be broken, but she was not defeated. And thanks to Andrea, she had a fighting chance to rebuild her life, claim her future, and finally, truly, be free. The light at the end of the tunnel, though distant, was undeniably there. And Harriet, for the first time in years, felt strong enough to walk towards it.

Chapter 93

Epilogue

When Harriet Hart swiped right on Arden Goldstein's profile, drawn in by a photograph that showcased not his smile, but his magical eyes. Big, deep brown eyes that seemed to hold galaxies within. His bio was basic, a line about being a finance bro, but his eyes spoke volumes. From that first tentative hello on the dating app, a current surged between them.

In real life, the effect was even more potent. She saw flecks of gold glittering within those depths, like stardust scattered across a velvet canvas. She saw swirling nebulae, entire universes contained within those brown irises. She saw herself reflected, amplified, idealized; her adoration, her yearning, painted in the rich gold of her burgeoning infatuation. It was intoxicating, a heady cocktail of lust and longing. He was her golden God, and his gaze was her sun.

Arden was initially hesitant. Harriet's world, filled with past trauma and vulnerability, felt a universe away from his typical New York life. But Harriet's gentle nature and the fierce intensity in her gaze, a reflection of the fiery passion in his own heart, broke down his walls. He found himself drawn to her quiet strength, her unwavering belief in his dreams, a belief he often lacked in himself. He saw the world through her eyes, her creative eye, her discerning eye, her intensely loving eye, and it broadened his perspective. The differences, once daunting chasms, became bridges, connecting two distinct worlds in a symphony of shared laughter and whispered confidences. He never explicitly understood the symbolism of the gold she saw, but somehow, he felt it too.

Their story wasn't without its bumps. But every time Fear crept in, Harriet would look into Arden's eyes on the photographs she had saved on her phone, and she would see not only her reflection but also the unwavering promise of the future, shining brighter than any gold. And Arden, looking back, saw a strength and a love as boundless and vast as the universe that shimmered within the depths of Harriet's captivating gaze. In the end, those golden flecks became a symbol of their enduring love story, a testament to two souls who found their way to each other despite the seemingly infinite distance that had separated them.

Love, as it turned out, wasn't enough. It took more than a swipe right, more than a pair of alluring eyes, more even than good intentions. It took genuine connection, raw honesty, and the courage to see the world and each other without filters. It was understanding that love wasn't a transaction, a strategic acquisition. It was a messy, complicated, and utterly terrifying leap of faith. It was about seeing someone, flaws and all, and choosing to love them anyway.

Harriet had always believed in the idea of love. The grand, sweeping romance of novels, the meet-cutes in rom-coms, the whispered promises under starry skies. She devoured these stories, projecting herself into each heroine, waiting for her own Prince Charming to materialize.

Harriet's heart, once a fragile porcelain doll, was now forged in steel. She never forgot the Monster, but he no longer defined her. He was a scar, a reminder of the darkness she had overcome. And that scar, that perversion of love, was now a badge of honor, a testament to the extraordinary power of a woman who dared to reclaim her own narrative. Her almost perverse version of love wasn't about finding a Prince; it was about becoming the Queen of her own life. And that was a kind of fairy tale, a real one, far more powerful than anything she had ever read.

She loved fiercely, not out of desperation, but out of abundance. She gave freely, not expecting anything in return, but because her heart overflowed with the kind of genuine, unadulterated love the Monster had never understood.

Arden was the lucky recipient of her unconditional love. *Whether he is ready for it remains to be seen.*

www.ingramcontent.com/pod-product-compliance
Lightning Source LLC
Chambersburg PA
CBHW030531120726
47904CB00005B/1716